Hanna!

Hi. I'm so glad your friend. Thanks a lot for reading my Christian viewpoint. I hope you are blessed and please let me know what you thought about the Book. I hope to chat with you on facebook.
Say hi to Athra for me
Blessings to u,
Pauly

Beyond the Veil

Randy L. Noble

©2010 Randy L. Noble. All Rights Reserved.

All characters contained herein are fictional. Any similarities to persons living or dead are purely coincidental.

Front cover picture courtesy of Dreamstime.com

3

Acknowledgements

To my Lord and Savior Jesus Christ, who calls us out from every nation, tribe and tongue to find Salvation in him through the power of the cross.

To my beautiful wife Becky. You are the love and inspiration of my life. And of course, Jezzie, you are, too! (Our dog)

To all Muslim women everywhere. I sincerely pray that you will be able to see the beautiful face of God, like Nadia did, that is beyond the veil.

To Christopher for his amazing technical support.

To both Maryam and Marzieh. I am very thankful to God for your freedom. Your courage and faith have inspired me to live more faithfully for Jesus.

To all my co-workers at Family Christian. Thank you for your support and prayers that made this project possible.

Table of contents

1. *The Dream*
2. *A Worldwide Compassion*
3. *A Living Sacrifice*
4. *A Crisis of Faith*
5. *The Letter*
6. *The Journey*
7. *The Visit*
8. *Kidnapped*
9. *Divine Deliverance*
10. *Into The Darkness*
11. *A New Beginning*
12. *Beyond The Veil*
13. *Counting The Cost*
14. *Five Years Later*
15. *Persecution*
16. *Broken Wings*
17. *Providence*
18. *Reunited*
19. *A Very Special Christmas*
20. *A prophecy Fulfilled*
21. *Saying Goodbye*
22. *Reconciliation*
23. *Letting go.*

You opened up the way
When your hands and feet were nailed
Now I can see your face beyond the veil
I want to touch your face
With these hands that are frail
I long to see your face beyond the veil.

Chapter One
The Dream

The panic stricken screams of a 15 year-old girl shattered the stillness of a cold moonlit night.
"Help me. They're trying to kill me!"
Terrified and gasping for breath, Nadia was running for her life. Two men armed with razor-sharp machettis had been chasing her all night. Nadia could faintly hear the ominous sounds of the machettis slicing through the tall weeds and brush not far off in the distance.
Grasping her bruised knee with one hand and trying to keep her balance with the other, Nadia struggled to continue running. The huge forest that she had wandered into was dark and deep and the only light that illuminated her way were the particles of moonlight spilling over the twisted tree limbs.
Suddenly, Nadia came upon a gravel path. She stopped and then quickly looked over her shoulder. "They're coming," she nervously muttered to herself. "I've got to keep going."
After limping ahead a few more feet, Nadia found herself near the edge of a cliff. Looking over the edge she could see a deep ravine in the pale moonlight. Quickly she ran to her left away from the cliff and found her way back on the path.
"Where am I?" Nadia desperately asked herself.
The pain from her bruised knee was excruciating. Exhausted and out of breath, Nadia didn't know how much longer she could continue running. She found a tree and leaned up against it. She looked up to her right and saw a hill. Her face glowed with excitement.
"A bridge!" Nadia shouted out loud. Just beyond the winding hill ahead and off in the distance was an old wooden bridge stretching above a raging river. Her heart pounding with

excitement, Nadia gasped for breath and began limping as fast as she could up the hill.

"There she is. Let's get her!" One of the men screamed from off in the distance.

Breathing heavily, Nadia reached the top of the hill, sobbing out loud in fear and agonizing in pain. Then, just as she started down, her foot slipped and her body hit hard against the side of the hill. Struggling to get up, Nadia grabbed her knee, screaming in pain and with all of her might, she managed to stand up again.

The entrance to the bridge was just a few feet away. Nadia grabbed her leg and began wildly limping toward the bridge. Reaching the entrance, she looked over the railing. The bridge stretched out five hundred feet across a deep ravine carved out by a raging river. Nadia began limping across the bridge in pain.

"I have to make it!" Nadia cried out, her voice trembling with fear and panic.

Then as she looked back to see how close the two men were, suddenly the bridge was engulfed in a wall of flames. A literal ring of fire ignited all around her, engulfing the bridge and stretching out across to the other side. Nadia was surrounded by a wall of flames. She let out a terrifying scream and fell to her knees. Clasping both hands tightly around her head, Nadia tightly shut her eyes and began coughing from the intense smoke and flames.

"God help me! Please help me!" Nadia screamed in desperation.

Then suddenly, the intense roar of the flames stopped. There was a hush, an ominous silence. A sudden abrupt end. The wall of flames had mysteriously vanished and the smoke cleared from all around the bridge. Nadia stopped sobbing. She slowly released her hands from around her head and began to open her eyes. She was still kneeling on the bridge.

The flames and the smoke were gone. It was quiet and peaceful. Nadia felt a calmness and a peace that she had never experienced before, flooding her soul. Suddenly, the night sky was enveloped by a blinding white light. There was a hush and an utter quiet in the midst of the dazzling white light. The lights rested peacefully like a brilliant aura overtop the bridge.

Nadia tried to look up in the light, but it was too bright and much too brilliant. She held her hands out in front of her face and tried to speak, but could not utter a word in the presence of the light.

"Am I dead?" Nadia wondered to herself.

Then suddenly from the midst of the light, a being emerged and began to slowly walk toward Nadia as she knelt on the bridge. Nadia began to tremble in fear and awe as the being drew closer to her. The being stood over six feet tall and was dressed in a long white robe with a golden sash tied around its waist. As the being drew closer, Nadia gazed into its face. The being's eyes were penetrating and staring intently at her. Nadia had a strong sense that the being knew her every thought. She could see the being's hands. They were outstretched before her. The face of the being was dazzling white and beautiful.

A peace and a calmness overtook Nadia. She had never felt so secure and as safe as she did now. All of the fear, the frustration, and the pain had melted away from her and was replaced by an indescribable tranquility that she had never felt before.

Then the being spoke to her.

"Nadia."

Nadia was immediately filled with awe and reverence. She fell forward onto the floor of the bridge prostrating herself in worship.

"Nadia," the voice echoed in her head with such authority and yet such tenderness. "Nadia. Don't be afraid. I am now with you. You are safe."

Her eyes flooded with tears of joy, Nadia slowly rose up from the floor of the bridge.

"Sir," Nadia said with her voice trembling and her body shaking, "Who are you?"

The being reached down and gently touched her face.

"I am Jesus, Nadia. You are safe and you now belong to me."

Nadia stared in Jesus in utter astonishment.

"Jesus?" Nadia murmured out loud, her voice cracking and stuttering with fear.

Jesus smiled back at Nadia. His face was aglow with love and kindness. Jesus reached into his robe and removed a beautiful silver necklace and gently placed it around Nadia's neck. The necklace dropped to her chest and glowed brilliantly in the light.

"Go in peace Nadia. You now belong to me," Jesus said.

The moment Jesus adorned her neck with the beautiful silver necklace, Nadia was mesmerized and overwhelmed with a sense of belonging unlike anything that she had ever felt before. She felt like a princess whose prince had just whisked her off onto his horse and rode off with her into the sunset.

Then suddenly, the dazzling, brilliant white light disappeared like the snap of a finger and Nadia fell limp back onto the floor of the bridge. She slowly awakened to a fog and waves like a dry mist rolling all over her. Nadia stood up. She couldn't see anything but the denseness of the white mist surrounding her.

"Where was the bridge?" Nadia thought to herself. She reached out with her hands through the mist. Then Nadia heard, faintly in the distance, the beautiful music of a piano softly playing.

Nadia started to walk forward, edging her way closer to the sound of the music. Suddenly, the mist parted and revealed a doorway. Nadia could see people in the distance with their hands raised, singing along with the instruments that were playing. The mist now completely cleared away and revealed the inside of a Church with stain-glassed windows and lavish carpeting.

"Where am I?" Nadia nervously muttered to herself.

The people continued singing. Their faces beamed with joy.

"Why can't they hear me? Why can't they see me?" Nadia wondered to herself. Yet in spite of the mystery, Nadia was overwhelmed with a sense of peace.

As Nadia began to walk down the aisle, she noticed a tall, wooden door. Quickly, she ran to the door and turned the doorknob. The door swung open. The music abruptly stopped and Nadia found herself standing outside her wooden hut. She was finally home again.

"I'm home!" Nadia cried out. "Mother, Father, Zak! Where are you?"

The door to the wooden hut swung open revealing her father, mother and brother. She raced toward them, but they couldn't see or touch her. They acted as if Nadia wasn't there.

Nadia's Father, Rashid, shook his head in anger. "How could she do this?"

Fatima, Nadia's mother, laid her head on her husband's shoulder, bursting into tears. Zak, Nadia's little brother, ran over to his mother and put his arm around her waist. His face was filled with sadness and confusion.

"What's wrong with you?" Nadia cried out. "Why don't you look at me? Why can't you hear me?"

Frustrated and filled with fear, Nadia ran over to her parents but couldn't touch them. It was like an invisible wall stood between them.

Then abruptly, the heavy white mist rolled in once again and Nadia's parents disappeared from sight. Filled with fear and frustration and unable to understand what was happening to her, Nadia collapsed into the heavy mist and fell into a deep sleep.

What seemed like hours had only been a few short minutes. Nadia awoke from her deep sleep and stood up in the ominous white mist that had enveloped her. As she walked forward, the mist parted again for her to walk through. This time she found herself in a dimly lit room and what she saw perplexed her. Over in the corner of the room was a man sitting in a wheelchair and staring out the window. It was raining outside and the man sat quietly gazing out the window deep in thought.

"Sir, may I help you?" Nadia offered.

Nadia slowly walked toward the man. He didn't answer, but continued to stare out the window. Nadia realized that he couldn't hear her. She felt a deep sense of compassion for the man. He looked extremely lonely and depressed.

Then, just like the snap of a finger, Nadia was once again enveloped by the ominous white mist. Nadia felt sedated and out of touch with reality. Her mind was spinning, grasping for answers as to what was happening to her. Feeling helpless and out of control, Nadia tried to push her way again through the mist.

Then suddenly, just like before, the mist parted like someone pulling back a curtain and Nadia found herself in the middle of a crowd of people in a courtyard. There were hundreds of men and women gathered looking toward a wooden stage. Nadia's eyes focused upon something hanging above the stage. There was a tall, wooden plank hovering over the stage and dangling below was a noose.

"What!" Nadia shouted out in disbelief. The noose dangling from the wooden plank was coiled and tied into a circle. Nadia suddenly realized that this must be a public execution.

Suddenly the crow erupted with cheers and raised their fists in protest. Off to her left, Nadia watched as four men dressed in military uniforms, escorted a tall, brown-haired woman in between them. They were headed toward the wooden platform at the center of the stage. The crowd continued cheering. Some were laughing, while others were hurling insults and still others were spitting at the woman as she passed by them.

Nadia could feel her heart pounding. "No! no!" she yelled, pushing through the crowd of people. It seemed like a sea of people were between her and the wooden platform.

"No! no, you can't" Nadia screamed in protest. She continued to press her through the crowd trying desperately to reach the platform.

The escort arrived at the platform. The four men who had escorted her to the hanging noose backed off to the side. The woman, dressed in a long blue, pajama-type uniform was left all alone in the center of the platform. The crowd continued to tantalize her by hurling insults and throwing stones.

Then a man approached the woman and held up his hand to silence the crowd. The crowd grew silent. The woman stared straight ahead and mumbled a final prayer. Then the executioner approached the woman from behind her and placed a black velvet bag tightly over her head. There was a moment of silence and then he placed the nylon noose firmly around her neck.

It was all that Nadia could stand. She pushed her way through the crowd, racing toward the woman on the platform and then-

Nadia sat up abruptly in bed, screaming and crying, drenched in sweat and her heart racing.

"No! no," she screamed.

The room was dark except for the silhouette of the tree limbs shining through the window from the full moon outside. The wind was howling and there was an ominous tap of the tree limbs against Nadia's window.

    Nadia tried to compose herself. She touched her trembling body with her hands. She was really at home in her own bamboo cot. Zak was sound asleep right next to her. Slowly her breathing returned to normal and she wiped the tears away from her eyes. She fell back down upon her pillow and breathed a huge sigh of relief. It had been only a dream, a very bad dream.

.

CHAPTER TWO
A Worldwide Compassion

Jason Ridgeway turned his car onto interstate 70 and sped past the Historic St Louis Gateway Arch. He was in a great mood today! The sun was shining brightly and a hint of spring was in the air. He had the top down on his convertible and the wind was whipping through his hair

Today was a very special day. It was his birthday. He was officially 35 and enjoying the perks of the single life. But even more importantly, Jason had just returned from the oncologist. He received some incredible news. He was cancer-free! After one year of chemotherapy, his doctor was able to pronounce him cancer-free and in remission. Jason had been battling colon cancer for over a year and had been in and out of the hospital for treatment and tests. Through much prayer and patience, God had been faithful to Jason bringing him through a very difficult struggle.

Today Jason felt as if a huge weight had been lifted off of his shoulders. What a great birthday gift! But not only that but also he was on the way to Alpha and Omega bookstore to have his new cd put out on the shelf. After almost six months of production in the digitally computerized studio in his home, he had successfully completed all of the overdubs and was ready to have it distributed. Jason was the worship leader and musician at the 5,000 member church, Spirit and The Word Outreach Center, located in West St. Louis County. Ever since he was five years old, he had been playing guitar and writing his own songs. Back then, of course, he was writing and playing rock and roll songs and playing the local teen hang outs. However, when he became a Christian at age 17 while in high school, he began writing contemporary Christian worship songs based on the various psalms in the Bible. Jason loved to compose songs that challenged his listeners to live a Godly life and also songs that emphasized the nature and attributes of who God was.

Today was a day to be thankful to God. Jason turned his car onto Riverview Boulevard heading for the bookstore. He slipped in his latest cd and cranked up the volume to the title track, "living sacrifice." In a few short minutes Jason turned his car into a gravel driveway and arrived at Alpha Omega bookstore. He grabbed his briefcase, walked through the door and up to the customer service desk. Dan Wheeler, the bookstore manager, smiled and shook hands with Jason.

Jason laid the briefcase down on the counter and took a deep breath.

"Wow, what a day this has been!" Jason said.

"You have the new music?" Dan asked.

"Yes," Jason said, smiling opening up his briefcase. He picked out a few copies and handed them to Dan.

"I'm really excited about this one, "Jason said holding up one of the compact discs. His face was beaming with confidence. "This was so challenging to produce while taking treatments-Oh," Jason stopped and looked up at the ceiling with tears of joy flooding his eyes.

"Are you alright," Dan asked with concern in his voice.

"Yes!" Jason shouted, his face beaming with joy, "I'm in remission!"

"Fantastic Jason," Dan shouted back in agreement.

"God is good," Jason said, wiping the tears from his eyes. He took another deep breath.

"Oh," Dan said, reaching down underneath the counter. "You're going to need these for tomorrow night."

Jason reached out his hand as Dan gave him a stack of child sponsorship packets.

"Absolutely," Jason said, opening up his briefcase, "Worldwide Compassion is a great organization. " The child sponsorship packets contained pictures, names and information about children and their families from all over the world. Worldwide Compassion was a Christian humanitarian organization committed to providing clean running water, food, medical and spiritual aid to poverty-stricken children and their families regardless of race, creed or color.

"Dan," Jason said with passion building up in his voice as he leaned on the counter.

"There's nothing more precious to my heart than to see these children taken care of and that's why we're having a very special night at the church tomorrow, so that every family can become financially involved in the lives of these needy people."

Dan nodded his head in agreement.

"You're right. That's why here at the bookstore I'm just as passionate as you to give our customers the opportunity to get involved, too."

"The church is far too materialistic, "Jason pointed out," We need to show our faith and love more. We need to get involved."

"I agree," Dan said, shaking his head once again in agreement.

"I'm going to sing the title track," Jason continued, "from my new cd tomorrow night to make this point very personal to everyone. It's much more than a worship concert."

Jason took a deep breath and chuckled.

"Sorry I got on my soapbox again."

Dan laughed. "Not a problem Jason."

"Got To go, Thanks for everything." Jason shook hands with Dan. He picked up the briefcase and headed out the front door.

Jason got in the car, put his briefcase on the seat and then took another deep breath. He put the key in the ignition and started out the driveway heading for the most important stop of the day, visiting his Mother. Jason was headed for Oak Lawn Nursing Home to visit his Mother who had been a patient there for over two years. Mrs. Ridgeway was admitted there when Jason's father died after a long battle with alcoholism. Shortly after that, his mother was diagnosed with Alzheimer's disease. The disease had quickly progressed and now she was suffering in the final stages. Jason's Mother was the love of his life and he made sure that he visited her every single day. It was a short commute from the bookstore to the nursing home. Jason glanced at his watch. It was 4:45 p.m. He wanted to see his Mother before dinner time, so he turned his convertible onto 1-270 highway and got off on Dorsett road.

Pulling up to the entrance, Jason parked his car, got out and headed for the gift shop. He walked out with a half-dozen bright red roses and quickly arrived at the nurse's station.

"I'm here to see Mrs. Ridgeway," Jason said. The nurse smiled at him and escorted him into her room. Jason peeked in. His Mother was sitting in a wheelchair next to her bed. Her head was down resting against her chest. She was asleep. Jason tip-toed up to her and leaned down gently kissing her on top of her head of silver hair. Startled, she sat up abruptly in her wheelchair and opened up her eyes.

"Oh," she said smiling," Say, you know, you're kind of cute."

Jason half-chuckled, smiling back at her, realizing that this was the disease talking. She didn't recognize him, but probably thought that he was an old boyfriend from her teenage years.

"You're not bad looking yourself," he answered back. "I've got something for you, mom." Jason pulled out the roses from behind his back and handed them to his mother.

"Oh, how beautiful." His mother's eyes lighted up as she grabbed the flowers from his hand.

"That's not all," Jason said reaching over to the compact disc player on the window sill. He lifted the lid and put his new cd inside. "New music for you, mom." She smiled back at him, still fascinated by the flowers that she was holding tightly in her hands.

"How are you?" Jason asked as he sat down on the bed. His mother continued to stare at the flowers. Jason intently watched her. It was very painful to see how the disease was progressing.

"I used to grow these all the time," his mother said, clasping the flowers tightly in her hands. Her eyes stayed fastened upon them. Then she let them drop in her lap and suddenly she sat absolutely still with her head bowed down.

"Mom," Jason asked reaching over to touch her. "Are you alright?" She didn't answer but sat there motionless with her head against her chest.

"Mrs. Ridgeway, time for dinner. Are you hungry tonight?" The nurse walked in the room and Mrs. Ridgeway lifted up her head.

"Huh," she said in a startled tone and then looked over at Jason.

"Jason," she said with conviction in her voice," I didn't know you were here."

"Yeah mom, "he said smiling. He leaned over and kissed her on the forehead and got up from the bed.

"You have a good dinner. I've got to get going."

Jason said good-bye to the nurse and hurried out the door. He quickly got in his car and sat there for a moment. Tears began to well up in his eyes as he started the car. It was time to go home and call it a day.

In just a matter of minutes, Jason pulled into his driveway. Grabbing his briefcase, he found his keys and unlocked the front door. It felt so good to be home. He flung his briefcase across the bed in the computer room and got into some more comfortable clothing. After checking his e-mail, Jason grabbed something to eat from the kitchen and then headed for his "sacred space" where he could write, reflect, pray and just be alone with God after a long day. This was a very special room with no clocks, no computers and no TV's. There was a small table in the corner of the room with a chair. Hanging right above the table was a beautifully painted picture. It was a picture of sunrise at a boat dock with an old wooden walkway surrounded by a beautiful blue lake. It was a clam and serene picture that quieted Jason's soul. Painted right above the picture in white letters was "Be still and know that I am God." On the table was a lamp that was dimly lit to add to the peaceful mood of the room. In the center of the table was one of the most important things in Jason's life, his journal. Every night at this time, Jason would conclude the day by writing a short synopsis of it. Sitting comfortably in his chair with some soft instrumental music playing in the background, Jason slowly collected his thoughts before he could start writing. He paused for a moment and then began writing.

Friday, September 7, 2004

If there is one word I could use to describe this day, it would be grateful. God I am grateful to you for the cancer being in remission. You have been faithful to me and answered my prayers. What can I say but thank you for your mercy and compassion? This day reminds me of the song I've been working on "I'm so grateful I belong to you. You heal all my hurts and pains and heartaches that I go through. And your mercy's like the morning dew. I'm so grateful I belong to you. "

Jason put down the pen and rubbed his eyes. It had been a long and busy day and he was tired. Tomorrow was going to be even more challenging with the special event at the church.

Just as he rose up to go to bed, Jason stopped and looked over at his briefcase. "Oh I forgot," he muttered to himself. He reached over to pick out a child sponsorship packet for himself. The rest of the packets were going to be distributed to the families at the church tomorrow night. Going through all of the packets, Jason picked out one and laid it back on the table. He looked down at the picture of a beautiful young girl with brown hair and blue eyes standing in front of a wooden hut. He began to read.

"Hello, my name is Nadia Mustafa. I am a Muslim. I am 15 years old. I live here in this village with my family in Dhaka, Bangladesh."

Jason continued to read and was moved with compassion over Nadia and her family's plight with poverty. It would be a privilege to sponsor her on a monthly basis so that her life could be rescued from the vicious cycle of poverty.

Removing his glasses, Jason carefully laid them down beside Nadia's picture. He turned out the lamp on the table and headed for bed. He needed a good night's sleep for the big day at church tomorrow.

CHAPTER THREE
A Living Sacrifice

"...k, check," Jason said tapping the microphone. The big ... at the church had finally arrived and Jason was going through a typical sound check. He walked over to his computer and tested the power point presentation on the big screen above. Everything seemed to be in working order. The other band members had arrived and were starting to set up their equipment.

Walking down from the stage, Jason caught a glimpse of his good friend Robbie coming toward him in his high-speed wheelchair. "Hey," Jason yelled with a look of glee in his eyes. They quickly high-fived each other. Robbie had become a paraplegic after suffering a spinal injury in a bicycle accident. Since then, Jason had been busy teaching Robbie how to play guitar. Robbie was always excited to see Jason and was full of questions on how to play guitar chords.

"Hey Jason, what are you going to be playing tonight?," Robbie asked.

Jason reached into his coat pocket and pulled out his new cd. He handed it to Robbie. "Awesome," Robbie said with his eyes lighting up.

"The band and I will be playing the title track, Living sacrifice."

Robbie gave a look of approval and then looked up to Jason.

"Will you come over and teach me the chords?" Robbie asked. Jason knelt down beside Robbie's wheelchair and looked up at him smiling.

"You bet I will." Jason stood up and gave Robbie's mother a big hug. "Hi mom," he said. Robbie's mother hugged him back.

"Got to go, God bless, "Jason said in haste and then proceeded to walk toward the stage. The church auditorium was quickly filling up. It was 7:15 p.m. The lights dimmed and a bank of lights illuminated the stage. There was hush and the people quickly quieted down as Pastor Willoughby stepped up to the microphone.

"Good evening and welcome to Spirit and The Word Outreach. Tonight is a very special night so let's begin with a word of prayer. "The auditorium grew quiet and Pastor Willoughby began.

"Father, we come to you in the precious name of Jesus and praise you for everything you have provided for us in Christ. Please pour out your blessings upon the music and the ministry that we will hear tonight. Give us a heart of worship and a heart of compassion for the millions of starving children and their families all over the world. This we ask in Christ's name, amen." Amen's resounded all over the auditorium and Pastor Willoughby left the stage and sat down in the front row. Jason stepped up behind the microphone with his band joining him in the background. He looked out over the mass of people. There was an ominous reflection from the blue lights over his fender Stratocaster guitar. Jason reached over to the table and picked up his Bible.

"The Apostle Paul admonishes us in Romans Chapter Twelve, vers1-2. " There was the sound of people turning the page simultaneously as Jason paused waiting for the people.

"Therefore, I urge you brothers, in view of God's mercy, to offer up your bodies as living sacrifices holy and pleasing to God, this is your spiritual service of worship. Do not conform any longer to the pattern of this world, but be transformed by the renewing of your mind. Then you will be able to test and approve what God's will is, his good, pleasing and perfect will."

Jason reached over and put his Bible back on the table. "This is what this song is all about." Jason began to softly strum his guitar, playing the opening chords with the keyboard player slowly blending in with him. The overhead video board lighted up with the first verse of the song. There was a slight pause after the opening chords as Jason began to softly sing the first verse.

I offer up myself as a Living Sacrifice. I want to be holy and acceptable in your sight. I want to love you Lord with all my heart and soul and might. I want to be like Jesus, I want to do what is right.

People began to stand up, some raising their hands in worship and others quietly singing along. Jason continued.

I lay down my life as an offering to you. Please melt my stony heart. Please cleanse it through and through. I lay my Isaacs down. I give them back to you. I want to be a living sacrifice for you

Some people touched and convicted by the lyrics began to kneel down beside the pews. Tears began to flow down the faces of some people and others began to sing louder with passion.

And I worship you as a living sacrifice of praise. I'm bowing at your altar; my hands and heart are raised. And I'll love you Lord all the rest of my days.

The song now began to build up to the chorus and Jason glanced back to his band with a musical cue.

I want to be a living Sacrifice. I'm bowing at your altar. I'm laying down my life. I surrender all my plans and dreams to you. I lay down all my Isaacs. I give them back to you.

The emotions in the auditorium intensified in response to the chorus. People clapped along and sang with conviction and passion. Jason's voice grew louder with emphasis. Now everyone was standing up and responding to the song.

And I live to worship you. Yes I live to worship you.

The band reached a crescendo on the last part of the verse and the song ended amidst a loud roar of cheering and many amen's. Just as the cheering from the audience was starting to subside, a young well-dressed lady approached the stage and picked up a lone microphone positioned in the corner. The microphone was strategically placed there for anyone who believed that they had a prophetic word from The Lord and wanted to share it publicly. Spirit and Word Outreach Church welcomed the display of spiritual gifts. Each prophecy was taken seriously and put to the test of Scripture to avoid error and confusion.

The church audience became quiet as young lady took a deep breath, relaxed and put the microphone up to her lips. Her body was trembling and her lips were shaking. She opened her mouth and began to speak.

"I am about to tear down all of the strongholds of religion among the Muslim countries, saith the Lord. My Spirit is about to open hardened hearts, to satisfy the hunger and thirst of every Muslim man, every Muslim woman and every Muslim child. My heart is moved with compassion to bring deliverance and salvation and freedom. My Spirit is about to move in Iran, In Iraq, in Bangladesh and in Saudi Arabia. I will use this Church to fulfill my holy purposes, saith The Lord.

I am raising up a young warrior and I will bring her among you. I will anoint her with the fire of Esther and the boldness of David to do mighty exploits for me to break down the strongholds in Iran and in Bangladesh. You must welcome her, bless her, equip her and train her and send her out in my name. I will use this church to send her out as a sheep amongst wolves. So fast and pray and prepare your hearts to reach the Muslim countries. I will bring freedom, Salvation and a revival amongst my Churches in the midst of great persecution. I am about to do a great thing so that your will know I am the Sovereign God of the universe, saith The Lord."

The young lady finished and put the microphone back on the stand and walked off the stage. No one moved or said a word. Jason looked over to Pastor Willoughby. He had a stunned look on his face. This had been one of the most powerful prophecies ever given at the church. Everyone sat still and pondered the prophecy, challenged by the powerful word they had just heard. Finally pastor Willoughby came up to the microphone.

"Thank you young lady for obeying God, "Pastor Willoughby paused for a moment.

"God has spoken powerfully to us tonight, first in music and now in this word. I have only one response: Lord, we humble ourselves before you and will obey what you have told us, amen." Amen's could be heard throughout the audience and then there was a rousing applause, as people stood to respond to the word. As the applause subsided, Jason walked over to his computer to begin the video presentation about Worldwide Compassion. All eyes were fixed on the overhead video screen. A picture with the Worldwide Compassion logo dissolved onto the screen and Jason walked over to the side of the stage wearing a microphone head set fastened around his jaws.

"Tonight in keeping with the song I performed earlier and also with the powerful, prophecy that we heard, we have an opportunity to put our faith into action as "living sacrifices." The next picture faded onto the screen showing a poor family standing in front of a wooden hut in Brazil.

"This is a typical scene," Jason said, "of the average family struggling with poverty. Worldwide Compassion comes into a typical village like this one and transforms the dirty infected water into clean drinking water."

The next slide showed two children in line at deep water well in a village.

"Once the water has been cleansed, families like this can safely drink the water without the fear of disease."

The next slide showed a team of Physicians attending to the physical needs of local villagers.

"Worldwide Compassion provides qualified doctors who give the basics of health care, including inoculations against deadly diseases."

The next slide showed some children sitting in a classroom with a teacher instructing them.

"Worldwide Compassion gives children a chance to get a decent education so that they can realize their dreams and break free from the vicious cycle of poverty. They also fund people who want to learn skills and trades, like carpentry or construction of churches like the one that we see here."

The screen went blank and the presentation had come to an end. The house lights came back on. "You have in your folders," Jason said, "a child- sponsorship package. I ask that you prayerfully consider a monthly child sponsorship that will make a tremendous difference in the life of the child. God has placed this beautiful boy or girl in your lap tonight and is asking you to become a "living sacrifice" for them. Thank you and God bless you."

There was a brief applause. The evening had come to an end. People stayed around for fellowship, while Jason began packing up his guitar. Then, just as Jason was starting to leave, Robbie showed up by his side in his wheelchair.

"Awesome song Jason," Robbie exclaimed.

"Thanks Robbie," Jason smiled and said, high-fiving him. Jason stepped down off of the stage and ran into Pastor Willoughby. The Pastor had a strange and perplexed expression on his face. Jason stopped and walked over to him.

"What are you thinking, Pastor," Jason asked. Pastor Willoughby gave Jason an intense look.

"I have a feeling that our lives are about to drastically change!"

CHAPTER FOUR
A CRISIS OF FAITH

The first few rays of dawn were peeping over the horizon and beaming down upon a remote village outside Dhaka, Bangladesh at the other side of the world.

Nadia Mustafa had awakened at five am as was her daily custom for prayer before she made the long walk to school with her little brother Zak. She stood in front of the mirror rubbing her tired eyes. She hadn't sleep well last night because of some unusual troubling dreams that had kept her awake.

Nadia and her family made their home here in the Radanovich Village
Project located 25 miles outside of Dhaka, the capital city of Bangladesh. The village project was part of the ongoing work of Worldwide Compassion, a Christian humanitarian organization providing the basics of life for those families living below the poverty line. Over 45% of the people of Bangladesh suffered below the poverty line with ½ of all children struggling with malnutrition. Frequent cyclones and floods raged through Bangladesh causing crop destruction and devastating farmlands creating situations where poverty becomes a way of life. Worldwide Compassion responded to the needs of the people by cleaning up the infected water system and providing deep tube wells to stop the spread of harmful disease.

The Mustafa's were among twelve other families that inhabited the tiny village that stretched out over a 1/4 mile. Nadia, her father Rashid, her mother Fatima and her brother Zak huddled together in a small three-room wooden and bamboo hut with a tin roof. They had lived together with the curse of poverty all of their life, barley having enough food and money to survive. However, when Worldwide Compassion came along, their lives began to change for the better and be enriched. Rashid was going to school now every day to learn a carpentry trade. Nadia and her brother

Zak now both had adequate school supplies so they could attend school and get a good education. While Nadia and Zak were at school, Fatima spent the day doing household chores and preparing meals for her family. Life was difficult, but now they had a chance to break free from the cycle of poverty and realize their dreams.

Nadia daily witnessed the devastation of poverty and saw how it made life so difficult for her and other families in the village. She was determined to do something about it. She wanted to be a nurse and work in the clinics like the ones here in the village and bring hope and healing to those in need. Everyday she watched Jeremy, a Christian representative from Worldwide Compassion play with the children at the playground. She was impressed with his genuine warmth and compassion and desired to be just like him. Nadia and Jeremy had many long talks and although she was not a Christian like him, she respected his kindness and warmth that he demonstrated to the village children.

Nadia had grown up as a Muslim. She had been one all of her life. Her father and mother had taught her everything that she knew. They were orthodox Muslims believing strictly in the five pillars of Islam. Nadia daily recited the foundational creed of Islam," There is no God but Allah and Muhammad is his messenger." Allah was the only true God and judge over all of mankind who had sent Muhammad as His final prophet to restore the truth of His message. In Islam, Jesus was considered only to be a prophet alongside of Muhammad bringing the true message of Allah to mankind.

Nadia also participated in one of the most important pillars of the faith: prayer. Prayer was central to her life as she dedicated herself to spending five times a day from sunrise to sunset in this pillar. Nadia was also taught to be involved in almsgiving. Even though they were poor, the Mustafa's would share what they had with everyone else in the village.

The next pillar was fasting. Living on a daily diet of rice, fish and vegetables, Nadia and her family observed the yearly fast of Ramadan occurring on the tenth month of the Islamic calendar. From dawn until dusk, they fasted and prayed reading a chapter together from the Quran. The purpose of the fast was self-denials and breaking sinful habits so they were prepared to meet Allah on judgment day. The reward for fasting was a complete forgiveness of all sins, wiping the slate clean before Allah.

The last pillar of Islam was the personal pilgrimage to Mecca, the birthplace of Muhammad. Muslims were required to take this journey at least once in their lifetime if they could afford it and were physically able. Nadia wanted to visit this place one day to worship Allah and pay honor to Muhammad. However with the circumstances the way they were, Nadia doubted this would ever happen, unless Allah took pity on her and her family and bestowed His blessings upon them.

Standing in front of the mirror, Nadia was preparing for the first prayer time of the day just after sunrise. Nadia stood 5'9" inches tall. She had beautiful curly brown hair and deep blue eyes. She had a smooth olive and Sunkist colored facial complexion that was typical of most teenage girls living in Bangladesh.

It was very important to spiritually prepare for this time of prayer. Before prayer, Nadia had to purify herself through what is called ablution. This involved washing her hands up to the wrists 3 times, rinsing out her mouth 3 times and washing her face and feet. Without doing this she was taught, Allah would not honor her prayers.

Being quiet and careful not wake Zak, Nadia reached down and picked up her hijab, a veil covering her hair that she wore during prayer time. Nadia wore this during prayer time and also for modesty reasons. The hijab was a protection for women, along with the burqa, to keep men from gazing upon them in lustful and sexual ways. To protect them from this abuse and degradation, the Muslim women wore this type of clothing to conceal their full beauty and also to make them aware that Allah judges their hearts and not their appearance.

Carefully placing the hijab over her hair, Nadia reached down underneath her above-ground bamboo cot where she slept and picked up her slippers and a tiny prayer rug. She tip-toed quietly past Zak. She knew that when she got home from school, Zak would be pestering her to play soccer with him. Nadia loved playing with her little brother, but wasn't very crazy about being the soccer goalie for him and absorbing all of his wild and up-close kicks.

"I will be back in time for school," Nadia said.

Her mother nodded and smiled. She walked over and hugged her father, Rashid who was also preparing for prayer time.

"I love you Daddy, "Nadia said smiling as she walked out the door of the hut. Nadia was on her way to her favorite sacred spot for morning prayer. She looked forward to daily going to this sacred secret prayer hideaway to spend 45 minutes alone with Allah. The sacred spot was a tiny piece of ground surrounded by trees next to a small creek about a ¼ mile away from the village. It was a peaceful and quiet place where you could hear the relaxing sound of the water gently flowing over the rocks amidst the playful noise of chirping birds. Nadia loved this place where she could pour out her heart in prayer to Allah and at the same time be connected to the beauty of nature.

The sun was shining brightly as Nadia began her walk to her secret hideaway. Some of the villagers were up early as well carrying their jars on their way to the deep tube wells to get some clean water. A little boy was chasing his sister and almost ran into Nadia. She abruptly stopped as they ran circles around her feet. Nadia laughed at them and then kept walking up the path toward a grove of trees. The bright sun was glistening through the trees and splashing on Nadia's face. The sound of kids playing in the village slowly began to fade behind her as she entered a forest path. Nadia loved the outdoors. The smell of fresh air and the sound of chirping birds brought a calmness to her soul. She took a deep breath and continued slowly walking along the path and gazing at the beautiful scenery that was all around her. In the distance Nadia heard the gentle sound of water streaming over the rocks. She got off the path and came upon a grove of trees lining the edge of the creek. She ducked down under some tree limbs that shaded her from the bright sunlight. She was only five feet from the bank of the creek.

Putting her Quran down beside her, Nadia opened up her prayer rug and carefully spread it out next to the trunk of the tree. Nadia could feel the soft touch of a gentle breeze. The sunlight was obscured by the tree limbs, but there was enough illumination for her to see the pages of the Quran.

"This is perfect," she whispered to herself standing next to the tree trunk. It was a beautiful day with the sun beginning to rise up in the sky. Nadia had enough time to pray before returning back home for breakfast and walking to school with Zak. Nadia stood still and took a deep breath. She closed her eyes to focus on Allah shutting out everything else that was around her. A gentle breeze blew against her hijab and the strands of hair that were protruding out. She raised both of her hands to the side of her head.

"All praise to Allah," Nadia declared out loud. She repeated this again. Next she changed the structure of her prayer and declared," Allah you are great." Nadia said this slowly, pronouncing every word very carefully until the words resonated perfectly from her lips. Nadia paused. Next she folded her hands over her lower chest with her right hand over her chest. The posture of prayer was important for every Muslim and yet even more important was the intent of the heart. Nadia now continued to the next phase of prayer by reciting out loud Surah 1 from the Quran.

"In the name of Allah, the most gracious, most merciful. Praise be to Allah, the cherisher and sustainer of the world. Most gracious, most merciful, master of the Day of Judgment, this do we-"

Suddenly, in the middle of her prayer her mind went completely blank. Nadia stumbled through her words and wasn't able to finish reciting the Surah. This was strange. This had never happened before. With her eyes still closed, Nadia began again.

"In the name of-"

It happened again. Her mind went completely blank. "What is happening" Nadia wondered to herself. She briefly opened up eyes and looked around her and then closed them again. Only this time, an image flashed on the screen of her mind's eye. She found herself kneeling on a bridge, when suddenly a figure approached her. His face was dazzling white and beautiful. He reached down to Nadia and gently touched her face.

"Nadia, don't be afraid, I am Jesus."

Nadia quickly opened up her eyes in fear and gasped. Then she remembered. This was the dream that she had last night. In desperation Nadia fell forward and prostrated herself on the prayer rug. Trying to suppress the vision in her mind, she cried out," In the name of Allah-"she couldn't finish the next sentence. She had a disturbing feeling of utter emptiness. Nadia struggled to continue. Her prayer seemed so rigid and ritualistic.

When she closed her eyes, once again the vision returned to her mind. She saw Isa (Jesus in Arabic) again! He came towards her and gently placed a silver necklace around her neck. Nadia shrieked and then closed her eyes. "Why is this happening to me?" She tried to stand up, but just then, just like in the dream, Nadia was overcome with a tremendous sense of belonging. She lay prostrate on the rug overwhelmed with such peace that she did not want to move.

Nadia was awakened by the the chirping of birds above her head in the tree limbs. She slowly rose up and gazed up toward the sky. The sun was shining brightly through the tree limbs that were gently swaying in the breeze. Everything looked different to Nadia. Everything seemed so peaceful. Nadia had a deep sense of tranquility as she stood up. The trees, the sky, the bright shining sun, filled her soul with such a profound sense of awe and wonder.

Then reality seemed to rob her sense of awe. "I'm late!" Nadia cried out. She grabbed her prayer rug and Quran and started running back down the path toward home.

When Nadia arrived back at the hut, Fatima was putting some rice and vegetables on the table for their breakfast. The kitchen consisted of a small wooden table in the center of the hut with a string of lights above powered by a central generator for the entire village.

"You're late," Fatima said As Nadia hurried past her to sit down. Zak was now awake and sitting down at the table.

"Did you have a good prayer time?' Fatima asked.

"Yes mother, "Nadia said nervously as she sat down. Fatima noticed the unusual expression on Nadia's face. Rashid sat down next to Fatima at the table.

"Nadia, would you say the prayer for blessing?" Rashid asked glancing over at Nadia. There was pause. Nadia looked down at the table.

"Nadia," Rashid asked again.

"No, Daddy, no," Nadia nervously said, stuttering," Could you please say the prayer?" Rashid gave Nadia a puzzled look and then bowed his head in prayer.

"Allah, most gracious and most merciful. We ask that you bless our meal this morning."

It was a short prayer and everyone began eating. Zak looked over at his sister. He could sense that there was something different about her this morning. Nadia hurried through her breakfast and quickly got up from the table.

"Zak, we need to go!" Nadia said grabbing her schoolbooks. Nadia quickly kissed her mother and father goodbye, grabbed Zak by his arm and hurried out the door. Rashid and Fatima glanced at each with puzzled looks on their faces.

Nadia didn't say a word to Zak all the way to school. Arriving at school, Nadia said hi to her teacher and went to sit down at her desk amongst the other students without saying a word. Zak went next door to another building for the ten-year old age group.

It was hard for Nadia to concentrate all day at school. She kept remembering the experience that she had during prayer. She was frustrated and confused and needed answers. Then as she looked down at her desk, a thought crossed her mind. "I need to talk to someone, but who..." Nadia was deep in thought. She stared down at the piece of paper lying on her desk. The thought of journaling had never crossed her mind until now, but she didn't have a journal. "Oh well, I can start with this piece of paper," Nadia reasoned with herself. As she began to write, she felt an intense connection with herself and the piece of paper as if she were pouring out her heart to her best friend.

September 15, 2004

Dear Sarah (Nadia decided to call her imaginary pen-pal Sarah. Sarah was a real person, her best girlfriend who had died from pneumonia a year ago)

How I wish you were really here Sarah so I could talk to you. I miss you so much. Sarah you know me so well and I can trust you.

You know how hard I try to please Allah and follow the teachings of Islam. I want to be worthy on Judgment Day so I can go to paradise. I'm afraid. I'm confused. I've been having dreams now during prayer time, Isa is appearing to me. He touches my face and puts a necklace around my neck. Why would he do this Sarah? Isa is only a prophet. I want to ask him, but I'm afraid of offending Allah and committing the sin of shirk. Allah is the only true God and he would be angry if I talked to Isa. Please help—

Nadia stopped writing as her teacher approached her desk.

"Nadia, what are you doing? I asked you a geography question and you didn't answer. You seem like you're in another world."

Nadia quickly brushed the piece of paper aside to try and hide it.

"I'm sorry Mrs. Edmonds. I'll try to pay more attention, "Nadia said with a sheepish grin on her face. Mrs. Edmonds nodded and then turned to the rest of the class.

"School is over for today. Have a nice rest of the day and I will see everyone tomorrow at 8:00am"

Nadia smiled at Mrs. Edmonds, grabbed her piece of paper and quickly walked out of the door.

Nadia and Zak walked home together after another long day at school. Once again there was no talking between them. Nadia was deep in thought and anxious to get home so she could resume her new-found journaling hobby. As they entered the village, Nadia stopped and stooped down looking Zak in the eyes.

"Do you mind, little brother, if we postpone any soccer playing for today? I have something important to do." Zak sighed and gave Nadia a disappointing look.

"Do you promise to play tomorrow?"

"I promise."

Zak cracked a smile and Nadia gave him a hug. Then, just as they turned toward the hut, Rochelle, a special translator for Worldwide Compassion met up with them.

"Hi, are you Nadia Mustafa?" Rochelle asked.

Nadia stopped and gave Rochelle a puzzled look. Rochelle was speaking Bengali. Nadia was very impressed.

"Yes mam, I am and this is my brother Zak, "Nadia said.

"I have a surprise for you today," Rochelle began, "here is a letter from an American gentleman who has agreed to be a monthly financial sponsor for you." Rochelle handed Nadia the letter. Nadia's eyes lighted up for joy.

"Mom, Dad," she yelled running to the hut. Rashid and Fatima rushed out the front door to see what all the excitement was about. "Hello, Mr. & Mrs. Mustafa, "Rochelle said. "I'm here from Worldwide Compassion and I have a letter for Nadia and for you as well, from an American gentleman who will be financially sponsoring you on a monthly basis."

Rashid looked over to Fatima with a smile of gratitude.

"Thank you, thank you," Rashid said.

"The letter was written in English. I have a copy of it for you in Bengali," Rochelle pointed out. She opened the envelope and pulled out the letter to read it. Nadia and Zak drew closer to Rochelle as she began to read.

Dear Nadia:

My name is Jason Ridgeway. I am an American living in St. Louis, Missouri. I would like to be your friend. Let me tell you a little bit about myself. I am a Christian. I play the guitar, write songs and lead worship at my church. Two weeks ago, we had a special service at my church and many families like me said yes to monthly sponsor families just like yours. I am sending you a picture of me, a picture of the famous St. Louis Arch and a picture of my church. I want to know all about you Nadia and

your family as well. Next time I'll be sending you and your brother Zak some pencils for school. You are in my prayers.
Your friend, Jason

"That is so nice, so wonderful," Fatima said wiping a tear away from her eye. Rashid nodded in agreement with a warm smile on his face.

"Sounds like a very nice man," Rochelle said as she pulled out the pictures that Jason had sent. Nadia ran over and grabbed the pictures out of Rochelle's hands. Zak pressed up against her to look at the pictures. Nadia
was very touched by what Jason had said and was glad that someone would be willing to help her.

Chapter Five
The Letter

It was a crisp and cool October morning in St. Louis. The trees were shedding their coat of colorful leaves marking the beginning of the autumn season. Every Saturday morning Jason invited Robbie over to his house for his weekly guitar lessons. For Robbie, this was the one day of the week that he really looked forward to. Robbie's parents had divorced two years ago when he was only nine years old. It had been a very difficult thing for Robbie to accept until Jason came along. They had been very close friends for two years and the fear and frustration that once had plagued Robbie was slowly disappearing.

Jason stood behind Robbie's wheelchair and helped him place his fingers on top of the strings of his acoustic guitar.

"Wow, that's a stretch!" Robbie complained as Jason helped him press down on the strings.

"The d-minor chord is a tricky little placement for the fingers," Jason pointed out, "But you'll need to learn this if you want to play my song."

Robbie looked over his shoulder and gave Jason a sarcastic look.

"No pain, no gain, right," Robbie said. Jason laughed.

"You've got it, pal. Let's take a break."

Jason walked over to his chair and picked up his acoustic guitar. Robbie watched with excitement and enthusiasm as Jason began strumming a few chords.

"Is that a new song," Robbie asked.

"Yeah, I'm working on a new song. It's called Reflection. I'll play and sing the chorus for you." Jason looked back down at his guitar and began singing and playing the chorus of the song.

We are a reflection of the Father's love and affection. A mirror that's reflecting the wonders of your Grace. We're on the way to perfection through your discipline and correction. A trophy of your affection. A reflection of your face.

Robbie looked over at Jason giving him a look of approval.

"Those are awesome words. They have a lot of meaning," Robbie said. Jason put down his guitar and looked intently at Robbie.

"Every song I write I try to have a Biblical message that points people to God's Grace and how he molds and shapes us through the good and the bad times."

Robbie nodded his head and stared down at his legs for a moment.

"Sometimes I get upset and ask God why you let this happen to me." The tone in Robbie's voice changed from excitement to fear. The countenance of his face changed to gloom and Robbie was grasping for the right words to express himself. Jason reached over and put his arm around him.

"I feel that way sometimes too, Robbie. I sometimes ask God why my mom has to go through this horrible disease."

Robbie could see Jason's face tightening up with frustration. There was a pause and Jason nodded his head and looked back intently at Robbie.

"Then I realize that God doesn't ask me to figure it out or to understand, but to simply trust Him. He is in control. He is sovereign."

Robbie's face glowed with approval and his eyes became a little misty.

"Yeah, yeah, I guess you're right."

Just then the phone rang and Jason got up to go into the kitchen. He was only gone for a few seconds and he returned wearing a blank expression on his face.

"What's wrong Jason?" Robbie asked.

Jason stood completely still. He was deep in thought, staring ahead with a confused look on his face. He turned to look at Robbie.

"We have to call it a day. The nursing home just called and wants me to come right away. There's been a change in my mother's condition."

Robbie's mother was quickly notified to come pick him up. She arrived in a matter of minutes. Jason gave Robbie a tight hug in his wheelchair and walked with them out the front door. The autumn leaves were slowly drifting to the ground and the air was becoming chilly as Jason hurried to get into his car. Jason was trying not to panic. This was a huge struggle for him. Almost all of his teenage years, he struggled with agoraphobia and panic attacks. This was a common problem that millions of people suffered with. Anxiety attacks had paralyzed him with fear and nearly caused him to be a recluse. Fear and worry had held him captive until Jason received Biblical counseling and was able to get his feelings under control.

"I love you mom," Jason whispered out loud as he turned his car onto the highway. He watched his speed limit and reassured himself that God was in control. After all, he thought, isn't that what he had just got through telling Robbie? Jason was determined to let God's word transform his thinking and not to allow circumstances to dominate his feelings and emotion. Turning into the entrance of the nursing home, Jason quickly found a parking space.

"God, I ask for your comfort and your peace to flood my mind," Jason prayed, please fill my mom with your grace and peace at this time."

Jason got out of the car and hurried to the front entrance and found his way to the nurse's station. Nurse Jenkins was already there waiting for his arrival.

"How is my mom?" Jason anxiously asked. Nurse Jenkins gave him a reassuring look.

"Things are alright for now, but your mom's condition is slowly deteriorating, Jason."

Jason gave a worried look. Nurse Jenkins began walking with him toward his mother's room.

"She has not been eating well and she's been sleeping a lot more than usual. This is typical when the disease is progressing. We began to notice this yesterday and when your mother wouldn't wake up for breakfast, we wanted you to know right away."

Jason stopped walking and gave Nurse Jenkins a panicked stare.

"Is my mom going to die soon?'

"That's hard to say, Jason. Alzheimer's is very unpredictable. If this trend continues for a prolonged time, say, 4 or 5 days, then it could be soon, but I believe she will wake up soon and will probably be hungry."

Jason looked a little relieved.

"Can I see her?"

"Yes, of course," Nurse Jenkins said. Jason quietly walked into his mother's room. He saw the empty wheelchair in the corner of the room next to the bed. The shades were drawn and the room was dimly lit. Mrs. Ridgeway lay quietly asleep on the bed. Jason pulled up a chair next to his mother's bed and gently gripped her hand, hoping that she would open up her eyes. He softly uttered a prayer and held tightly his mother's hand.

"Mom, I love you," Jason softly said trying to hold back the tears. He held her hand and continued praying for a few more minutes. Satisfied that she wasn't going to wake up yet, Jason slowly got up and walked over to the nurse's station.

"Thank you so much for informing me. Please call me when my mom wakes up." Jason said to Nurse Jenkins. Nurse Jenkins smiled at Jason.

"Of course, don't worry," she said touching his hand.

Jason turned and headed out the door.

The postal carrier was just leaving the mailbox as Jason pulled into the driveway. Jason yelled hello and walked up to the mailbox. "Credit card bill, electric bill," Jason muttered as he fingered through the mail on his way through the front door. Then one letter stood out amongst the rest of the mail.

"Worldwide Compassion," Jason muttered to himself as he closed the door behind him. Jason set the other letters down on the kitchen table as he sat down in the chair. He reached for his glasses and put them on. There was a two-page insert letter on the inside written in Bengali. Jason's eyes lit up with interest as he began to read the letter inside that was translated into English.

"Oh," Jason said, It's a letter from Nadia," the young girl he was sponsoring. Jason placed the letter written in Bengali next to the one translated into English. He began reading.

> October 13, 2004
>
> Dear Jason:
>
> My name is Nadia Mustafa. I am fifteen years old and I live here in Bangladesh with my parents and my brother Zak in this tiny wooden shack. I am very thankful that you are my sponsor. In your letter you asked if you could be my friend. I would be very happy to be your friend. You said you were a Christian. I am a Muslim. I have been one all of my life. I hope that does not keep you from being my friend.
>
> Our life here is very simple. My father is learning to be a carpenter at trade school. My mother works hard to take care of us. Someday, I want to be a nurse and help all of the people that are suffering around me.
>
> I have a question for you, Mr. Ridgeway. Since you are a Christian, you would know more about this than I do. As a Muslim, I worship Allah as the one true God. Allah is great and there is no one like Him. Lately, I have been having some very strange dreams and in them Isa appears in each of them and tells me not to be afraid. As a Muslim, we believe Isa is only a prophet like Muhammad was. My question is this, Why is Isa appearing to me in my dreams? I hope since you are a Christian, you could help me find out why. Thank you for your time, Mr. Ridgeway. I am happy to be your friend. Here is a picture for you. Please write back soon.   Nadia

Jason put down the letter and removed his glasses. He was deeply touched to the core of his being. He was not expecting such a warm and personal letter with such a question. He expected a very general letter and a paragraph or two about their home life, but this had truly taken him by surprise. Nadia's letter had warmed Jason's heart. Today had been a difficult day with his mother's condition worsening, but this letter had rejuvenated his heart and soul. Jason was moved with compassion for Nadia that she would reach out to trust someone she barely knew with such an intimate question.

"I must write her back right away," Jason reasoned within himself.

Then he stopped and pondered the situation carefully. "What if," he reasoned to himself," Nadia is searching for answers, but her parents and her brother are unaware of this. I better not send a letter to hear and they find out what we're talking about. This would cause great strife and contention for her."

Jason paused and thought for a moment.

There is another way; he thought to himself, it would be more involved, but safer for Nadia's sake. Jason decided to personally deliver the Letter to Nadia himself. This would involve contacting a representative from Worldwide Compassion and arranging for a visit to Bangladesh. It would take a couple of weeks to obtain a passport and make all of the arrangements.

Jason reflected on the heavy responsibility and the delicate privilege he had been given. He was not interested in engaging Nadia in an intellectual, apologetic debate over Islam vs. Christianity, but instead he desired to respectfully communicate the wonder and awe of who Christ was. Christ, according to Jason, is the one who satisfies the spiritual thirst and hunger of every single human being, the one who brings fulfillment to the restless heart. If Nadia was searching for answers, than Jason was prepared to present the beauty and the love of Christ, those qualities which have drawn countless people for over 2,000 years. Jason desired to answer Nadia's question by helping her discover who Jesus is. It was now a little past 7:30 pm. Jason left the kitchen and returned to his "sacred space" to compose a response to Nadia. This was the joy of his life, telling people who his songs were all about. Jesus was the treasure of his life and Jason wanted Nadia to discover him in a very personal way too, just as he had done many years before.

In his customary fashion, Jason turned on some soft, instrumental music, dimmed the lights and sat down at the table.

> *Friday, October 27, 2004*
> *Dear God,*
> *Today, I've been struggling with fear and panic attacks again when I learned about mom's condition. I opened the door again to fear. Forgive me God for taking my eyes off of you. I know you are in control of everything. I know you will take care of mom like you always do.*
>
> *Thank you God for blessing me with the awesome privilege of sharing Christ with Nadia. It boggles my mind that in your providence you're giving me the privilege of telling her about you when she lives on the other side of the world! You're amazing God, so amazing!*

While it was 7:30 pm in St. Louis, it was approximately 7:15 am in a small village outside of Dhaka, Bangladesh. All alone in her sacred grove by the tiny creek that flowed through the woods, Nadia had paused from her daily prayer time to write in her journal, It was an exciting adventure for her, a new hobby that allowed Nadia to pour out her feelings to someone she could trust. Even though Sarah had died last year, Nadia trusted her as a best friend and was using her as a pen-pal to confide her deepest feelings. A gentle breeze blew past the tree limbs and across Nadia's face as she collected her thoughts and began to write:

> *Saturday, October 28, 2004*
> *Dear Sarah: Today, I made a new friend. His name is Jason Ridgeway. He is an American Christian who plays guitar, singing about his faith. I've written him a letter*

Sarah and told him about my dreams. I asked him to help me to understand why this is happening to me. I didn't tell him everything. I really don't know him at all. But Sarah, I can tell you everything. You remember all of the talks we used to have. Remember I asked you why the Quran talks about Isa performing miracles, but Muhammad did not. That had always bothered me.

Sarah, I don't understand why every time I pray, I feel so empty inside. I ask Allah, but He doesn't answer me. He seems so far away. I'm afraid to tell this to mom and dad and Zak. What would they think? But Sarah, I can tell you everything...

Nadia stopped writing and laid down her pen. Her lips began trembling and tears flooded her eyes. She understood far too well the implications of what she was admitting. Nadia was terrified. She was afraid of the consequences of doubting her faith. However, she could no longer suppress or deny the deep convictions that were tearing at her soul.

Nadia needed answers.

CHAPTER SIX
THE JOURNEY

Jason sat on the edge of the bed with his Bible in his lap. His mother sat right across from him in her wheelchair. There was good news. Mrs. Ridgeway had awakened from her two days of prolonged and excessive sleeping. Besides that, her appetite had returned and she was now eating. His many prayers had been heard and Jason was spending the afternoon with his mother before the long trip to Bangladesh in the morning.

"Psalm 27: verse 4, your favorite psalm, Mom," Jason announced as he opened his Bible. Mrs. Ridgeway's eyes sparkled with eagerness to hear Jason read. She moved her wheelchair a closer to the bed.

"One thing I ask of The Lord. This is what I seek. That I may dwell in the house of the Lord all the days of my life. To gaze upon the beauty of the Lord and to seek Him in His temple."

Jason finished and put down his Bible. Mrs. Ridgeway had a glow about her face. She seemed to be in another world. Her eyes were fixed, looking past Jason. Suddenly, it was if she woke up and returned to reality. She looked intently at Jason.

"I had a dream last night," she said.

Jason stared back at her giving her his full attention.

"Yes mom," Jason said.

Mrs. Ridgeway grinned and gave Jason a peculiar look.

"Jesus came to me, "she said with excitement. "He said, I'm coming to take you home with me real soon."

Jason leaned closer to his mother with a perplexed look on his face.

"Jesus told you that."

"Yes." Mrs. Ridgeway answered with an emphatic tone in her voice.

"Now, don't be sad," she reached over touching Jason's hand.

"He said everything would be alright."

Jason sat completely still. He tried to maintain his composure and not show any sadness or fear for his mother's sake.

"I know it will be alright, Mom," Jason said as he got up. He leaned over to his mother and kissed her on the forehead.

"I promise I will be back real soon and we'll talk again."

Jason walked out the door and stopped by the nurse's station to see Nurse Jenkins.

"I'm leaving for Bangladesh at 6: oo am in the morning. You have my cell phone number. Please call me if anything happens."

"Sure," Nurse Jenkins said smiling back at Jason. "Just relax; your mother is fine for now. Have a safe and enjoyable trip."

"Thank-you," Jason said.

It was 2:00 pm and Jason had some presents to buy before the trip. Tomorrow was going to be a very long day.

Jason reached over to shut off the alarm. It was 3:00am. He sat up on the edge of his bed for a moment. The room was pitch black except for a tiny ray of light streaming across the floor from the bathroom night light.

Slowly, Jason made his way to the bathroom and turned on the shower. Gazing straight ahead at the mirror, he yawned and stretched out his arms, thinking about the long flight ahead of him. He would arrive in Dhaka, Bangladesh in a little over 32 hours from now. That calculated into over a day from now! Jason would be boarding Flight 232 at approximately 6:20am this morning at Lambert Airport. He would be taking off at 6:45 am bound for Newark, New Jersey. The 737 would be landing at 9:10 am at Newark Liberty International Airport, where he would spend a very long 7-hour layover. Then at approximately 4:10 pm, Jason would take a short hop to JFK Airport where he would board Air India Flight 6212 at 5:30 pm. Air India would fly him nonstop to Mumbai Airport in Maharashtra, India, landing at 9:00 am the next morning. From there he would take Air India flight 7052 to Dhaka, a 2-hour and 45-minute flight that put him on the ground at approximately

12 noon. He would then check in at the Best Westin La Vinita Hotel in downtown Dhaka and spend the day resting from his long journey and taking in the sights of the city. Then the next morning, he would be picked up by Rochelle, The Worldwide Compassion representative and interpreter and drive 25 miles to The Radanovich Village Project to meet Nadia and her family. Just thinking of the over 10,000 mile trip was overwhelming to say the least and Jason wondered if he was physically up to the task. Today was Wednesday, November 21, 2004. He would not be at his destination in Dhaka until Thursday afternoon, November 22.

After a quick shower, Jason proceeded to make his way to the kitchen. It was 3:30 am. He sat down to a small bowl of cheerios and a glass of orange juice. Knowing that the short flight to Newark would probably not offer any meals, but just peanuts and soft drinks, Jason decided to have a quick breakfast.

After putting the dishes in the dishwasher, Jason hurried back to bedroom and got dressed. He went down a checklist as he put the luggage on the bed. One duffle bag with gifts, check. One suitcase, check. One overnight bag with bathroom accessories, check. One acoustic guitar in a black case, check. Jason paused and thought for a minute. He turned on his cell phone and looked around to make sure that he had packed the charger. "Oh," he said tapping his shirt pockets with his hand. "Airline tickets," he laughed, "now that's kind of important, check." He checked around the house and turned on some lights, checked the doors and then started taking the luggage out to the car. It was pitch black outside except for the porch light which came on as he walked out to the car. He put the luggage into the trunk and placed his guitar in the back seat and started up the car. Finally, he was on the way! In just a few short minutes he had turned onto 1-270 heading west to 1-70 and Lambert International Airport. Jason turned on the radio and listened to the weather report. The high today was going to be 50 degrees, but where he was going at this time of year, the temperature would be soaring in to the mid-eighties.

It was 4:15 am when Jason turned into Lambert Airport. He found the long-term parking garage and quickly found a parking space. He was greeted by a sky cap as he made his way to the

terminal. The sky cap took his luggage and his guitar, while Jason carried his duffle bag over his back. Jason walked into the airport terminal at 4:30 am for a security check-in. Thanksgiving was right around the corner and already this early in the morning, there was a long line of people forming lines at the customer service counters. Walking up to the Continental customer service counter, Jason gave the representative his tickets. The Customer service rep took his suitcase and guitar, weighed them and handed him back his tickets. "Have a nice flight," The agent said as Jason found his way back to the lounge area. It was 5:15 am. His flight would not be boarding for another hour. He took his seat next to gate 26 and decided to relax and listen to his I-pod to pass the time.
    "Your attention please, Continental Flight 232 bound for Newark, New Jersey is now boarding at gate 26."
    Jason looked down at his watch. It was 6:00 am. The sun was starting to come up and peer through the glass windows of the terminal. He grabbed his duffle bag, put his I-pod away and headed toward the security checkpoint. People were starting to crowd into the airport as Jason watched lines of people forming at each customer service counter. Jason passed successfully through security and boarded the huge Boeing 737.
    "Good Morning sir, "The flight Attendant said greeting him. "Morning," Jason said back smiling as he walked back down the aisle toward the coach section of the plane. Jason found seat 32 and proceeded to store his duffle bag in the compartment above his seat. He grabbed his Bible out from the bag, closed the compartment and then settled down in his seat next to the window.
    In a few moments people were getting settled in their seats. Parents with their children, older couples and single men and women were arriving at the last moment to find their seats. It was 6:20 am. The Flight Attendants began their emergency preparedness presentation, showing the passengers the exits to take in case of a fire. The oxygen masks were deployed and the attendant discussed the proper usage to the passengers. As they were finishing up, a tall, well dressed man in a two-piece suit sat down next to Jason. He wore glasses and had a beard.
    "Hello, I'm Edward Bannister," he said extending his hand.

"Jason Ridgeway," Jason said shaking his hand.
Edward leaned back in his seat.
"We're you headed?" He asked.
"Dhaka, Bangladesh," Jason replied.
"Wow, that's a long way, Pal." Edward answered him leaning over his seat to pick up a newspaper. The Attendants came by and asked both Edward and Jason to fasten their seta belts. Then The Boeing 737 pushed the gate and began to slowly taxi down the long runway. Jason glanced down at his watch. It was 6:25 am. There were running just a few minutes behind. The 737 came to a stop awaiting clearance from the control tower. Then two minutes later the 737 roared down the runway picking up speed. The roar of the engines became louder and the cabin began vibrating from the speed and the thrust. The 737 finally lifted up off the runway and began slowly climbing toward its cruising altitude of 30,000 feet.

In just a few minutes, the 737 reached its cruising altitude of 30,000 feet and the Flight Attendants began to come around for drink orders.

"I'll have some coffee," Edward told the flight attendant. She then looked over to Jason.

"Give me a soft drink, please."

Edward reached down and picked up a newspaper. Jason leaned a little more back in his seat and opened up his Bible. He began thinking about his visit with Nadia and her family. It was important to Jason that he behaved in a way that would bring honor and glory to Christ.

He turned to Colossians 4:5:

"Live wisely among those who are not believers and make the most of every opportunity. Let your conversation be gracious and attractive so that you will have the right response for everyone."

The words, 'gracious and 'attractive caught Jason's attention. He paused for a moment and meditated on the meaning of the words and their implications.

Jason then turned to 1 Peter 3:15.

"Be ready to speak up and tell everyone who asks you why you're living the way you are and always with the utmost courtesy." The word courtesy stood out to Jason. He thought about the words gentleness and respect in relationship to the word courtesy. The Flight Attendant returned with the coffee and soda.

"Thank you," Edward said as he took the cup of coffee from the attendant.

"Thank you," Jason said taking the soda from her hand.

Edward glanced over and noticed the Bible sitting in Jason's lap. He rolled his eyes and gently shook his head.

"You believe that," Edward said with a snobbish tone in his voice.

Jason looked up at Edward.

"Yes I do, "he respectfully replied and then looked back down at his Bible.

Edward leaned his head back and stroked his beard.

"You would agree," Edward began saying while looking straight ahead. "That we live in a highly scientific and technological age. "

Edward now turned his head and looked straight at Jason.

Jason nodded his head in agreement.

Edward rubbed his nose and leaned closer to Jason pointing down at his Bible.

"Don't you think that God and The Bible are irrelevant for our time? If we want answers to life, science and technology will tell us what we need to know. Don't you agree?"

Edward leaned back, straightened his tie and took a sip of his coffee, confident that Jason would not be able to refute him.

Jason thought for a moment and then responded.

"Let me see if I understand you. You said that we don't need God or the Bible, they're irrelevant because science gives us the true knowledge about reality, right?'

Edward nodded his head in agreement.

Jason leaned over closer to Edward.

"You want to be scientific in your thinking."

"Yes, I do," Edward replied, leaning over to put his cup of coffee down.

"Then why don't you believe the Bible?" Jason asked.

Edward gave Jason a perplexed look.

"What?"

"Did you know Edward, science points toward the existence of God, rather than away from it.?"

Edward laughed sarcastically and shuffled in his seat.

"Oh, come on," he said, starting to chuckle.

"Let me give you an example, "Jason said, "Genesis 1:1, in the beginning God created the heavens and the earth. Good rational science demonstrates the truthfulness of that claim."

Edward rolled his eyes and leaned his head back in his seat.

"No way, "he said with an arrogant tone in his voice.

Jason leaned closer and pressed his point.

"Okay, are you familiar with the law of causality?"

"The law of what," Edward answered with a smirked look on his face.

"The law of causality states that everything that comes to be, that is everything that has a beginning, has to have a cause."

Edward began shifting in his seat; He cleared his throat and leaned over to get his coffee.

Jason continued.

"The universe had a beginning. Therefore, the universe had a cause."

"So," Edward answered with a sarcastic tone.

"Most atheists believe that the universe is eternal. That it wasn't created. But the second law of thermodynamics, the law of physics, states that the universe is not eternal, but is running out of usable energy, like an hourglass tipped on its head, it's running down toward disorder."

Jason shifted in his seat to get more comfortable. He continued.

"According to this second law, the universe will one day die a 'heat death' demonstrating that it had a beginning. So Edward, isn't it logical
to conclude that the universe had a beginner?"

Edward took a sip of coffee and was quiet for a moment. Then he sat his coffee back down.

"Wasn't there a big bang," he asked looking sharply at Jason.

"Yes there was and that actually supports my point that the universe came into being. That is, at a point in time, the universe came to be since we know out of nothing, nothing comes, there had to be a beginner."

Edward smacked his lips. He had a perturbed look on his face.

"Whatever," He replied.

Jason leaned back into his chair.

"Edward, take for instance this plane that we're flying on. Do you think this plane resulted from a tornado going through a junkyard or was it the result of a designer?"

"Your point?"

"My point is, we're trying to be scientific, right?"

"Right."

"Did you know forensic science looks at specified and complex causes and points to an intelligent designer as the cause?"

"Go on."

"The reason they do is, our experience tells us that natural laws have never produced specified and complex systems such as books, computers, etc."

Edward rubbed his chin.

"Really," he said with curiosity in his voice.

Jason took a quick drink of his soda and continued.

"Forensic science operates on the principle of uniformity which states it's reasonable to assume the origin of the most specified and complex systems in existence must be the product of an intelligent being rather than mindless, purposeless natural laws or time, random chance and natural processes."

Edward reached into his pocket and wiped off his forehead.

"Let me give you an example, Edward. Would you believe that an explosion in a print shop could cause a book?"

Edward twisted his head a little and looked ahead. He struggled for an answer.

"Or, "Jason continued. " Take Mount Rushmore. The sculptured heads of the Presidents. Was that the result of millions of years of wind and erosion or the result of a sculptor and his tools?"

Edward once again shifted in his seat.

"It seems to me Edward, that the universe and everything around us screams intelligent design. Scientific laws and the laws of logic demonstrate this in a big time way. So I think true, rational science points to the existence of God rather than away from it."

Jason finished his presentation and took a sip of his soda.

Edward sat quietly. He thought for a moment and then took a deep breath.

"Well, all of the data or evidence as you say has to point to the existence of God, but doesn't that data or evidence have to be interpreted. In other words, is this not just your interpretation, Jason?"

Edward took a sip of coffee, leaned back in his chair and relaxed. Jason thought for a moment and looked back at Edward.

"The Bible makes it clear that what can be known about God is plain to us, because he has clearly shown us the evidences that I've shared with you. The problem is not with God but with us. In our sinfulness to live the way we want, we close our eyes to the evidences. As the Bible says, we suppress that information and therefore we have no excuses."

Edward became quiet again, picked up his newspaper and muttered something to himself. He paused for a moment and then looked over at Jason.

"It's been an interesting conversation. I really enjoyed talking with you," Edward said. Then he gazed back down at his newspaper.

The Flight Attendant leaned over.

"Can I get you anymore to drink?"

"No," Edward answered. He took a deep breath and returned to reading his newspaper. Jason leaned back into his seat and began reading his Bible again.

"Your attention please. This is your Captain speaking. We will be landing in Newark in fifteen minutes, where we will have a seven hour layover before proceeding on to JFK Airport. Thank you for your attention."

The Flight Attendant came by and leaned over the seat looking at Edward and Jason.

"Please fasten your safety belts. We'll be landing very soon now."

Edward laid down his newspaper. Jason put away his Bible and fastened his safety belt. The 737 began rapidly descending and reducing its speed as they approached the airport.

Time quickly passed and the 737 touched down on the runway and taxied onto the orange concourse.

Edward slowly got up and grabbed his newspaper, not saying a word and walked quickly ahead of Jason. Jason reached up and got his duffle bag from the overhead compartment. Walking into the airport terminal, Jason stopped and glanced at his watch. It was 9:45 am. He had seven hours to kill before the short hop to JFK which didn't take off until 4:15 pm.

Jason glanced around the airport terminal and spotted a café. Now was a good time for breakfast. He was starving and some pancakes and eggs sounded good to him right now. Jason quickly found a table and sat down placing his duffle bag next to him on the floor. A waitress came and took his order and Jason leaned back in his chair sipping on some orange juice. He bent over to begin reading his Bible when suddenly heard a familiar voice.

"Hello." It was Edward.

Jason looked up from reading his Bible. He was pleasantly surprised.

"Mind if I sit down here," Edward asked motioning toward a chair.

"Not at all," Jason replied sitting down his glass of orange juice.

"I won't be long. I'm meeting some relatives here and I'll be leaving soon. I won't be going as far as you." Edward looked up as the waitress came back.

"I'll just have some coffee," he said.

The waitress nodded and walked away. Jason could see the serious look on Edward's face. Edward took a deep breath and looked over at Jason.

"I want to apologize for my rudeness and arrogance on the plane. That was totally inappropriate," Edward said with a look of humiliation in his eyes.

Jason looked at him with compassion.

"Apology accepted. I too am sorry in my zeal to make a point if I offended you." Jason said.

Edward looked down at the table. The waitress returned with his coffee.

"Thank you, mam," he said as he tore open a package of coffee creamer. He began to stir his cup. His eyes were fixed upon the spoon. He laid the spoon down and folded his hands, laying his elbows on the table.

"I remember as a kid. My Father was a strict disciplinarian. He hated every type of religion. Especially Christianity. He said Christianity was a stupid religion for the weak."

Edward took a sip of his coffee. Jason's eyes followed as he put the cup back down on the table. He listened intently.

"So, growing up, I was taught that you had to make it on your own. You had to work for and earn everything without depending on some wimpy religion or any so called deity. When I was in college, I surrounded myself with other skeptics or atheists like myself and we spent most of our waking hours ridiculing all this religious superstition."

Edward paused and took another sip of his coffee.

"I've talked to a lot of Christians and I have to say that you are the only one who has taken the time to listen and to try to answer my questions. I don't agree with your answers, but I respect the way you articulated your answer."

Jason smiled politely at Edward.

"Thank you Edward." Jason leaned closer across the table toward Edward.

"I'm passionate about what I believe, because I believe Christianity answers the basic needs of the human heart. It tells us who we are, why we're here, why there's evil and suffering and where we're going. It's much more than a religion. It's a relationship with the living God through Jesus Christ."

Edward leaned back in his chair and nodded his head. Then he leaned forward resting his elbows back on the table. He was quiet for a moment and begin to think about what Jason had just said.

"You're very sincere Jason. I can tell you've done a lot of research."

Edward stood up and pushed his chair back into the table. He extended his hand toward Jason. Jason got up slowly and shook

Edward's hand. Edward reached into his pocket and left a dollar bill tip on the table.

"I'll give some thought to what you've said."

Jason smiled and nodded his head.

"That's all I can ask."

Edward waved good-bye and walked away. Jason stood and watched Edward as he walked away, feeling a sense of compassion and understanding for him.

The long lay-over seemed to pass by quickly. Jason awoke from a short nap after hearing the overhead page for his flight. It was 4:30 pm and the 737 made the short trip to JFK in less than thirty minutes. Arriving at JFK, Jason promptly went to the ticket counter to secure his tickets for Air India flight 6212 nonstop to Mumbai. The holiday crowds packed out the terminal at JFK. There were excessive long lines everywhere. It was noisy and very busy and Jason was feeling tired already. After walking in circles, Jason found a secluded seat next to the window where it was much quieter. He laid down his duffle bag and collapsed!

What seemed like hours had only been twenty minutes and Jason was awakened by the overhead page.

"Air India Flight 6212 nonstop to Mumbai is now boarding at Gate 11."

Jason stood up shaking off his tiredness and ran quickly to the gate. He passed the security check point and made his way through the galley door to inside the huge Boeing 757. It was 5:15 pm. Jason patiently waited through the line and found his aisle seat in the coach section. He placed his duffle bag above him in the overhead compartment and brought down his journal and his Bible.

At 5:30 pm, the 757 pushed the gate and taxied onto the runway. After being granted clearance, the 757 gathered speed down the runway and took off smoothly into the air, rising quickly through the clouds and leaving the city lights of New York behind.

Air India reached its cruising altitude of 33,000 feet. Jason could hardly believe it. He was finally on his way to Dhaka. In over fourteen hours he would be landing in Maharashtra, India at Mumbai airport and from there travel to Dhaka. The cabin lights had been dimmed so that the passengers could sleep. Dinner would be served a little later. Jason turned the light on above his seat. He made himself comfortable and took out his journal. He wasn't in his sacred space like at home, but he was closer to God some 33,000 feet above the earth. It was quiet except for the soft hum from the plane's engines. Jason peered out the cabin window. It was pitch black except for a few traces of white clouds. He leaned forward to begin writing.

> Wednesday, November 21, 2004
> Dear God:
> What a day! Here I am at 33,000 feet above the earth and closer to you! I can't believe it. Tomorrow I will be in Dhaka and then the next day I'll be visiting Nadia and her family. This is a dream and a prayer come true! Thank you God for your provision. What a privilege to be your representative to a Muslim family all this way across the earth.
>
> Thank you also Lord for the privilege of witnessing to Edward. It was amazing how you enabled him to open up his heart to me. Lord, I pray that you would give him a hunger and thirst for your truth; I pray that his heart will be always restless until it finds its rest in you! Please give me a sensitive and respectful heart when I meet Nadia. I know you have been at work in her heart. It is so exciting to be a part of your plan to reach the hungry, thirsty souls of the world. Please draw Nadia to yourself, Lord. Please help her to see that you are the real treasure that her heart is longing for.

Jason finished the last line and rubbed his tired eyes. It had been a very long day. He turned out the light above him and curled up next to the pillow in his seat. He needed plenty of rest to endure the long journey still ahead of him.

The bright sunlight beamed through Jason's cabin window as he put on his seatbelt. It was 8:50 am and they were circling for a landing at Mumbai Airport. It had been a very long flight. Jason stretched in his seat. He had slept for many hours and even though he was well rested, his body and mind were getting weary from the long journey.

The 757 touched down a few minutes past 9:00am at Mumbai Airport and taxied to the debarking concourse. Jason grabbed his duffle bag
from the compartment above and headed into the airport terminal. It was a beautiful day in Mahararastra, India. The temperature was a balmy 90 degrees. He had time enough to grab a bite to eat and tour the terminal before boarding Air India flight 7052 to Dhaka the last leg of his long journey.

Chapter Seven
The Visit

Jason climbed out of the taxi cab and stood in front of the Best Western Lavinci Hotel in downtown Dhaka, Bangladesh. He tipped the driver and then laid down his luggage on the sidewalk.

"I'm finally here! I made it!" Jason cried out with his arms outstretched in front of him.

It was Thursday afternoon, November 22, 1:45 pm. He had begun his journey, yesterday morning at 6:20 am, some 32 hours ago!

Jason grabbed his luggage, walked through the revolving door into the lobby and up to the front desk. He secured a door card and a bell hop carried his luggage as they took the elevator up to the fifth floor. The bell hop carried his luggage to the door. Jason promptly tipped him. He inserted the card into the door, turned the knob and walked in.

He spotted the bed right away. Without hesitation he flopped onto the bed and laid there for a minute. He took a long, deep breath. Jason was extremely tired, feeling the effects of Jet lag. Yet he knew he had a full day of sightseeing before being met by the representative from Worldwide Compassion tomorrow morning.

Jason slowly rose up from the bed. He went over to the window and pulled back the curtains. Surrounding the hotel and extending far down the street were tall, high rise buildings and skyscrapers. Jason looked down at the busy and crowded street below. He saw people swarming in every direction gathered by the many shops that were sandwiched together and lining up and down the street.

Dhaka has an estimated population of over 7,000,000 people. The population was predominately Muslim, with a smaller percentage of Hindus and Buddhists. Besides the many small shops nestled next to each other up and down the streets, Jason observed the many rickshaws carrying tourists amongst the cabs and other automobiles crammed against each other. Dhaka was a very crowded and busy city.

Jason quickly changed into some appropriate clothing for the weather, a blue muscle shirt, a pair of blue jean shorts and some comfortable sandals for his feet. He took the elevator down to the lobby floor and walked out the front door of the hotel. Walking outside, Jason immediately felt the temperature change. It was a steamy 91 degrees in Dhaka in the middle of November! He stepped onto New Market Daher Road and took a deep breath. The sweet smell of BBQ invaded his nostrils. Outside of the various retail shops, there were grills set up to attract the tourists. Jason could smell fish being cooked on the grill. It had a very spicy and appetizing aroma!

Jason began walking amongst the crowd of people. He passed by shops that were selling jewelry, leather products, shoes, books, clothing and many other assorted items. The noise of cabs honking, people talking and the many rickshaws filled the street that Jason was walking on. Off to his left was the Café Mango followed by a Pizza Hut and a Kentucky Fried Chicken. Dhaka was known as the City Of Mosques because of its large Muslim population. Jason kept walking and came upon an alleyway. In the distance he could see one of the many mosques that were spread out all over the city.

Suddenly, he heard a voice shouting in English," Jesus is more than a Prophet. I can tell you as a former Muslim that Jesus is God. He is my Lord and Savior." The young man than repeated it in Bengali. Jason turned away from looking down the alley and noticed a young man standing on top of some boxes and preaching through a megaphone to a small crowd of people who had gathered around him. Some of the people yelled back at him in anger and scorn for what he was preaching.

"Come to Christ now. He will save you from your sins," the young man yelled boldly back to the crowd. Many people in the crowd became enraged and angrily shook their fists at him. Jason impressed with young man's courage made his way through the crowd of disgruntled and angry people and approached him. He lowered the megaphone down from his mouth and looked intently at Jason.

"Excuse me sir. Please listen to me," he said with a look of urgency in his eyes.

"Jesus died for your sins and rose again."

Jason leaned closer to the young man. The crowd began to disperse so that it was only Jason and the young preacher.

"What is your name sir, my name is Abdullah," he said stretching out his right hand.

Jason firmly shook his hand. Their eyes met.

"I admire your courage Abdullah, "Jason said slowly releasing his hand from Abdullah's.

Abdullah smiled.

"Jesus went to the cross for me. It's the least I can do for him."

Jason nodded his head in agreement. Abdullah looked around at all of the people swarming up and down the street browsing at the many different shops.

"Some days," Abdullah said, now looking back at Jason. He jumped down from his platform of boxes and stood next to Jason.

"People spit at me. Some throw bottles and rocks. Some threaten me. " Jason looked at Abdullah with great admiration. Abdullah continued.

"The city of Dhaka claims in their constitution to not discriminate against anyone's religion, but that's a lie," Abdullah said giving Jason a look of disgust.

"I know some people who are placed in prison cells and tortured because they left Islam and became Christians. The city constitution is a lie,"
Abdullah said emphatically. He looked down and shook his head. Then he looked back straight at Jason thumping his finger into his chest.

"The day you accept Jesus as your Savior is the day your life is marked by the Government."

Jason bit his lip and slowly shook his head.

"Becoming a Christian here is costly," Jason said.

"It is," Abdullah agreed.

"Which Church are you from?" Jason asked.

"It is the Church of the Living Word," Abdullah replied with excitement.

"Almost everyone who attends were once Muslims. We are all ex-Muslims for Jesus," Abdullah said with a smile.

"Wow," Jason said, his face beaming too with excitement.

"And you, Jason?" Abdullah asked.

"I am a worship leader at Spirit and Word Outreach in St. Louis." Jason then reached into his pants pocket and handed Abdullah a copy of his latest cd.

"This is for you, Abdullah. Songs of worship to motivate you as you street preach."

Abdullah's face broke out with a grateful expression.

"Thank you brother. I can't wait to share it with the others."

"You know, "Abdullah began. He looked intently into Jason's eyes.

"As a Muslim, all of my life, I was taught to perfect myself to pray, to fast, to give alms, to be obedient to Allah. I had no peace, no joy, I had no assurance I would even make it to paradise. This was all religion ever done for me."

Abdullah paused as tears welled up in his eyes.

"Then one day, I met Jesus."

Abdullah's face beamed with joy.

"I found out the difference between religion and relationship. Jesus came to perfect me, to pay a sin debt I could never pay and give me His righteousness in exchange for my filthy rags of sin. Now I know Jason I will be in paradise. I have a real assurance."

Abdullah finished and wiped away the tears from his eyes. Jason embraced him with a hug and then backed away looking at him closely in the eyes.

"Your dedication and your love for Christ inspires me," Jason said.

"Yours, too," Jason said.

Then Abdullah climbed back up on his platform of boxes and began preaching again. Jason disappeared into the crowd. He looked back at Abdullah and contemplated the cost of following Christ in Dhaka.

After having a quick dinner at the Club Mango consisting of a delightful chocolate milkshake and a blt sandwich, Jason decided to head back to the hotel. He was tired and wanted to take a shower after enduring the sultry summer-like day in Dhaka. Jason toweled off as he left the shower. "Ah," he sighed. The shower was a welcome and delightful conclusion to a long and tiring day. Jason looked at the clock on the table. It was 8:50 pm, which meant, it was 8:50 am in the morning back in St. Louis.

Jason drew back the curtains and sat on the bed. He gazed out the window admiring the distant lights coming from the apartment buildings. They provided an appropriate backdrop against a beautiful sunset evening in Dhaka. Jason reached over and picked up his acoustic guitar. All day, the words to a new song had been flowing through his mind and into his heart. He had been working on a new song and now, digesting the events of the day, Jason felt inspired to write the verses to "reflection." Reflection was a song about growing in God's Grace as a Christian, reflecting his holiness in every day life.

Jason began strumming his guitar, opening with an a-suspended chord and going down the fret to a g-suspended. He reviewed the chorus he had written and then jotted down the first verse.

I lay down all my wounds and my scars
And I offer up my life to you
You give your beauty and replace all my shame
You erase all my pain
You are faithful and true

Jason paused and wrote down the interlude.

Mold me, shape me, and transform me
Into the likeness of you
Cleanse me, fashion me, purify me . Into a heart that's in awe of you.

"Yes," Jason exclaimed, satisfied with what he had wrote. He then launched into singing the chorus.

We are a reflection of the Father's love and affection.
A mirror that's reflecting the wonders of your Grace. We're on the way to perfection through your discipline and correction. A trophy of your affection. A reflection of your face.

Jason stopped playing and put his guitar back into his case. Exhausted, he crawled into the bed and turned out the light. He would be meeting Rochelle, The Worldwide representative early in the morning at 8:00 am. He needed a good nights sleep for the very special visit tomorrow.

"Welcome to Dhaka, Jason." Rochelle stood 5'10" up against her Suv parked in front of the Hotel. She brushed back her wavy blond hair and extended her hand toward Jason.

"Hello, Rochelle," Jason said shaking her hand.

"Ready for a short trip?" Rochelle asked.

They both hopped into the blue suv and started down the street, dodging the many rickshaws busily passing in front of them.

"Dhaka is a busy place," Rochelle pointed out as she turned the corner past the numerous store crowded together on both sides of the street.

"So I gathered," Jason chuckled. They both laughed.

"Oh, "Rochelle said. She pulled out an envelope next to her in the seat and gave it to Jason.

"That is the letter you wanted to give to Nadia. It's been translated from English into Bengali."

"Thank you," Jason smiled and put it into his shirt pocket.

The Suv merged from the busy city street onto a two-lane highway that would take them out of the city heading toward the Radanovich Village Project, a distance of 25 miles.

"I promise to make an awkward situation for you as smooth as possible. Just listen closely and follow what I say when I translate," Rochelle said.

"Yes I will," Jason said nodding his head.

"Relax; this is going to be one of the most memorable experiences of your life, Jason. The Mustafa's' are nice people. Nadia and Zak are very intelligent children. They're a great Muslim family."

Rochelle could tell that Jason was a little nervous. Jason leaned back against his car seat.

"I'm really looking forward to this. I can't wait," Jason blurted out nervously.

"I've lived in Dhaka for five years now. It's a challenging and sometimes dangerous place to live. There are drugs, gang's wars that go on, not to mention human trafficking, where young girls are kidnapped and sold for a price on the sex slave trade market. And if you're a Muslim that converted to Christianity, you can be bodily attacked and persecuted, especially if you're street preaching. But I love what I do Jason. I love helping the poor and I wouldn't trade it for anything in the world."

Rochelle stepped on the brake to allow a rickshaw to cross over in front of them to the other side of the road.

Rochelle continued.

"I really feel I've grown in The Lord living amongst the poor in the village. I really see how good we've got it back home and how much we take our lives for granted."

Jason looked at Rochelle and nodded his head in agreement.

"Ever since the plane landed here in Dhaka, my heart has been heavy because I have the overwhelming desire to just do everything I can to make life better for people like Nadia," Jason said, his voice echoing with passion and conviction.

The suv turned right onto a gravel road and the ride became bumpier. The suv ascended up a small hill and emerged on the other side. The landscape had changed from a dirt road to a large green field stretching out in the distance. It was a rice field stretching out past the hill into the distance. Jason could see people amongst the rice plants in the field working in the blazing sun. It was a balmy 88 degrees in the middle of November. They came upon a small wooden bridge that spanned over a creek. The suv slowed down to cross. On the other side of the bridge was a long fence surrounding a village. Above the fence gate was a white sign. It read "Radanovich Village
Project" in black letters.

"We're here Jason" Rochelle said as she drove onto the complex past the gate.

As soon as they passed the gate, Jason could see wooden and bamboo huts sitting next to each other. Looking to his left, he saw a deep tube well at the top of a small hill and a line of people waiting to draw the clean water from it with their buckets. Looking to his right, Jason saw a playground with swings and children playing soccer running up and down the grass field. The suv drove past two women busy working in a garden, while two children walked past them escorting a goat. They looked up at Rochelle in the suv and waved. Rochelle waved back and then turned the suv into a dirt road by a tree. She parked it, took the key out of the ignition and pushed her sunglasses down on her eyes.

"Let's go see Nadia." Rochelle said.

Rochelle and Jason walked down a gravel road that passed by the children's playground. Jason dobbed the sweat off of his forehead with a handkerchief. The intense heat and humidity was bearing down on him. It was 90 plus degrees and Rochelle seemed to be somewhat immune to the sultry temperatures after living in Dhaka for the past five years.

The gravel road made a turn to the right. Jason and Rochelle walked slowly down a hill and crossed over a small bridge that led straight to Nadia's hut.

"Here we are," Rochelle said.

A small wooden hut structure, 42 feet in length and 12 feet in height with a tin roof was home for the Mustafa family. Rochelle tapped on the door. A short, stocky lady dressed in a burqa answered. Rochelle pointed over to Jason, speaking in Bengali. The lady nodded her head and spoke back looking at Jason. She became excited and moved away from the door motioning for Jason to walk in.

"Fatima, Nadia's mother, says, welcome to our home," Rochelle said to Jason. Jason acknowledged Fatima's welcome and walked in with Rochelle following behind. Jason felt a slight cool breeze as he stepped inside the small wooden hut. Ironically, there was a small electric fan mounted in the window to his right. The village generator powered fans and light bulbs for each hut. This was one of the few modern conveniences that the village people enjoyed together.

Standing in the corner next to a table was Rashid, Nadia's father. Rashid was also short and stocky, 5'8" tall. He was bald with a gray beard wearing brown pants and sandals. Rochelle spoke in Bengali introducing Jason. Rashid extended his right hand toward Jason. Jason shook hands saying "hello" to Rashid. Next to Rashid stood a tall, thin young boy with a soccer ball in his hands.

"This is Zak, Jason," Rochelle said, introducing him.

Zak was almost 5'11" tall with wavy brown hair and brown eyes. He put down his soccer and said something in Bengali. Rochelle laughed and looked at Jason.

"Zak wants to know if you'll play soccer with him."

"Sure, tell him, I'd be glad to," Jason answered smiling back at Zak.

Rochelle repeated his answer to Zak. Zak gave Jason an enthusiastic look and picked up his soccer ball. Rashid and Fatima looked over at Jason laughing and muttering something in Bengali to each other.

As the laughter died down, Nadia emerged from the bedroom section of the hut. Nadia was dressed in a dark gray burqa, without the veil that covered her face, lining the outside of her face and extending down her legs to her ankles. Her thick and curly brown hair was tucked up underneath her hijab. In her hands, Nadia was carrying a sweet rice cake. She walked up to Jason and stopped. She looked up at him smiling with a look of excitement and joy beaming from her deep blue eyes. Nadia cupped her hands together. In the center of her hands was the sweet rice cake. She smiled and motioned to Jason with her eyes to take the cake. Nadia kept her eyes fastened on Jason and said something in Bengali. Rochelle listened closely and then looked at Jason.

"Nadia says, welcome to my house. Would you like to have a sweet rice cake? She says she made them especially for you."

Jason was touched. He gazed back to Nadia with a look of gratitude and carefully took the sweet rice cake from Nadia's hands. He slowly took a bite of the cake.

"M—mmm," Jason said, delighting in the taste of rice, coconut and brown sugar.

"Delicious," Jason said, finishing the piece of cake. He gave an approving look toward Nadia.

"Thank you," Rochelle translated back to Nadia.

Nadia's face suddenly turned red as she blushed. She began chuckling out loud. Zak also joined in chuckling out loud. Rochelle began chuckling too and looked over at Jason.

"Nadia says you have crumbs all over your mouth."

"Oh," Jason laughed back and quickly wiped off his mouth with his handkerchief.

The humorous incident with the sweet rice cake was very therapeutic putting everyone at ease and more relaxed. The laughter and the silly-faced expressions broke up the awkwardness of trying to communicate because of the apparent language barrier. Jason and the Mustafa's had found a way to break the ice and be more comfortable with each other.

Rochelle composed herself after laughing and spoke in Bengali to Zak. Rashid and Fatima came over to Rochelle and also said something in Bengali. Jason followed them closely with his eyes. Rochelle, using her hands to communicate, looked over to Jason

"Rashid and Fatima are going to start preparing dinner. Zak wants to know if you will play soccer with him."

Zak grabbed his soccer ball and shot an excited look at Jason. Nadia looked at Zak with a silly grin.

"And, Rochelle continued, Nadia would like to give you a little tour of the village, Jason."

Nadia looked at Jason with an anxious and adventurous smile on her face.

"I would be honored to take your tour," Jason politely said to Nadia, and then he looked at Zak." I would love a good soccer match with you." Zak filled with excitement grabbed his soccer ball and Jason followed behind Nadia as they walked out the front door. Rochelle followed close behind them acting as their interpreter.

Just a few feet beyond the front door and off to the side of the hut, Nadia led Jason to a small standing water pump protruding up from the ground. She looked at Jason and pointed to the pump saying a few words in Bengali.

"Nadia says, this is where we wash the dishes every day after eating," Rochelle said to Jason.

Nadia pushed on the handle and some clean running water gushed out. She put her left hand underneath the flow, smiling back at Jason. Nadia then reached down and picked up a cup lying next to the pump. She pushed the handle with one hand while holding the cup in the other. The water gushed out into the cup. With water spilling over the top of the cup, Nadia chuckled and steadied the cup. She looked up to Jason and smiled, offering him a cool drink. Jason reached out and took the cup with both of his hands. The cool refreshing taste of the clean water was soothing to Jason in the intense Bangladesh heat.

Nadia laughed and wiped her hands of on her burqa and continued walking. They came upon a small playground filled with children from the village. There were two swing sets, a merry go round and two makeshift soccer nets. A few children were busy playing soccer, laughing, kicking the ball and shouting out to one another. As Nadia walked up to the swing set, two little girls and their brother ran up to her. Nadia bent down and pointed over to Jason. Their faces lighted up and they drew closer to Jason. Rochelle looked at Jason.

"Nadia wants you to meet her friends, Sue and Leah." Jason bent down and shook their hands.

"Hi, "he said smiling at the two little girls.

As Jason stood up, he could see Zak running out onto the field. The other children playing soccer vacated the field leaving only Zak in the center.

"Zak would like you to play goalie, "Rochelle said to Jason.

Nadia giggled and shook her head grinning back at Jason. Jason ran out onto the field and positioned himself in front of the net. He bent down and held out his arms in the official capacity of a goalie. Zak began moving the ball up the field, while Rochelle and Nadia stood on the sideline laughing and watching on. Zak came within six feet of the goal, making a couple of tricky moves and blasted the ball past Jason. Jason dove to his left as the ball flew past him. Rochelle and Nadia clapped and laughed on the sidelines. Jason got back up with a humiliating look on his face and threw the ball back out to Zak.

"I'm getting too old for this "Jason laughingly admitted as he gasped for breath. Before he could compose himself, Zak once again booted the ball. Jason dove to his right this time. But it was too late. Home team 2 and visitors 0.

"That's all," Jason shouted and came back over to the sidelines. Zak quickly came over. Jason met him and held up the palm of his hand. Zak gave him a puzzled look. Jason pulled his hands toward his and said, "High five."

Rochelle translated this to Zak. Zak looked back to Jason. He lifted up his hand laughing and they high-fived each other. Nadia looked on with interest as Zak and Jason seemed to hit it off so well together. It delighted her heart that her little brother was getting along so well with her new found friend.

While Zak lingered behind them playing some more soccer with the rest of the village children, Nadia continued walking with Jason with Rochelle following close behind. She asked a question in Bengali. Rochelle turned to Jason interpreting it for him in English.

"Nadia wants to know if you're married."

Jason blushed a little and looked over at Nadia grinning.

"No, I am not married. I have no plans at this time."

Rochelle quickly translated and Nadia shook her head. She then asked her next question as they stopped to sit down on the ground next to a tall tree. Nadia sat down in front of Jason, while Rochelle sat next to Jason.

"Nadia writes poetry and wants to know how you write your songs?"

Jason stared up at the sky and thought for a moment. He then looked back down and sated back over to Nadia. His face was glowing with delight. Jason loved to explain the inspiration and motivation behind his songs.

"Well Nadia, "Jason began. Nadia had an expression on her face of yearning and eagerly wanting to know. Her eyes were fixed on ever word that Jason said.

"When I think about Jesus and how he loved people, how he healed people and forgave their sins, how he showed compassion to everyone. When I think about his unconditional love, the songs just flow out of me. My songs are based on the love of Christ and how he demonstrated that to everyone who came to him."

As Rochelle slowly translated, Jason could see the glow on Nadia's face. She listened intently, her face brightening up and reacting to every word that Jason had used to describe who Jesus was. There was a hunger and thirst in her eyes and Jason could clearly see it.

Nadia then reached into her pocket and pulled out a piece of paper handing it over to Jason. Rochelle turned to Jason.

"Nadia would like you to read a poem that she wrote." Jason gently took the piece of paper from Nadia's hand and began to read.

Allah you seem so far away. I need to hear your voice today.
Allah I feel so empty inside. Don't you see the tears that I've cried?
I need some answers in my life; I want to be free from the pain and strife
Please send me an answer for today. Please send me a good friend to me, I pray.

Jason finished reading Nadia's poem and looked back over to her. His heart overflowed with compassion and love for the emptiness that Nadia was feeling. He wanted desperately for Christ to bring peace and rest to her restless heart. He truly was touched and was fighting back the tears. Nadia's face had an expression on it that was crying out for answers.

"That is beautiful, Nadia," Jason softly whispered back to her. Nadia's face broke into a gentle smile. She gave a look of gratitude that Jason had taken the time to read her poem.

"We have to head back, "Rochelle announced. They stood up to brush off their clothes.

"Dinner will be ready soon."

The walked back to the hut and entered through the front door. Rashid and Fatima were busy sitting dishes on the table. There were five pillows carefully arranged around the bamboo table, which sat upon a large, brown fluffy rug. On the wall, above the table, Jason saw a clock and calendar for every month of the year. There was a family picture of Nadia, Zak, Fatima and Rashid hanging on the wall next to the calendar. Below the picture were some of Nadia's drawings and poems. There were colorful drawings of flowers, trees and a sketch of the playground where they had just came from.

Each of them removed their shoes and sat down on the pillows. Jason crossed his legs and made himself comfortable. Above his head was a string of lights for later in the evening. Since it was still early in the day, Fatima bent over and lit the two candles in the center of the table. Fatima had prepared, rice, fish and vegetables for their dinner this afternoon. After getting situated and comfortable, Rashid spoke and Rochelle interpreted back to Jason.

"Rashid is going to recite the Fatiha, the first suarh of the Quran as a prayer of blessing on our meal. He wants to know if you will follow him with your prayer as well."

Jason gestured back over to Rashid with a look of approval. Everyone became quiet and bowed their heads. Rashid began reciting Surah One from the Quran.

In the named of Allah, the merciful, the one who gives mercy
The Lord of two worlds, the merciful, the one who gives mercy

Owner of the Day of Judgment, to you we worship an to you we ask help show us the straight way, the way of those whom you have given grace, those who have no wrath on them, and who do not go astray.

"We thank you for bringing Mr. Ridgeway to us. We ask for your blessing upon him and upon the food we are about to eat."

Rashid paused. He was finished reciting. There was silence for a moment. Jason cleared his throat and began to pray:

"Heavenly Father." Jason paused and allowed time for Rochelle to translate. Nadia lifted her head up and opened her eyes. She stared at Jason with a stunned look on her face. She was fascinated and intrigued by Jason calling God, 'heavenly father." Nadia had never heard anyone ever address God as Father in prayer before. Jason continued:

"I thank you for Rashid, Fatima, Zak and Nadia. They are a beautiful family. Thank you for their wonderful hospitality and their kindness. Please shower your abundant blessings upon them and provide everything that they need. I pray that they will know your love and your grace today in a very special way. Amen."

Jason lifted up his head. "Thank you, thank you, Mr. Ridgeway," Fatima said smiling as she poured some tea into his cup. The food began to be passed around. Rashid wiped his mouth and looked over to Jason.

"Mr. Ridgeway."

"Jason," Jason interrupted and said smiling at Rashid.

"Jason" Rashid affirmed. "We are glad that you came to visit us. Most Americans, since the attacks of 9-11, are afraid and suspicious of all Muslims, thinking that every Muslim is a terrorist."

Rashid finished his point and filled his plate with some rice. Jason took a drink of tea and looked back at Rashid.

"Mr. Mustafa, I understand what you're saying and I would simply say that I certainly don't think of every Muslim as a terrorist."

Rashid nodded his head in agreement. He had a relaxed look on his face.

"There are extremists on both sides," Jason continued." Take for example the crusades. The crusaders believed that they were Christians doing God's will, when they were really being disobedient to God's will, by killing in the name of God."

Rashid nodded his head in agreement. Nadia leaned closer and looked intently at Jason.

"Killing in the name of God, is wrong, it is sin on both sides, "Jason said emphatically.

Fatima handed him a plate of fish.

"I hope you're not uncomfortable, Jason, sitting on the pillows," Fatima said.

"Not at all," Jason squirmed a bit and adjusted his legs.

"I hope that you like the fish," Fatima said.

"It's delicious," Jason answered.

"What is your favorite food?" Fatima asked.

"I love spaghetti!" Jason exclaimed. He wiped his mouth off with his napkin.

"I also love pizza and hamburgers and all that American fast food. I need all the energy I can get to be a soccer goalie," Jason said with a chuckle and a grin on his face. Zak and Nadia broke into laughter thinking back to the little soccer match that they had over an hour ago.

Everyone finished up their meal and were digesting and making some small talk. Jason leaned over and whispered into Rochelle's ear.

Rochelle tapped her cup on the table. Everyone became quiet.

"Jason has a little surprise for us. He brought along his guitar and is going to teach us a little song."

"Oh," Nadia said with excitement. She turned to Fatima with a look of glee on her face. Jason excused himself and grabbed his acoustic guitar out of his case and returned to sitting on his pillow. Zak's eyes widened as he slowly rubbed his hand against the guitar.

"I need a little group participation from all of you," Jason explained. He then began to clap his hands rhythmically.

"Follow me and clap like this." Jason explained. Soon everyone was clapping in unison and Jason began strumming his guitar and singing:

This is the Day. This is the Day. That The Lord has made, that the Lord has made. We will rejoice. We will rejoice and be glad in it. And be glad in it. This is the day that the Lord has made. We will rejoice and be glad in it. This is the day. This is the day that the Lord has made.

Zak and Nadia were clapping together. Their faces were aglow with excitement. Rashid and Fatima were chuckling at each other because they had lost the rhythm and had gotten behind clapping.

"Let's sing it again," Jason said and started again from the chorus. Rochelle finally stood up and Nadia and Zak followed. Everyone was having a jubilant time. Jason's music had filled every corner of the little hut.

"Great singing everyone," Jason said as he paused and then began to play an instrumental, one of the first songs he had composed when he was just a teenager. Nadia followed with her eyes every chord that Jason played and looked up at him in admiration. There was a lively applause at the conclusion of Jason's song. Rochelle finished clapping and looked at her watch.

"It's almost time for us to go," she said with a little sadness in her voice. But Jason has a special surprise for us."

Rashid and Fatima gave each other a puzzled look while Zak and Nadia looked up to Jason. Jason reached into his duffle bag and brought out a bag of presents. He looked at Zak and Nadia. His face was beaming with gratitude. He then looked over to Rashid and Fatima.

"Today has been a day that I will never forget for the rest of my life. I want to thank you for your kindness and hospitality. I have really enjoyed learning all about you and I admire you all for being such a close family in spite of your hardships and difficulties. I have learned a lot from you and I want to give you something to remember this day by."

Rashid and Fatima's faces glowed with appreciation. They were touched. Nadia and Zak kept staring at Jason with excitement in their eyes. Jason handed Rashid and Fatima a bag.

"Thank you," they both said and together opened their bag.

"Oh," Fatima exclaimed. Pillows!"

Rashid laughed out loud. "New pillows to sit on. Thank you Mr. Ridgeway."

"For you Zak," Jason said handing Zak a bag. Zak quickly tore open the wrapping. He got a huge smile upon his face.

"A new soccer ball! "He cried out. Nadia clapped her hands and began laughing.

As Nadia calmed down from laughing, Jason reached into the duffle bag and handed her a present. Jason didn't say a word. She gently took the present from Jason's hand and sat down on the pillow to open it. Zak looked on in curiosity. Brushing aside the paper, Nadia lifted out a brown-colored journal.

"Thank you, Mr. Ridgeway," Nadia said with gratitude filling her voice. She opened up the journal and sifted through its pages. Her face was radiant.

She looked down at the journal with awe and wonder. Her eyes fell upon the special letter that Jason had written to her. Nadia held the journal in her hands as if it was the most important possession in her life. Then she noticed an inscription on the first page beautifully engraved in gold in Bengali:

Jeremiah 31:3 – I have loved you with an everlasting love.

Nadia's eyes were drawn and fastened onto the Bible verse. The atmosphere became very quiet and still. Nadia looked up at Jason. Her blue eyes were filled with wonder and fascination. Jason looked deeply into Nadia's eyes with compassion. Then he looked down to the bag and handed Nadia a little black box.

"Another gift for me?" Nadia asked Jason looking puzzled.

"Yes," Jason said softly back to Nadia.

Nadia took the box from Jason's hand. The hut became very still once again. She slowly opened the lid and peered into the box's contents. Suddenly Nadia stopped. She didn't move. Her eyes were fastened on the contents inside the box. Then very slowly she lifted up a silver necklace from out of the box. Her eyes grew wide and her mouth fell open as she held up the silver necklace. Nadia had an astonished look on her face. For an instant, the images of the dream she had flashed before her face. She immediately remembered the scene in her dream when Jesus placed the necklace on her. Only now, in reality, she was holding one in her hands.

"Nadia, Nadia, are you alright?" Fatima asked as she reached out to touch her.

Suddenly, Nadia flinched and came back to reality. She was shaken and at a loss for words. Tears began to fill her eyes. She turned and looked at Jason.

"I don't know what to say. It's very beautiful. Thank you."

Rashid drew closer to Nadia. Zak climbed over the pillows. They both gazed intently at the necklace. Fatima gave Jason a look of surprise.

"I hope that you like it." Jason said speaking up in all of the surprise and excitement.

Nadia stared down at the necklace and then back up at Jason. Her whole body began to shake with nervous excitement. She shook her head in agreement.

"I do like it. Thank you Mr. Ridgeway" She then broke into a chuckle, "I mean, Jason."

Rochelle stood up. Jason stood up as well. Nadia stood up from the table.

"I don't like to break this up, but we must be getting back." Rochelle announced.

"Mr. Ridgeway has an early flight tomorrow morning."

Nadia had a heartbroken expression on her face. She laid down her journal and necklace on the table and ran over to Jason hugging him tightly. Jason looked surprised while Nadia held onto him tightly. Rashid and Fatima came over to shake hands.

"Thank you for coming, Mr. Ridgeway," Rashid said, "We really enjoyed your visit!" Zak walked over to Jason with his new soccer ball.

"When you come back, you get to play goalie again."

Nadia walked to the front door with Jason and Rochelle. She was wearing a very sad expression on her face.

"I hope that I answered your question, Nadia." Jason said as he stood at the front door. Nadia cracked a little smile. She understood exactly what he meant. Nadia stood at the door waving good bye to Jason and Rochelle as they walked to the SUV. She closed the door behind her, picked up her new journal and disappeared into the bedroom section of the hut.

"I think you hit it off very well with the Mustafa's today, Jason," Rochelle remarked as they drove across the bridge leading out of the village. "Especially with Nadia. I got the impression that she looks up to you as a Father-figure."

Jason remained quiet for a moment, absorbing and reflecting on what Rochelle had just said to him.

"You may be right Rochelle. Nadia is very special to me."

Rochelle gave Jason a look of agreement. Driving down the hill, the suv left behind the village and turned onto the main highway.

It was only a forty-minute drive back to the hotel. Jason thanked Rochelle for being such a good interpreter. He picked up his guitar and duffle bag and took the elevator up to his room. He opened the door to his room with his card and set down the luggage.

Exhausted, Jason flopped down on the bed and took a deep breath. Today had been one of the most incredible days of his life.

Chapter Eight
Kidnapped

The Air India 757 climbed toward its cruising altitude of 31,000 feet. Jason leaned back in his seat and turned on his I-pod. Meanwhile, far below, Nadia was preparing for prayer time at her sacred grove. It was a quiet and beautiful morning with the rays of the sun glistening on the leaves of the trees. Before putting herself in the proper posture for prayer, Nadia instead reached into her journal and pulled out the letter that Jason had written her. The relaxing sound of the water gently flowing over the rocks in the distance caught Nadia's attention and she took a deep breath and opened the letter. It had been translated from English to Bengali. Nadia unfolded the paper and began to read:

Dear Nadia:
You asked me in your letter, why is Isa, that is Jesus, appearing to you in your dreams? That is a very good question. First of all, I have never had that happen to me. I would be thrilled and honored if that ever happened to me. There is a purpose for Jesus appearing to you in your dreams as you described to me. God has a special purpose for that. He wants you to discover who Jesus is!

Jesus is the reason for all of my songs, Nadia. His love and forgiveness has so captivated me that I want everyone to know. I want you to know Jesus, too. I can tell you truly Nadia; He is so much more than a prophet. In the Bible, Jesus brings healing to the sick, He gives life to the dead, and He has compassion on the weary and brokenhearted. He teaches with great authority and exposes every false religious leader. He comforts the hurting and the downtrodden. He says "Come to me, you who are weary and heavy laden and I will give you rest." He tells the hungry, I am the bread of life. He tells the thirsty, I will quench your spiritual thirst. Jesus says to you," I have come that you might have life and life more abundantly.

Nadia, Jesus knows everything about you and me. He forgives all of our sins and wrongdoings. If Jesus is appearing to you in your dreams, don't run away and be afraid. Instead run to Him in prayer. He will listen and understand. I hope this has helped answer your question. Please write again soon,

    Your friend.
    Jason

Nadia put the letter down. The words that Jason had used to describe Jesus penetrated to the very core of her being. Her heart had been longing for truth and these words spoke powerfully to her spirit. Nadia knelt down. She raised her arms out in front of her. Tears began streaming down her face. She closed her eyes.

"Please show me the straight path, "Nadia cried out in desperation. In an instant, Isa was there. Nadia could see His splendor shining brilliantly against the darkness of her mind. Isa knelt down and gently touched her face.

"Nadia, I am the straight path. I am the way, the truth and the life. Come and follow me."

Nadia fell forward completely prostrate on the prayer rug. Her entire body was shaking. Her tears of frustration suddenly became tears of joy.

"I will, Isa. I will, Isa," she cried out.

Nadia completely surrendered. Everything around her suddenly became still. The birds stopped chirping and the cool morning breeze seemed to vanish away. In a moment, it was all over.

Nadia sat down on the bank of the creek and watched the ripples in the water as it flowed effortlessly over the top of the jagged rocks. It was so quiet and so peaceful today. Nadia watched as a beautiful yellow-spotted butterfly peacefully glided across the creek and landed softly on top of a rock. Taking a deep breath, Nadia lay back on the grass and gazed up into the deep blue sky. Never before had she experienced such a feeling of tranquility, such a presence of the divine. For the first time in her life, Nadia felt loved and accepted. She kept reflecting on the scene in her mind, when Jesus reached down and touched her face. It was a wonderful touch of affection that had melted away all of the fear and frustration that had tormented her soul.

Nadia could feel deep down inside of her the creative juices beginning to flow. She turned onto her left side and picked up her journal. She once again read the inscription that Jason had put on the title page," God says in Jeremiah 31:3, I have loved you with an everlasting love." Nadia paused and meditatively reflected on the meaning of that verse. She had never read the Bible before. This verse had opened up her soul to the truth and loveliness of God. Nadia closed her eyes and almost instantaneously she heard the voice of Christ. It was a voice of authority and yet gentleness. Nadia sat up once again on the bank and took the pen in her hands. She began to compose in poetic form what she heard the voice saying to her. The thoughts and images raced across her mind and Nadia began to write down the passion that was flowing out of her heart.

I made you with this purpose in mind. That one day you would seek and find and know me. This is your purpose in life.

Nadia paused and stared down at the words. She was awestruck in what she was writing!

I shaped and formed and set you apart. That your hunger and thirst would lead to my heart and love me. This is your purpose in life.

It felt like a river bubbling up out of the core of her being. Nadia continued to write.

You were made to worship and to make my name known. You were made for me. This is your purpose and passion in life and your destiny.

Nadia put down her pen and rested. Her heart was resonating with awe at the beauty of Jesus. Jesus had become to Nadia the treasure of her life. Yet in the corner of her mind, Nadia hesitated and felt the enormous weight of the consequences for what she now believed. She was guilty of Islam's most heinous sin. She had committed the sin of shirk, that is, assigning partners to Allah. Most specifically, by believing that Jesus was God, she had alienated herself from both her family and Allah.

Nadia was already feeling the pressure and weight of what it would cost to follow Jesus.

"Give me that ball," a little boy yelled out to his sister on the playground. The early morning air was alive with playful noise of the village children having fun on the playground.

Jeremy Bradenmore laughed out loud as he wrestled in the sand pit with the children. They were very playful and sometimes very aggressive, pulling at his hair and jumping on his back. Jeremy loved children and was enjoying his lifelong dream living amongst the poor and poverty stricken.

Jeremy had missed Jason's visit to Nadia by one day. He had just returned from England where he was visiting his parents for two weeks. Working for Worldwide Compassion was a dream come true for Jeremy. His life long vision was to emulate his Lord and Savior Jesus Christ by living amongst the poor and demonstrating the love of God.

In the distance, Jeremy could see Nadia emerging out of the woods and walking on the path toward the playground.

"Hey," Jeremy shouted as he stood up from his wrestling match. The village children paused from their activities and looked up toward the path.

"Jeremy, is that you?" Nadia shouted back. She began to break into a
run, clutching her journal in one hand and her prayer rug in the other.

Jeremy met her half-way and gave her a big hug.

"Good to see you!"

Jeremy had studied the Bengali language in school and was very conversant with it. This broke down the awkwardness of the communication barrier as he lived among the villagers. He looked closely into Nadia's eyes and could see a joy that he had never seen before. He reached down and tugged at the silver necklace around Nadia's neck. Nadia's face lit up and turned red from blushing.

"What's this?" Jeremy asked.

Nadia turned her head for a moment and then looked back at Jeremy.

"Sit with me on the picnic table," Nadia replied pointing to the table under the tree.

The kids started laughing and tugging at Nadia's hijab. Nadia smiled and bent down saying hello to them and then followed Jeremy to the picnic table. Jeremy brushed his crusty blond hair aside from his forehead as a cool breeze swept by the table. Nadia laid her journal down and laid her elbows on the table. She wore a very serious expression on her face. She looked down at the table for a moment and then looked back at Jeremy. Jeremy could see tears beginning to fill Nadia's eyes. He reached over with his hand to dry them.

"What's wrong Nadia? " Jeremy's voice was filled with concern.

Nadia touched his hand in gratitude and wiped the tears away from her eyes.

"I don't know how to explain it." Nadia began as she stared down at the table struggling to find the right words.

"I was praying today as I always do, well- I," Nadia stuttered.

"You have to keep this secret. My mother and father can never know," Nadia said emphatically with a look of fear and desperation in her eyes. Jeremy looked stunned and anxious to hear Nadia's story.

"My sponsor, Mr. Ridgeway came to visit me while you were away," Nadia continued.

"Before he left, he gave me a letter, answering my question."

"Yes, "Jeremy said looking perplexed.

"I asked him to explain to me why he thought Isa was appearing to me in my dreams."

Suddenly, Nadia's face brightened up with joy. Tears began to flood her eyes.

"This morning, I asked Allah, show me the straight path."

Nadia's lips began to tremble and the tears began to flow.

"I saw Isa. It was like a vision. I don't know," Nadia said struggling to explain.

"He touched my face, Jeremy!"

Nadia could barely control herself. Jeremy reached over and gently held her hands.

"Isa told me, I am the way, the truth and the life, follow me Nadia."

Nadia's voice cracked with emotion. Jeremy's face beamed with joy. His eyes were filled with tears.

"I told Isa, I will follow you."

Jeremy rose up from the table and embraced Nadia. Nadia completely broke down in tears. Jeremy held her tightly and rejoiced.

"I am so happy for you," Jeremy said holding her tightly. He let go of Nadia and sat back down wiping the tears from his face. Nadia composed herself and looked intently at Jeremy.

"Jeremy. I am so afraid. My parents will hate me and disown me. I will never see them and Zak ever again," Nadia said trembling with fear. Jeremy looked back at Nadia trying to reassure her.

"Nadia. We will pray right now. I will be there for you. I will help you."

Both Jeremy and Nadia bowed their heads together. They prayed fervently together asking for God's strength and Grace. Nadia suddenly got up.

"Thank you Jeremy. I have to go."

Jeremy watched with concern as Nadia hurried back to her hut. He understood the dilemma she was facing.

All through dinner, Nadia barely spoke a word. Fatima and Rashid observed her as she quietly ate, looking down at her plate. They looked at each other and were concerned. Finally, Fatima spoke up, breaking the silence.

"Nadia, don't forget your homework after your prayer time."

Nadia looked up, nervously staring at Fatima.

"Yes mother," she finally said.

She hurriedly cleaned her plate and rose up from the pillow. Nadia kissed her mother and father, grabbed her journal and headed out the front door of the hut. It was 8:00 pm. Sunset would be in forty-five minutes. This was the fourth prayer watch of the day and Nadia couldn't wait.

There was a touch of coolness in the evening air as Nadia found her way to her sacred spot near the creek and grove of trees. She stretched out her prayer rug. This time she didn't assume the strict postures for her ritualistic prayer. Instead, she sat down on her prayer rug and quieted herself. Her mind raced with the events of the day. Fear and anxiety gripped her soul, yet Nadia knew deep down inside that the decision she had made to follow Isa was the right one. For the first time in her life she knew her life had a purpose. Nadia was consumed with a real sense that God loved her. The sense of God's love for her had gripped her heart and enabled her to say yes to Isa even though she realized what it was going to personally cost her.

Closing her eyes, Nadia lifted her chin up and released the enormous heaviness she was feeling in her spirit.

"Isa," Nadia cried out.

She couldn't believe what she had just said.

It wasn't Allah she was crying out to, but Isa. Yet when she called out to Isa, she felt a very personal connection for the first time. It didn't feel rigid or ritualistic, but very intimate and very personal. Nadia felt like she was crying out and confiding in her very best friend.

"Isa," Nadia repeated.

"Isa do you understand? Do you understand that I will lose my family? My friends? I might even lose my life!"

Nadia paused. The tears began to stream down her face. She couldn't hold back the passion that was filling her soul.

"I said I would follow you. What should I do? What do you want me to do? "Nadia cried out.

There was calm and a stillness that invaded her whole being. From deep inside Nadia heard a voice speak to her.

"Trust me, Nadia and I will show you what to do."

Immediately, Nadia calmed down on the inside. She didn't have a Bible. She knew very little about Christianity except that the writings of the New Testament supposedly were corrupted overtime until Muhammad received the true revelation about God from the angel Gabriel.

In spite of this, Nadia felt she could trust the voice within her soul. She picked up her journal and began to write the thoughts and impressions flooding her being. In the midst of her turmoil and fear, the voice encouraged her to be still. She could hear the inner voice tell her, "I am with you. Do not fear, for I am here, I am with you."

A peace transcending her understanding flooded her soul. Nadia continued to write:

I am with you. I'll be your shelter in the storm. Don't be afraid of what they do. I will carry you in my arms.

Nadia dropped the pen and raised up both her hands above her head. An overwhelming sense of love and gratitude penetrated her soul. Nadia felt safe. She felt protected.

"I will trust you Isa. I will trust you," Nadia gently whispered in response to the voice.

Even though Nadia sensed that there would be some dark and difficult days ahead, she relaxed and let go of the anxiety that was gripping her body and soul.

Time seemed to quickly pass by. It was nearly 8:15 pm. The burning red and beautiful glow of the sunset painting the clouds was a sight to behold. It was getting dark and Nadia knew she had to head home to do homework. Refreshed, she picked up her journal and prayer rug and left her secret sacred spot for the last time of the day.

Suddenly, from out of the shadows, seemingly out of nowhere, a hand reached out and fastened tightly around Nadia's mouth. Startled, Nadia tried to turn her head to see what was happening, when a second hand wrapped itself around her waist, squeezing her tightly. Shocked and terrorized, Nadia tried to lift her body off of the ground, when a tall man dressed in a gray muscle shirt, pushed himself up against her, grabbed her chin and tapped her mouth tightly shut with a piece of gray duct tape. Nadia's heart was pounding with fear. She tried to scream and began kicking the man in front of her. The man behind her tightened his grip around her waist. Nadia felt an intense pressure. She felt suffocated. It was hard to breathe. She wrestled and tried to scratch her way free. The man in front of her grabbed her by the ankle and lifted her body up off the ground, while the man behind her maintained his tight grip around her waist. The man in front forcefully bound her ankles together tightly with a piece of rope. Then the two men together quickly carried Nadia a few feet off the path to a waiting car. A third man, who was waiting, quickly opened up the trunk. The two men carrying Nadia dropped her inside the trunk, slammed the lid down and quickly drove off. The brilliant and colorful orange sunset had faded into the shadows of the dark night. As the car drove off, a gust of wind and dirt from the spinning tires tore open some pages from Nadia's journal laying behind on the ground.

CHAPTER NINE
DIVINE DELIVERANCE

Jason sat up in his bed. He had been abruptly awakened from a deep sleep. He felt his heart pounding in his chest. He was grasping for breath. Beads of sweat were pouring down the cheeks of his face. The early morning rays of sunlight peaked through the blinds of his bedroom window. The clock next to the bed read 9:00 am. The images and shadows of the frightening dream were still fresh in his mind. He had seen a girl. She was trapped in a dark place frantically screaming. He remembered hearing her call out his name for help. He recognized the girl's voice. It was hauntingly similar to that of Nadia's!

Jason stared around his bedroom trying to collect his thoughts. He looked down at his hands. They were shaking. He had never experienced a dream like this before. Wiping the sweat from off his face with his hands, Jason threw off the blankets and fell to his knees by his bed. He began praying feverently in the spirit for Nadia.

"Nadia's still not home," Fatima said with a worried tone in her voice. Rashid walked over to his wife. The clock on the wall of their hut read a little after 9:00 pm.

"She is never this late," Fatima nervously said.

She looked at Rashid with a frightened look on her face. Rashid put his arm around her.

"She's a big girl now, mom," he said trying to console her.

Fatima pulled away from her husband and opened up the door. She spotted Jeremy sitting on the picnic bench adjacent to the playground.

"Jeremy, Jeremy!" Fatima yelled.

Jeremy put down the book he was reading and hurriedly made his way to the hut.

"Yes, Fatima. Is something wrong?" Jeremy asked.

Fatima gave Jeremy a blank stare. She was at a loss for words. She composed herself and finally spoke up.

"It's after 9:00 pm. Sunset was over a half hour ago and Nadia's' still not back yet."

Jeremy moved closer to Fatima trying to console her.

"Maybe she had a lot to pray about."

Fatima abruptly interrupted Jeremy.

"She is never late."

Fatima was starting to panic and Jeremy knew he needed to act quickly.

"Okay. Look. I'm going to go up the path and find Nadia. I'll be right back."

Fatima's eyes beamed with hope as she watched Jeremy take off running toward the path leading out of the village playground.

It was a darkness that Nadia had never experienced before. It was pitch black. The air was rustic. It was hard to breathe. The trunk she was in was like a steel coffin with no escape.

Nadia struggled to break free from the ropes she was bound with. She tried screaming through the tape on her mouth but had to stop after struggling to breathe. Every few feet her body bounced and shook from the car hitting bumps in the road. Sweat was pouring down her cheeks. Nadia's heart was racing along with the terrified thoughts in her mind. This was a nightmare! Who were these men? Are they going to kill me, Nadia asked herself!

Then suddenly, the car came to a stop. Nadia could hear them turn off the engine. Then she heard the doors opening and closing. The lid of the trunk was flung open and two men, their faces covered up by the dark night, reached down toward her with a flashlight. Nadia's body tightened up with fear. She tried to break loose from her bonds. One of the men reached down with his hand and squeezed open her mouth. Nadia tried to fight it off but found herself helpless. The man pressed two fingers down her throat and forced a capsule underneath her tongue. He then snapped her cheeks together. Nadia fought fiercely to regurgitate the capsule.

The more she fought, the tighter the grip became over her mouth. She could taste something bitter underneath her tongue. It was awful! She began choking. Her whole body tightened up. Nadia tried to rise up in the trunk, when suddenly her body collapsed back inside the trunk. Everything seemed to slow down. She felt weak and helpless. Her breathing began to slow down. Her body relaxed. The fight was over and Nadia finally surrendered and went to sleep.

Zak emerged from the bedroom rubbing the sleep away from his eyes. He had been awakened from his nap by the talking going on in the living room area of the hut. Fatima and Rashid stopped talking when they saw Zak come in.

"What's going on?" Zak asked with a puzzled look on his face.

Fatima looked at Rashid. She was speechless. Rashid walked over to Zak.

"Nadia has not come home from prayer time yet and we were a little worried."

Zak turned to look at Fatima and then back at Rashid. He knew there was something wrong by the tone in his father's voice.

"Why don't we go to the sacred grove? It's not that far away?" Zak suggested. He was anxious and beginning to get worried and upset. He started toward the front door.

"Wait," Fatima blurted out. Zak stopped abruptly and turned looking at his Mother.

"Jeremy has gone to look," Fatima explained.

"Zak, did you notice anything unusual about Nadia today?" Rashid asked.

Zak thought for a moment shrugging his shoulders.

"Nadia seemed a little quiet today. She seemed like something or someone was on her mind," Zak offered.

"Zak, has she said anything to you?" Fatima anxiously asked.

Zak gave his mother a confused look.

"No, what would she say-"

Just then, there was a knock at the front door. Fatima raced to answer the door. Jeremy stood at the entrance. He had a perplexed look on his face. Fatima saw a book and a rug in his right hand. Jeremy finally broke his silence.

"I found these along the path."

Jeremy slowly revealed what he was holding in his hand. Fatima suddenly shrieked and broke into an uncontrollable sob. Rashid and Zak hurried to her side at the front door.

"What, what did you find Jeremy? Where is Nadia?"

Rashid cried out gazing at what Jeremy was clutching in his right hand. His eyes couldn't believe what they saw. It was Nadia's journal!

The images were blurry and the air was damp and musty smelling. There were voices in the background and a cell phone was ringing. Nadia moaned as she slowly awoke from unconsciousness. Her eyes were struggling to focus. She couldn't mover her head or her hands. Above her a ceiling fan was slowly rotating. Slowly lifting up her head, she began to look around. Nadia was lying on an old, dirty mattress in the corner of the room. A light bulb with a pull string was shining over her head. As she became more conscious, panic and fear began to set in. Nadia's breathing accelerated and started to become erratic

"Help, help, help!" Nadia managed to cry out and her head exploded in excruciating pain. She felt dirty and violated. Her body was racked with soreness and pain. In the blur of her semi-conscious state she could see scratch marks up and down her legs. Her hid jab had been ripped from her head and her curly brown hair draped down over her shoulders. Nadia began to audibly moan.

"Isa, Isa," Nadia half-whispered. Her head pounded with pain.

In the other room with the two other men, Ravi paced back and forth as he talked on the cell phone. He crushed a cigarette out in a styrofoam cup and sat down on some boxes.

I've got a good one," Ravi explained, "She'll do just fine." He paused as the person on the other end of the cell phone spoke.

"What time is the rendezvous?" Ravi asked.

"Uh, huh," he said shaking his head. Ravi began pacing up and down again.

The sex slave trade business had paid Ravi well. He had been the contact kidnapper for over two years in Dhaka, abducting young girls and selling them for profit to become prostitutes. He had been casing the village for over two weeks observing Nadia's daily routine.

"A half-hour," Ravi said.

"Gotcha," he agreed and then hung up the cell phone.

"Isa, Isa," Nadia murmured out loud as she struggled to wake up. Ravi turned to the other men.

"We need to be ready in a half-hour."

Ravi looked at his watch. It was almost midnight.

At first, Nadia thought she was only dreaming. But it happened once again. The bed on which she laid began to violently shake. Dust and particles began to fall down from the ceiling and onto the mattress. The shaking intensified. Nadia ferverently tried to free herself. She heard loud voices and shouting coming from the other room. The walls surrounding Nadia looked as if they were rocking back and forth and moving. The intensity of the shaking was becoming unbearable. There was a loud muffled roar accompanying the shaking that pierced through her whole being. The mattress that she was laying on was vibrating and shaking with such force that Nadia felt like it was going to swallow her. The ceiling above her started to crack. Pieces of wood and plaster were plummeting down next to the mattress.

"Help me!" Nadia screamed and fiercely tried to undo the ropes tied around her hands and feet.

Nadia let out a scream once again and then suddenly the intense vibrating and shaking mysteriously stopped. Dust from the debris filled the air swirling around the room. Nadia began coughing. It was very hard to breathe. Then, it became strangely quiet. Nadia lay completely still. Her eyes shifted from side to side. There was no sign of her kidnapers. Nadia began to shake. As the smoke from the dust began to dissipate, a feeling of calmness and tranquility overtook her. Nadia found herself sitting up on the mattress. She looked down at her wrists. She could move them. The ropes were gone! They had vanished. Nadia flexed her wrists. She stared at them in unbelief. She looked down at her ankles. She could move them. Then she noticed the duct tape was no longer covering her mouth. She could speak. Nadia's face beamed with joy. She began to laugh out loud. She raised her arms up and began weeping out loud.

"Thank you, Isa! Thank you Isa!" Nadia exclaimed.

She continued to stare at her hands and legs in astonishment. Nadia than got up from the mattress and stumbled against the rubble feeling dizzy. No sooner had she regained her balance when suddenly, the room was engulfed with a white and blinding light. Overcome, Nadia fell to her knees and covered her face with both of her hands.

"Nadia, Nadia," a voice called out to her.

Trembling in awe, Nadia looked up. In the center of the glorious light, a man appeared. His face was radiant and glowing in a brilliance that Nadia could not bear to watch. Unable to speak, Nadia fell prostrate on the floor.

"Do not worship me," the voice commanded.

Nadia continued to lay outstretched on the floor.

"I am an angel sent from the throne of Isa. Stand up blessed one!"

Nadia slowly rose up from the floor, trembling in awe and fear. She tried to gaze into the light but squinted from the overwhelming brightness.

"Nadia, you are now free," the angel said, "Do not fear, your kidnapers have been subdued, but you must hurry. They will try to catch you but they will not succeed, so do not be afraid. You must leave this place and run into the woods. I will be with you and illuminate the way,"

Nadia looked down at her feet. She was wearing sandals. She looked at her brown dirt-stained dress.

"But how will I run through the woods wearing these clothes?" Nadia asked. The angel smiled back at her.

"Jesus will be with you. He will illuminate your way. He has foiled the evil schemes of your kidnappers, so it is not a great thing for him to make your pathway safe."

Nadia was filled with confidence and assurance. She looked around the room. Everything was in shambles and rubble and yet she was unharmed without a scratch.

"Come, we must go quickly," The angel insisted. Stepping over the rubble, Nadia followed the angel through the bedroom door and out into the dark night. They walked past the car to a gravel road and into the moonlit night. The air was slightly cool. Nadia gazed up into the sky and marveled at the full moon.

Walking onto the gravel road, the angel pointed to a path that led into the dense forest.

"You must hurry Nadia. Your attackers will soon be behind you. But do not fear. The Glory of God will light your way."

The angel gave his final instruction to Nadia and then disappeared. Nadia gasped and was startled.

"Where did you go?" Nadia turned from side to side in panic and fear. Then she looked in front of her. She saw a clear path leading into the forest. Nadia was terrified. Then she looked up at the full moon. The moonlight spilled onto the trees ahead of her. She had no idea where she was. Remembering what the angel had told her, Nadia began to run, her sandals bouncing on top of the rocks in the gravel road. She stopped and looked back at the ruins of the house and then disappeared into the deep, dark forest.

Nadia was lost. Looking up at the trees, she could make out traces of moonlight reflecting off of the limbs. She looked down at her sandals. Her feet pained from the straps twisted and torn from her struggle with the kidnappers. Nadia looked directly ahead. The path seemed to wind along the bank of a creek that was shrouded with more tall and twisted trees. Before she could take a step, Nadia could feel a strange but comforting feeling inside. It was a strange and subjective inclination that she instinctively knew what direction to take. It was difficult to comprehend, but somehow Nadia knew exactly what route to take through the dense woods. This was a confirmation of what the angel had told her. Jesus had promised to be with her and illuminate her way. Despite the fact that it was late at night and the woods Nadia was traveling through was both dense and dark, she could see a distance of ten feet in front of her. Mysteriously, the moonlight shining through the trees was acting like a lantern to guide and illuminate her way.

Then, as Nadia began to walk forward on the gravel path, suddenly the moonlight glistened down upon her shirt. Nadia stopped walking and looked down at her chest. An exhilarating feeling of confidence and courage filled her whole being. The moonlight was reflecting off of the silver necklace around her neck. The silver necklace was still there! In spite of the intense struggle she had with her kidnappers, the necklace had remained unharmed. Nadia couldn't believe her eyes.

"Thank you Isa," she whispered out loud and then started walking again back down the path.

Up ahead, Nadia could see a hill. The path took her up the hill and winded along another tiny creek that was flowing through the woods. As she walked, the moonlight peeked through the trees and illuminated her way. As she passed along the creek bed, Nadia suddenly stopped. She thought she heard voices.

"That can't be," she muttered to herself.

There were flashes of light ricocheting off of the tree limbs. Startled, Nadia turned around and looked behind her. In the distance she could see shadowy figures and tiny specs of what appeared to be flashlights.

The peaceful walked had suddenly turned into a nightmare! The kidnappers were in pursuit of her.

"Yet how could this be, weren't they injured by the earthquake?" Nadia reasoned within herself. She had to quickly find a way out of the dense woods and into safety.

"There must be a town or village up ahead with someone who can help me," Nadia anxiously muttered to herself as she ran.

The terrain was rocky and full of twist and turns around trees and broken tree limbs. It was very difficult to run in sandals.

She came to a clearing through the trees. Nadia saw a field up ahead and beyond that an old wooden bridge stretching across a river. The voices were getting louder and closer. Nadia watched the beams of their flashlights dancing across the tree limbs.

Sensing freedom was within her grasp, Nadia ran faster! Sweat began pouring down her face and her heart pounded faster. Her legs quickly became tired and racked with pain as she ran faster.

Nadia reached the top of the hill and raced toward the entrance of the bridge. The bridge towered fifty feet above a raging river. The moonlight ominously spilled over the choppy river waters below. Nadia felt very weak. She was tired and hungry and overcome by panic and fear.

Without looking down at the river below, Nadia raced across the bridge. In a matter of seconds, she reached the other side. Exiting off the bridge, she looked quickly to the left and ran up the hill. Below the hill was a gravel road. Nadia looked down the road hoping to spot a car and get help.

Then, just as she began to walk down the road, her head began to throb with pain. She felt dizzy and disoriented. Her whole body seemed to go limp. Her vision became blurry. She couldn't see anything in front of her. Exhausted and afraid, Nadia dropped to her knees. Everything seemed to become dark and silent. With no strength left in her, Nadia collapsed alongside the gravel road.

Chapter Ten
Into the Darkness

Jason sat down in front of the television with a bowl of cereal in his lap. He was hungry after a long prayer session. His mind was still spinning from the thoughts and concerns about Nadia's safety. Flipping through the channels with the remote, Jason finally clicked on the world news.

"In international news this morning." The newscaster began and then the screen dissolved to a picture of a map.

"The city of Rangpur in Bangladesh last night was hit by a small earthquake. A few homes and businesses suffered slight damage. Ten people were injured or trapped by falling debris. The earthquake could be felt 125 miles away in the capital city of Dhaka. Rangpur is 125 miles away from Dhaka in the southwest corner of Bangladesh and a distance of only 25 miles from the border of India."

Jason looked mesmerized at the television screen. He dropped his spoon into the bowl. Was this a coincidence? Was this somehow connected to his dream about Nadia? These scenarios and thoughts raced through Jason's mind. He laid the bowl of cereal down on the table in front of him. At that moment his cell phone rang. Jason felt a shockwave of fear surge through him.

"Hello," he began, almost afraid to answer his cell phone.

"Jason."

Jason quickly recognized the voice. It was Rochelle.

"Rochelle, is that you?"

"It's me."

"Is this about Nadia?"

"How did you know?"

"It doesn't matter, Is Nadia alright?"

"Nadia is missing."

There was an eerie moment of silence.

"Missing, what happened?" Jason demanded.

There was another moment of silence.

"We don't know."

Jason stood up and pulled the cell phone tight against his face. "What do you mean, you don't know?"

"Nadia didn't come home from prayer time after sunset." Rochelle paused.

"We-"

Jason interrupted. His voice was filled with panic.

"Did she run away? Was she kidnapped?"

There was silence on the other end.

"We, that is Jeremy, went to look-"

"And" Jason interrupted.

"Jeremy came back with her journal."

Jason became silent. The words ripped through his whole being and left him paralyzed with nothing to say.

"Her journal?" Jason's voice cracked with emotion.

"Yes, her journal was found. We have called the Dhaka Police. I wanted you to know this right away. Keep us all in your prayers. I'll be in touch."

Rochelle hung up. Jason slowly sat down on the couch in shock. All he could think about was the dream.

Collecting his thoughts back together, Jason looked down at his watch. It was 10:15 am. He had to be at Church by 11:30 am for a special prayer meeting followed by rehearsal for the Christmas musical.

Jason cupped his hands over his nose and rubbed his face. He took a deep breath. He was not in the mood for rehearsals and meetings today. Especially since it was a prayer meeting, Pastor Willoughby had asked him to briefly share about his recent trip to Bangladesh. How could he explain this to them now with Nadia missing?

Without wasting any more time, Jason put the dishes in the dishwasher and made his way to the shower. While in the shower, Jason realized that the prayer meeting he was going to actually was occurring at the perfect time. There would be some intense praying for Nadia's safe return.

Jason quickly dressed, grabbed his cell phone and guitar and hopped in the car. He turned on some music and headed for 270 highway. It was only a distance of six miles and he would be at Church. Watching his speed limit and keeping his anxious thoughts in check, Jason turned into the parking lot at Spirit and The Word Outreach Church. There were several cars there already. Jason quickly got out of the car. He gazed down at his watch. He was already five minutes late. He ran through the front door into the Church foyer, down a flight of steps and walked through some double doors. Catching his breath, Jason walked into a small, carpeted and dimly lit room where the prayer meeting was being held.

There were a dozen men and women sitting on fold-up chairs chatting with each other.

"Jason," Pastor Willoughby shouted.

He stood up from his chair. The other Church members smiled and said hello.

"Welcome home," One lady smiled and said getting up from her chair to greet him.

"Thank you," Jason answered and then took a seat.

The chairs were arranged so that the entire group was sitting next top each other in a large circle. The room became quiet as the talking ended. Every eye was now fixed on Jason. Jason sat back in his chair and relaxed after taking a deep breath.

"Visiting Nadia and her family was one of the most profound experiences of my life." Jason stopped and dropped his head. After a few seconds, he looked back up at everyone. Tears filled his eyes.

"Nadia is a Muslim, as you all know. But she is very empty inside. I know. She is hungry and thirsty for the truth. In so many ways, she told me that. She wrote me a poem which I will treasure for the rest of my life."

Jason paused to wipe away the tears. A few Church members quietly said amen and were touched by Jason's story. Jason continued.

"Last night, I had a terrible dream. I saw in my dream a girl terrified and trying to get out of a dark dungeon or box that she was in. She called out my name in the dream and I recognized her voice as Nadia's. I immediately woke up and knew that the Spirit of God was awakening me to intercede for Nadia. She was in trouble."

All eyes were fixed on Jason. They were fascinated with his story.

"About an hour later, when I was watching television, there was a report of a small earthquake in Rangpur, which is 125 miles from where I was in Dhaka. Then, just as the report ended, my phone rang. It was Rochelle, the Worldwide Compassion representative and my interpreter when I visited Nadia. She called to tell me-."

Jason's voice cracked with emotion.

"Nadia was missing. They had found her prayer journal along the pathway where she goes for prayer on a regular basis."

Jason paused again overcome with emotion.

"I know, I know beyond any doubt that God is going to do mighty things in this little girl's life. I know, I believe she is going to become a Christian."

There were resounding amens throughout the room. Pastor Willoughby reached over and put his arm around Jason. He then leaned forward and looked straight in the eye of every person in the circle.

"How many of you were here about two and a half months ago when a young lady gave a powerful prophecy at our Worldwide Compassion night?" Pastor Willoughby asked. Every hand went up.

"Listening to what Jason has just told us, has really impressed me that Nadia could very well be the girl that the Spirit of God told us would come to this Church so that we could train her and send her out."

Jason looked over at Pastor Willoughby. His face shined with encouragement. There was a chorus of amens and unanimous agreement.

"This young lady who gave this prophecy has never been seen since then. Satan is trying to thwart God's plan, but he will fail. We need to pray for Nadia and forget about time constraints and cares and focus on God's purposes in this little girl's life."

Pastor Willoughby grabbed Jason's left hand. Jason's hand dropped in his.

"Let's all join hands and seek God's face and intercede for Nadia."

The atmosphere in the little prayer room became still and quiet among everyone huddled together. Then Pastor Willoughby broke the silence as he started to pray.

"Almighty God, your sovereign plans cannot be thwarted. Your purposes will be accomplished."

There was a chorus of amens as Pastor Willoughby voice became louder and bolder in declaring God's truth.

"We stand in agreement here today that every demonic stronghold arrayed against Nadia is broken and cast down in the name of Jesus. We declare that Satan's purposes be thwarted while your purposes God be accomplished. We command every demonic force broken over this young girl. We declare that she is covered by your precious blood and that you send your angels to help her, for they are ministering spirits for those who are heirs of salvation."

The excitement of the prayer brought everyone to their knees. Some of the men began to kneel down and rest their elbows on the chairs while continuing to pray. Some of the women began walking and pacing up and down praying while Pastor Willoughby continued.

"Lord, we ask that you supernaturally protect and defend Nadia. Bring your people, other Christians to her that will declare your holy word to her so that she sees your unconditional love in Christ and is saved."

There was a responsive roar of clapping and shouting in response. Jason stood up raising his hands high over his head in praise to God. Pastor Willoughby continued.

"We thank you, Lord, no matter where Nadia is that you protect her and keep her safe and bring her to us as you promised. Your Word cannot return void. Your Word and your promises cannot fail because they are true."

Once again there was a tremendous applause amidst the shouting and crying as Pastor Willoughby concluded his prayer. Everyone hugged each other and rejoiced that God would keep Nadia safe.

The rest of the day was spent in rehearsal for the Church musical. It was almost 4:30 pm before everyone called it a day. Jason left the Church free from all of his worry and depression.

Climbing into his car, he sat still for a moment, reflecting on the time of prayer. He started the engine and was about to drive away, when his cell phone rang. Jason picked it up. He recognized the voice as Nurse Jenkins on the other end.

"Jason, please come quickly. Your mother has slipped into a coma. Things are not looking well."

It was almost as if someone had popped a balloon and let all of the air out of it. Jason's heart sank. He was devastated.

"I'll be right there," he nervously replied and sped out of the parking lot.

Racing toward the exit to the highway, Jason sped past a line of cars and flew around the corner ignoring the speed limit. He raced through a yellow flashing light and barreled onto the highway to avoid the rush hour traffic. Jason muttered a quick prayer out loud and pounded on the steering wheel in frustration.

"First Nadia and now my mother," Jason yelled out loud racing past a slow moving car in the passing lane.

Within a few minutes, Jason arrived in the nursing home parking lot. He grabbed his keys from the ignition and ran into the front entrance toward the nurse's station.

"I got here as soon as I could," Jason shouted nearly out of breath.

Nurse Jenkins greeted him and Jason stood still for a moment to compose himself. Sweat was pouring down his forehead and Nurse Jenkins could see how upset he was.

"Jason, I want you to calm down and try to relax."

Jason began to tremble with nervousness.

"Can I see her?"

"Of course," Nurse Jenkins replied as they walked toward Mrs. Ridgeway's room. They both stopped at the door. Nurse Jenkins looked into Jason's eyes.

"Your mother is comatose. Her entire body is shutting down. Her breathing is labored. Congestion is filling her lungs and throughout her body. When she breathes, she makes a gurgling sound. It is part of the dying process."

Tears began to stream down Jason's face. Nurse Jenkins handed him a Kleenex.

"I am really sorry Jason. I know how difficult this must be for you. We both knew that this day would come."

Jason nodded his head.

"Yes, yes, I know," Jason said trying to fight back the tears.

Jason turned and entered his mother's room. Mrs. Ridgeway was lying flat on the bed. Her breathing was very labored. The constant gurgling sound from the congestion was a frightening sound to Jason's ears. He slowly walked over to her bed and pulled up a chair.

"Mom, mom, "Jason quietly whispered.

He gently put her hand in his and bent over closer to her face.

"Mom, mom, I'm here with you," Jason said with voice cracking.

Mrs. Ridgeway slightly jolted after Jason spoke and coughed. Nurse Jenkins came up behind Jason and gently tapped him on the shoulder.

"If you need anything, I'll be right here."

Jason turned his head and smiled with gratitude. Tears streamed down his face.

"Thank you, I will."

Jason turned back around and looked down at his mother. He knew that she might be able to hear him in spite of being comatose, so he decided to carefully choose his words.

"You were right, Mom, when you said Jesus appeared to you in a dream, remember?"

Jason began to gently stroke his Mother's hair.

"You said, Jesus would be coming back real soon to take you home."

Jason gripped his Mother's hand a little tighter.

"He has come just like you said he would. I guess, I wish you could stay a little longer."

Jason could hardly control his emotions. He finally broke down crying and laid his head on his Mother's chest.

"I'm going to miss you, mom. I love you," he said keeping his head on his mother's chest. At that moment, he felt his mother's left hand slowly touch the back of his neck. Her hand was cold and damp and shaking. The touch of her hand brought incredible comfort to his soul. Jason began to sob uncontrollably.

"Jesus is with us, mom."

Jason reached into his pocket and pulled out his cell phone to call Pastor Willoughby. Excusing himself from his mother's room, He found his way to the hallway and took a break. It was 6:00 pm. Jason felt helpless. He had never been on a death watch before. It was so difficult to watch his mother suffer.

As Jason lifted up the styrofoam cup to finish the last drop of water, he saw Pastor Willoughby out of the corner of his eye walking through the front door. He walked over and gave Jason a big hug.

"How are you holding up, Jason?" Pastor Willoughby asked looking deeply into Jason's eyes.

Jason bit his lip, trying to fight back the tears. Pastor Willoughby hugged him once again, trying to ease his pain.

"I'm trying to hang in there," Jason replied, his voice trembling and cracking with emotion.

Suddenly, Nurse Jenkins rushed over to them.

"Come quickly, she's slipping away from us fast."

Jason tossed his cup on the floor and they both raced into Mrs. Ridgeway's room.

The horrifying sound of gurgling and choking met their ears as they both entered the room. Pastor Willoughby stood back as Jason ran to his mother's bedside. He quickly sat down in the chair and grabbed hold of his mother's hand.

At that moment, Mrs. Ridgeway gasped for breath and her chest rose up for the last time. The choking and gurgling sounds stopped. The room became quiet. Jason stared down at his mother with tears streaming down his face. He slowly let go of his mother's hand. Her cold and clammy hand went limp. Nurse Jenkins slowly walked over and put her stesiscope down on Mrs. Ridgway's chest. After a moment, she lifted up her stesiscope and looked Jason in the eyes.

"I'm really sorry, Jason, but your mother has passed."

Jason stared back at Nurse Jenkins. He was devastated. He couldn't utter a word. His face was drenched in tears. Pastor Willoughby came over and placed his hand on his shoulder.

"Heavenly Father, he began to pray, we thank you for putting an end to Mrs. Ridgeway's suffering and welcoming her home with you in your kingdom today. We ask now for your comfort and your peace upon Jason. Please bring healing and wholeness to his pain and sorrow, in Jesus name, amen."

Jason bowed his head and sat completely still. He didn't feel a thing. His pain and sorrow had turned into numbness. He felt as though he had fallen into the darkness.

Chapter Eleven
A New Beginning

The blazing white light slowly pulled Nadia toward the center. She felt as if she was floating along effortlessly. It was a wonderful feeling of euphoria and total surrender.

Then suddenly, Nadia felt the pull toward the center gaining momentum. The light grew closer and brighter. It felt like she was about to be swallowed up into the brightness.

"Mother, Father, Zak!" Nadia screamed in desperation. The momentum and the intensity increased drastically.

"Help me!" Nadia screamed again.

Almost immediately, Nadia faintly heard the sound of a voice that she didn't recognize.

"Can you hear me? Are you alright?" the voice asked her.

The brightness of the light was overwhelming Nadia. She clasped her hands over her eyes and-

The sweet smell of fresh air blew gently across her nose. Nadia slowly opened up her eyes. The bright sunlight beamed down upon her face. She slowly lifted up her arms. They felt extremely heavy.

"Just relax," the voice instructed her.

Nadia turned her head to the right. The face of a girl loomed above her.

"Here," the girl said as she turned her head, "Give me a cup of water."

"Drink this slowly," the girl instructed her as she gently propped up the back of Nadia's head with a folded-up blanket.

Nadia tried to raise herself up but quickly fell back down from the dizziness. She was lying on her back next to a gravel road just a few feet away from a wooden bridge.

"Where am I?" Nadia asked.

She felt groggy and sore all over her body.

Suddenly, two other faces appeared above her.

Nadia jerked and shrieked in fear trying to get up but fell back down once again. Her head was spinning from dizziness.

"It's alright. You're ok. You're safe now." The girl reassured her.

"Who are you? Nadia asked.

"My name is Leah. What is your name? "

Nadia paused for a moment to gather her thoughts.

"Nadia."

"That's a beautiful name," Leah answered.

"Nadia means, rare, precious,"

Nadia managed a little smile. When her eyes focused she peered into Leah's face. Leah had attractive brown eyes and short, curly dark blonde hair tainted with golden highlights. Her eyes seemed to gaze right into Nadia's soul.

"Let's try to set up again," Leah said.

One of the men with Leah carefully helped Nadia into a sitting position.

"Oh, Nadia, this is Abdullah." Leah said pointing up at Abdullah.

Nadia managed to sit up. She saw a tall, black-haired man kneeling next to her, wearing a warm and gracious smile.

"Nadia," Abdullah said, "We are glad that you are alright. We are thankful to God we saw you as we drove by."

"It is a miracle that we found you."

A tall, slender girl dressed in a blouse and tan kakis knelt down and stroked Nadia's hair.

"You're beautiful," the girl said admiring her.

"My name is Aisha."

Nadia managed a smile in her weakened condition.

"Do you think you can walk?" Abdullah asked as he helped Nadia to her feet.

Nadia very slowly rose up from the hard, cold ground next to the gravel road. As she stood up, her legs felt rubbery and her stomach ached from lack of food. Nadia was nearly dehydrated and weak.

Abdullah got on one side of Nadia and Leah on the other as they slowly climbed up the hill from the gravel road toward an old, gray bus that was parked on the shoulder of the highway.

Reaching the shoulder of the road, another man came up to them to assist. He was short, bald-headed and wearing glasses with a thin black beard across his face.

Abdullah and Leah let go of Nadia, as then man helped her climb up the steps to the inside of the bus.

"Hello Nadia, I'm Ali. I'm here to help you. You're going to be alright."

Ali gently helped Nadia up the steps of the bus, with Aisha, Leah and Abdullah following behind. There were several other young men already sitting on the bus. They stared at Nadia with faces of joy and gratitude as Ali helped her to a seat.

As Ali let go of her arms, Nadia dropped back into the seat. She was exhausted and hungry.

"You must be very hungry," Ali observed looking into Nadia's eyes with concern.

"I will get you some food from the cooler," Abdullah offered as he walked back down the aisle toward the back of the bus.

Leah took a seat right behind Nadia. Abdullah quickly returned with some slices of banana and oranges. Nadia reached into Abdullah's hands for the slices of fruit. She quickly grabbed them from his hands and stuffed them into her mouth. They tasted fresh and delicious melting over Nadia's tongue. Food. It was such a welcome sight. Nadia took a quick swallow of water and looked up at Abdullah with gratitude.

"Thank you. Thank you, kind sir!"

"It's Abdullah, Nadia and you are quite welcome."

As Nadia sat busily devouring the fruit, Aisha came over to her with a cup of tea.

"Would you like some tea, Nadia?"

"Oh yes, thank you. Thank you."

Nadia reached up and put the cup to her mouth, quickly gulping down the tea.

She stopped for a moment and took a deep breath. The fruit and tea was beginning to give Nadia much needed strength that had been drained from her by the terrible ordeal she had suffered through.

Nadia turned and looked back at Leah.

"Leah, is that your name?"
"Yes, that is right," Leah answered.
"Where am I?"
"You are outside the city limits of Rangpur."

Nadia's eyes widened. Living in the village most of her life, she was not aware of many places or cities in Bangladesh.

"Nadia," Leah asked, leaning up against the back of Nadia's seat, what happened to you? Where are you from?"

Nadia stared back at Leah with a blank expression. She was still feeling exhausted and her mind was unclear from the effects of the drug she had ingested from her kidnappers. Leah saw tears beginning to well up in Nadia's eyes. Nadia bit down on her lower lip and looked up past Leah, struggling to find the words to answer her question. Leah got up from her seat and sat next to Nadia and held her. Nadia broke down sobbing, dropping her head into Leah's shoulder.

"It was horrible!" Nadia cried out, her voice cracking with emotion.

"It's alright Nadia," Leah said trying to console her. She hugged Nadia tightly.

After a few moments, Nadia lifted her head up from Leah's shoulder. She composed herself and then looked back over at Leah. Everyone's eyes were fixed on Nadia as she began to tell her story.

"I live in a small village outside of Dhaka. It's a wonderful place provided by Worldwide Compassion for families struggling with poverty. I live there with my mother, father and my brother Zak."

As Nadia said the name, Zak, she broke down crying once again.

"They're probably terrified, not knowing where I am. I miss them so much, Leah."

Leah reached over and held Nadia tight once again seeing the pain and anguish in her eyes.

Leah looked Nadia in the eyes.
"If this is too painful, you don't have to tell it, Nadia."
Nadia shook her head.
"No, no, I need to tell somebody. I can't hold this in."
There was a moment of silence. Nadia composed herself.

"Every time I pray, I go to a very special place, a sacred grove, about a quarter of a mile from our hut."

Nadia's face glowed with excitement as she described her secret prayer place.

"Just before sunset, last night, I took my Quran and my journal and went up to the secret place. It was a very special prayer time."

Nadia stopped and looked around. She was reluctant to share what happened because she didn't know the men and women on the bus well enough to confide in them.

"When prayer time ended, as I was getting up to walk home-"

Nadia stopped. All eyes were fixed on her. She began to tremble. Struggling to continue, Nadia dropped her head down fighting back the tears.

"I felt a hand grab my mouth. I tried to scream and another hand grabbed me and then-"

Nadia's face was twitching and her hands were shaking. The trauma caused by the kidnappers was almost too much to bear. Leah reached out and gently held Nadia's hand.

"They forced me into the trunk of a car and then made me take some pills and it was horrible and so dark-"

Nadia screamed out loud, breaking down again.

Abdullah gave a shocked look at Leah. Aisha shook her head as tears streamed down her face. Nadia continued.

"I remember waking up and hearing them talk on a cell phone to someone to meet them in a half-hour."

"Oh, no!" Abdullah suddenly burst out exclaiming.

He shot an angry stare at Pastor Ali and then looked directly at Leah who was absorbed in Nadia's story.

"This must have been a human trafficking ring," Abdullah bluntly said with anger in his voice. Leah shot a frantic stare at Pastor Ali. He acknowledged her facial expression by bowing his head. Ali knew what Leah was thinking.

"But," Nadia continued. "You will think I am crazy, but," Nadia paused. For the first time, a jubilant smile broke over her face.

"Just when I thought I was going to die, there was an earthquake-"

"That's right!" Abdullah shouted. Everyone on the bus gasped.

"Remember?" Abdullah continued, "How we were awakened by a huge tremor!"

Leah's face turned white with shock.

"Go on, Nadia"

Nadia could hardly contain herself.

"The whole house began to shake and I heard the man in the next room screaming and shouting in fear and then, an angel appeared right in front of me. I looked at my wrists and feet and the ropes were untied and laying on the bed."

Nadia grew more excited as she continued.

"I was terrified at the beauty and the brightness of the light and yet I felt safe and at peace. The angel told me not to fear and said Isa had foiled their evil schemes."

Leah eyes were flooded with tears of joy. Pastor Ali's face glowed with gratitude. Aisha raised her hands in the air in praise to God.

"Then the angel led me out of the house and told me to run into the woods saying Isa would illuminate my way. Then as I started to run, I heard the kidnappers coming in pursuit of me, so I ran harder and harder until I couldn't run anymore and then-"

Nadia stopped. She was out of breath. Her face beamed with gladness from sharing her story.

"Then I woke up and you, all of you were there!"

There was a rousing applause as Nadia finished her story. Everyone stood to their feet and shouted praises and thanksgiving to God for bringing Nadia to them.

Nadia looked around at everyone. She was at a loss for words.

As the excitement began to die down, Leah overcome with tears of joy looked at Nadia.

"Nadia, what those men meant for evil, God meant for good."

Immediately, there were shouts of joy throughout the bus. Nadia stared at everyone on the bus. She had a perplexed look on her face.

"Thank you, thank you for saving my life. I, I don't know what-" Nadia stopped as if she was deep in thought. She looked over to Leah.

"I know some of your names, but I really don't know who you are. Why are you riding in an old school bus? Is this-"

Leah interrupted Nadia. Suddenly, it grew very quiet.

"Nadia, all of us are former Muslims. We are Christians. We have a Church in Rangpur, Called the Living Word."

Leah then drew closer to Nadia, looking intently into her eyes.

"Are you a Muslim?"

Nadia nervously bit her lip and looked down.

"It's okay. We're not here to judge you or pressure you. We're so thankful to God that he brought you to us," Leah said seeing the apprehension in Nadia's eyes.

"We want to be your friend, Nadia. We are here to help you. No one is going to condemn or hurt you."

Nadia felt a little more at ease. She nodded her head.

"You asked me if I was a Muslim"

Nadia paused. She looked confused and intimidated.

"I'm not sure I know what I am, Leah."

Leah nodded her head giving Nadia a reassuring look that told her that it was alright.

Nadia drew a deep breath and rubbed her eyes.

"I don't wish to be rude, but I'm really tired and I think I need a nap."

"Sure" Leah answered back. "No problem."

Leah immediately got up and walked to the back of the bus. She came back with a pillow.

"Here, Nadia just lay back," Leah said stuffing the pillow behind Nadia's head. Nadia dropped her head back and then turned to the left staring out the window. Her eyes quickly closed and she was fast asleep.

Pastor Ali started up the bus.

"Let's all head home," he said turning the bus from off of the side of the road and back on the highway.

Leah watched as Nadia drifted off to sleep. Already, she felt a very special bond with Nadia. She laid her head back against the seat and relaxed as the bus picked up speed and headed toward the outskirts of Rangpur.

"We're here," Leah shouted.

Startled, Nadia straightened up in her seat. She looked out the window. The bus had stopped in front of a red, three story-brick building. Stretched out over top of the door was a long white banner with large blue letters saying, "Living Word Outreach."

Leah came over and sat next to Nadia. Nadia stretched out her arms in front of her and yawned.

"Excuse me."

Leah laughed.

"You have a good nap?"

"Yes thank you. Where are we?"

"This is our Church, Nadia. We are in the outskirts of Rangpur."

Both Nadia and Leah stepped off the bus into the bright, sunshiny day. It was 2:30 pm, Sunday, November 25. It had been less than a day since Nadia's dreadful ordeal. Nadia took a deep breath, taking in the fresh air and enjoying the penetrating rays of the sun.

"We picked the location for safety purposes," Leah explained.

"Safety purposes?" Nadia said, squinting from the bright sun.

"Yes," Leah said as they walked away from the bus and toward the entrance of The Church.

"Muslims do not like us. To them we have dishonored Allah, committing the sin of apostasy. We are outcasts and from time to time they come over from the city and yell accusations at us. They stand outside here and throw stones and tell us we're going to hell."

Nadia looked astonished.

"I thought Muslims are supposed to be peaceful."

"Most Muslims are, Nadia. There are some who take the Quran very seriously. For instance, the more radical ones interpret Surah 9:123 very literally. "Believers, make war on the infidels who dwell around you."

Leah stopped and looked intently at Nadia.

"We are considered apostate infidels worthy of death."

Nadia was stunned. She stared at Leah in disbelief.

"There is a real cost in following Christ, especially if you are a former Muslim living here," Leah pointed out with a serious look on her face.

Leah and Nadia stopped at the front door of the Church. Nadia stood still. She felt awkward and out of place.

"Nadia, while you slept, all of us talked about your situation. We believe we should take you to the police. You need to report what these men did so they can be caught and be kept from doing it to another girl."

"No, no, I don't want to do that," Nadia protested.

"Alright, "Leah answered, trying to calm Nadia down. She could see the fear and panic in her eyes. The cool breeze blew Nadia's curly brown hair into her eyes. Leah could see she was still traumatized.

"Okay, Nadia, okay." Leah reassured her, gently touching her on the arms.

"Why don't you stay with us for a couple of day's ands then we'll drive back to Dhaka on the bus and you can then return home to your parents?"

Nadia looked up at Leah and brushed her hair aside. She nodded her head in agreement.

"Until then, "Leah said, opening up the front door of the Church," Would you like to take a tour of our little Church? It's nothing fancy, just an ordinary meeting place."

Leah's face glowed with enthusiasm. Nadia nodded her head once again as Leah opened the door. They both walked inside. Leah switched on the lights. Nadia stood near the front door and gazed around the room. In the very back of the room was a large stage standing three or four feet off of the floor. In the center of the stage was a podium. Off to the left of the podium was a piano and microphone stands. Sitting on the stand in front of the stage was an acoustic guitar. Behind the guitar was a set of drums and cymbals Surrounding the stage and extending back half-way to the entrance was a row of chairs.

Nadia looked up toward the ceiling. Lining the left side of the room, above the windows, was a white banner with black letters.

"I have engraved you on the palms of my hands"
Isaiah 49:7

Above the center of the stage, near the ceiling was another banner, in blue lettering reading:

"We love because he first loved us."
1 John 4:19

The banner right in front of Nadia captivated her attention. She looked intently at what it said. Her eyes lit up.

"I have loved you with an everlasting love"

"The verse on my journal," Nadia quietly said to herself. Her eyes were riveted to the banner. Leah followed Nadia's eyes to the banner.
"Are you familiar with that verse?"
Nadia's head jolted. She stopped staring and looked at Leah.
"Mr. Ridgeway put that verse on my journal," Nadia explained.
"Who's Mr. Ridgeway" Leah asked with curiosity.
"Mr. Ridgeway is my financial sponsor. He lives in the United States. He came to visit me just this past Thursday, "Nadia answered with a smile.
It was the first time Nadia had smiled since they met and Leah took notice of it.
"He must be a very special man."
"Yes, "Nadia replied, blushing. Suddenly, her face turned gloomy.
"Oh, no!"
"What's wrong?"
Nadia looked panicked and frustrated.
"My journal, that's right, I dropped my journal!"
"You mean when you were kidnapped?"
"Yes."
Nadia looked traumatized again. Leah walked over to her.
"Let's go, I'll show you the kitchen and the sleeping room."
Together, Leah and Nadia walked toward the front door. Leah switched off the lights and Nadia followed behind her.

"Would you like some lunch?" Leah asked Nadia as they walked next door to the adjacent one-story brick building.

"Yes," Nadia replied.

Together they walked through the front door. Inside the building was the Church kitchen. There were several tables and chairs arranged in a circle. A book shelf stood in the corner to the right adjacent to the restrooms. There was a long table in front of the kitchen area displaying paper plates, knives and forks.

"Hello, Nadia," Aisha said as she walked back into the kitchen with Fatwa. Hakeem and Jubbar were quietly sitting in the corner of the room reading. Leah led Nadia into the kitchen area. Pastor Ali was busy dishing up some plates for the other Church members. He was wearing a long white apron and dipping a spoon into a huge bowl of rice.

"Nadia, we're having roti, a delicious flatbread that you will enjoy," Ali said handing her a piece. Nadia took the roti from Ali's hand and sampled it.

"Ummm," Nadia said smiling at Ali with a look of approval. "Very good."

"We're also having beef and broccoli," Ali said as he dished up a huge portion on her plate.

"Thank you," Nadia said.

"Here's some chai" Leah said, handing her a cup of delicious, milky sweet tea.

After filling their plates, Nadia followed Leah to a remote table in the corner of the room. It was a little more quiet and relaxed away from the noise of the other people.

As soon as Nadia and Leah sat down, Pastor Ali stood in the center of the room. There was silence as Ali said the blessing. Nadia followed Leah as they both together bowed their heads.

"God, we thank you for providing this delicious food and especially for bringing Nadia to us. We praise you for saving her life and freeing her from the men who kidnapped her. God we ask that you would forgive these men for their evil acts and bring them to justice swiftly so they cannot harm anyone else. We ask this all in Jesus' name. Amen."

There was a responsive chorus of amen's and everyone began to eat. As Leah took a bite of her beef and broccoli, Nadia looked up.

"Leah, I feel very awkward around the other men. Do you have a hijab that I could wear? I feel very ashamed and out of place."

Leah looked back at Nadia and nodded her head.

"Yes, I can help you with that. I personally no longer wear it, not because it is wrong. I agree wearing it for modesty reasons is a good thing. The reason I don't wear it is because it reminds me too much of the tradition and rituals of Islam. Now that I'm a Christian, I have freedom. I no longer am bound by customs or traditions."

Leah noticed Nadia's face after she finished her explanation. She looked perplexed and confused. Nadia looked down at the table for a moment. She picked up her tea and took a sip. She laid her cup back down on the table and looked Leah directly in the eyes.

"Leah, do you mind if I ask you a personal question?"

Leah put down her fork and wiped her mouth with her napkin.

"No, not at all, what's on your mind?"

Nadia adjusted herself in her chair, working up the courage to ask her question.

"Why did you leave Islam?"

Leah looked up from the table at the ceiling for a moment, trying to relax and gather her thoughts. She wanted to answer Nadia's question very carefully.

"I have to tell you something, Nadia," Leah began. Nadia's eyes were transfixed on Leah.

"Nadia, I'm Jewish."

Nadia didn't move. Her eyes were riveted on Leah.

"I was born in Tel Avis, Israel. I grew up in a very abusive household." Nadia could see the pain in Leah's eyes as she recounted her life.

"My parents were extremely strict with me. We were very orthodox Jews."

Leah stopped and took a sip of tea. She relaxed a bit and then continued.

"I remember when I was eighteen. I decided I had enough. So, and you have to remember in all of this abuse, I was crying out for love and attention."

Leah paused. Her eyes began to well up with tears.

"Sorry," Leah said, half-laughing and wiping her eyes.

"I hated my parents and I wanted to do the one thing that would enrage them. So I met with some local people who were Muslim. I returned home one day and told them that I had converted to Islam."

Nadia's eyes grew wide. She couldn't believe what she had just heard.

"Instead of getting their attention and sympathy, they called me a blasphemer and told me to leave. So, I did. To make a long story short, I really did convert to Islam and believed I had found the truth. I won't bore you with all the details, Nadia, but through many circumstances, I ended up living in Dhaka."

Nadia couldn't take her eyes off of Leah. She kept looking at Leah intently while sipping her tea.

"One day, about five years ago, I was going to the market in Dhaka. There was an American Christian street evangelizing. As I passed by him, he asked me if I would read a New Testament, if he gave it to me. I looked at him and said no. Well, he was very persistent in a respectful way, so I eventually gave in and took a copy of the New Testament from him. A few days later, I heard that he was attacked by a mob of radical Muslims and violently killed."

Leah stopped. She looked angry and saddened at the same time. Then she continued.

"While I did not agree with what he was preaching, I thought, why did they have to kill him? Doesn't he have a right to believe what he believes? So, one night, while I was reading the Quran, a verse caught my eye. I had read that verse many times before, but, thinking about what happened to the Christian, the verse suddenly took on a new meaning for me.

.

Surah 8: 12
I will cast terror into the hearts of the infidels. Strike off their heads: strike off the very tips of their fingers. That was because they

defied God and His   Apostle. He that defies God and His Apostle shall be sternly punished by God.

    Leah shook her head and looked adamantly at Nadia.
    "The Christian man was killed because he disagreed with the message of the Quran. It was at that moment that I knew I could no longer be a Muslim. Although most Muslims are peace loving people, I knew I could no longer be one after that incident."
    Nadia's eyes were glued to Leah. She wore a blank expression of disbelief on her face.
    Leah continued. Her eyes then lit up with joy.
    "Then one day, another group of Christians came through Dhaka. As I walked through the market place, they began to engage me. This time, I was open to their message."
    Leah's eyes filled with tears of joy.
    "They told me about God's love and forgiveness. That Jesus would forgive all of my sins and I could have assurance of eternal life. They talked about how Jesus taught to love your enemies and pray for those who persecute you."
    Leah grew more excited and laid her hands on top of Nadia's hands.
    "I had never heard anything like that before. I was taught as a Muslim, just like you Nadia, that on the Day of Judgment, we could only go to paradise if our good deeds, outweighed our bad deeds. Instead of that, they told me, that God would wipe my slate clean if I accepted Jesus and that salvation was a gift that could never be earned."
    Nadia looked stunned as Leah continued her testimony. She was drawn to what Leah was describing. Everything within her was thirsting and hungering for the excitement and joy of what Leah had.
    Leah paused and noticed Nadia was speechless and deep in thought. Suddenly, Nadia emerged from her temporary drift in thought and refocused her attention on Leah.
    "I'm sorry if I've gone on too much," Leah said.
    Nadia interrupted her.
    "No, no, that's alright. I'm happy for you Leah, really-"

Leah interrupted, looking Nadia intently in the eyes.

"What about you, Nadia?"

Nadia dropped her head for a moment. She grew nervous, wanting to leave. She got up.

"I'm feeling tired, I think I'll go and lay down."

"Sure, sure, "Leah agreed. She got up from the table.

"I'll show you your room."

———————

Nadia awoke and sat up on the bed, stretching her arms. She looked out the window. It was almost 7:00pm and nearing sunset. As she turned back from the window, Leah walked into the room. She reached into her shopping bag and revealed some clothes. Unfurling it before Nadia's eyes, she held it up and smiled.

"Do you like it, Nadia?"

Leah was holding up a cotton, grey shirt with an attached scarf and a pair of dark gray pants. Nadia looked with wonder, smiling back at Leah.

"It's a burqa," Leah said enthusiastically.

"While you were sleeping, I went to the clothing store in Rangpur."

Nadia stared at the burqa. She didn't know quite what to say.

"You can wear it tonight," Leah said walking over to Nadia. She laid the burqa down on the bed.

"Tonight?" Nadia said with a puzzled look on her face.

"Yes, tonight Nadia. Would you like to attend our Church service?" Leah asked.

Nadia picked up the burqa from off the bed and held it lengthwise against her body.

"Alright, yes," Nadia answered as she laid the burqa back down on the bed.

"Thank you, thank you for your kindness and respect." Nadia said. She was silent for a moment, deep in thought and then looked back at Leah.

"You remind me so much of Sarah, Leah."

"Sarah?"

"Yes, she was the best friend I've ever had. I could tell her anything."

"Thank you," Leah replied with a look of glee in her eyes.

"I want us to be friends," Leah said clasping both of her hands on Nadia's arms.

After a hot shower and some quality beauty time, both Leah and Nadia were ready.

"I want you to go and just relax, Nadia," Leah explained to her.

"We are your friends. I hope you realize that by now," Leah said, reassuring Nadia.

Nadia looked very content and beautiful, dressed in her new unwrinkled, dark grey burqa. She glanced over at the mirror and stared intently at herself and looked back over at Leah.

"You have been so good to me, Leah. I could never repay you for your kindness."

Leah, touched by what Nadia said, looked at her with compassion in her eyes.

"I want to be good to you, Nadia. Please let me. Don't worry about repaying me either. It's my gift to you."

Nadia saw the sparkle in Leah's eyes. Nadia smiled with joy as they both walked out the door of the sleeping area.

It was just a few feet to the Church door. Leah walked through the front door of the Church building. Nadia followed with a little apprehension in her step.

Inside, the worship band was tuning and warming up on the main stage. Young men and women were mingling and talking to each other.

"Great to see you!" Aisha said, seeing Nadia and Leah walking together. Leah was dressed in a white blouse and a gypsy-type skirt. She greeted Aisha with a hug. Then she turned to Nadia.

"Nadia, I sing and play tambourine with the worship band. So, please find a chair and make yourself comfortable. I'll be back in twenty minutes."

Nadia smiled at Leah approvingly. Just then, Abdullah and Hakeem walked over.

"It's good to see you, Nadia," Abdullah said, "Hope you have a good time."

Abdullah jumped up on the stage and grabbed his acoustic guitar. Walking to the center of the stage, Pastor Ali stopped at the pulpit and tapped the microphone with his finger.

"Test, test."

Everyone began to quiet down.

"Welcome to Living Word Outreach, I'm Pastor Ali Saleeb. We welcome you in the name of our Lord and Savior Jesus Christ. If you're here for the first time, we are so happy. You're our very special guest."

Pastor Ali looked directly at Nadia with a warm smile.

"We are going to begin now with some music. The words are above me on the screen."

Ali gestured above himself. He then looked down at Fadi who was working the overhead projector.

The music began. It was a jubilant song with Leah singing and playing her tambourine in unison with the rhythm of the song. Several men and women around Nadia began singing enthusiastically and raising their hands.

The music, the atmosphere, the joy, the sound of the instruments was all very new to the eyes and ears of Nadia. People began clapping their hands. Some were dancing jubilantly in place at their chairs. Nadia glanced up at the words above her on the screen.

> You are my everlasting joy. You fill my heart with songs of praise.
> You set my feet on higher ground. You are my everlasting joy.

The words and the music penetrated Nadia's soul. She felt refreshed and whole and some of her uneasiness was beginning to disappear. She looked around and noticed everyone forgetting about their problems and instead behaving as if they had been transported to another world.

Then, without warning, Nadia felt as if she had been here before. Suddenly, the joy was being sucked away by an ominous and uneasy feeling. Her whole body began to shake. She felt trapped. She looked for a door. Turning around, she saw a polished wooden door at the rear of the Church and then suddenly, she remembered the dream.

Riveted with fear, Nadia shrieked out loud in the middle of the song and turned to run out the door. The sudden rush that had invaded her body was compelling her to run and to escape.

Leah watched Nadia run out the door. She motioned to Abdullah. Abdullah shook his head in agreement. Leah swiftly exited off the stage and followed Nadia out the front door.

Nadia was standing outside with a dazed and confused look on her face. Leah slowly walked over to Nadia. Nadia acted as if Leah wasn't there. She kept looking in the opposite direction as if she was in another world.

"Nadia," Leah said walking over to her. "What's wrong? What happened?"

Nadia didn't answer. She remained completely still and subdued. She dropped her head, struggling to speak.

"The dream." She finally said.

"The dream? What dream, Nadia?"

Nadia finally turned and faced Leah.

"I never told you."

Leah edged closer to Nadia. She gave her a look of comfort and concern, touching her on the shoulder.

"You said that I reminded you of your best friend Sarah."

Nadia nodded her head and looked down at the sidewalk.

"Then, you can tell me anything," Leah said, encouraging her.

Nadia turned and looked at Leah once again.

"One night, I dreamt I was being chased by two men, just like the ones who kidnapped me. As I kept running, I noticed a bridge, so I ran across it and then-"

Nadia's voice changed from a panicked tone to a tone of ease and delight.

"The most beautiful being I have ever seen came to me and called me by name. He said," Nadia, don't be afraid. You are safe. You belong to me."

Nadia stared at Leah with a look of awe in her face.

"He said, I am Jesus."

Leah looked stunned.

Then, "Nadia continued," He put a silver necklace around my neck."

Nadia pointed to the silver necklace that she was wearing.

"Like this one. I have never felt so peaceful and secure like that before."

Nadia's eyes beamed with joy and delight.

"Every time, I went to pray, I saw Isa, but-"

Nadia's expression changed to despair.

"Isa is only a prophet. Why was he appearing to me? I was afraid of committing the sin of shirk."

Leah nodded her head, understanding Nadia's dilemma.

"Then, when I wrote a letter to Mr. Ridgeway, I asked him since he was a Christian; would he help me understand why Isa would be appearing to me in my dreams? Well, Mr. Ridgeway came to visit me and left me a letter to read. In the letter he told me all about Isa and said the reason he was appearing to me is that he wanted me to discover who he is."

Leah's heart was intrigued and touched by the story Nadia had just told her. She glanced out toward an open courtyard adjacent to the sleeping dormitory just a few yards from where they were standing.

"Nadia, I'd like to take you to a special place, a lot like your secret prayer grove. We can sit and talk for awhile. Would you like to come with me?"

"Yes, I'd like that," Nadia answered.

IT was almost 7:30 pm. In the distance, the orange rays of the sun were slowly disappearing beneath the horizon. It was nearly sunset. The beauty of the approaching sunset was breath taking to watch as Leah and Nadia walked into the Church courtyard. The courtyard was a quiet and secluded grassy area behind the Church. There were two trees outstretched along a gravel pathway. Underneath the trees was an old wooden bench. A few feet away stood a tall, ten-foot wooden cross. The cross stood ominously beneath the tall trees and its shadow loomed over the wooden bench. The evening sunset rays seem to careen off of the beams of the cross as if to beckon the weary traveler to come and sit down and be a peace for a little while.

As they approached the wooden bench, Nadia stopped. She stood, captivated, staring intently at the bare, wooden cross protruding out of the ground. She stood still and kept silent. Leah stared at the cross with tears in her eyes.

"This is the greatest statement of love the world has ever known," Leah said, pointing at the cross.

"Islam and all other religions try to reach up to heaven to earn their own righteousness. But in the cross, God stepped way down from His royal throne in heaven and freely purchased the free gift of righteousness in Jesus, for us."

Leah paused and let the words that she had spoken sink into Nadia's heart. Nadia turned from staring at the cross and looked back at Leah.

Leah continued.

"It's very hard, when you're striving every day to please Allah, to accept what God longs to do for you."

Both Leah and Nadia sat down on the wooden bench under the trees. Leah adjusted her body and got comfortable on the wooden bench seat, leaning over to talk to Nadia. Nadia sat comfortably next to her, desiring to hear more.

"Can I tell you a story about Jesus, Nadia?"

Nadia nodded her head in agreement.

"The story of Jesus and the woman at the well is the story that drew me out of a religion of duty and works and into a loving relationship that transformed my whole life."

Nadia quickly interjected her point.

"Ever since I was a young girl, Leah, I have had a longing, a desire, a curiosity, to know more about Isa, but I was afraid that I would offend Allah."

Nadia's facial expression changed from frustration to delight, an anxious longing to know more.

"Tell me Leah; tell me what you have learned about Isa."

Leah saw an anxious expression of longing on Nadia's face that delighted her heart.

"Well, "Leah began." When I read about Jesus meeting the woman at the well, in the Bible, for the first time in my life, I encountered God's love. The amazing thing about this story is Jesus deliberately went into Samaria. The Jews despised the Samaritans, because they intermarried after the kingdom split.

Well, here comes Jesus to Jacob's well. He's weary from his journey. Along comes a woman. She comes alone to draw water from the well. Why did she come alone? Probably she had to because she was a woman of ill repute. Yet, Jesus speaks to her, asking for a drink from the well. That is amazing, because it was against social customs of that day for rabbis to speak to a woman in public, much less one of ill repute. Yet this is exactly what Jesus did.

The woman was taken back by all of this and in essence said, "Jews don't have dealings with the Samaritans, why are you asking me for a drink of water?"

So Jesus reiterates the point. He says:

"If you knew the gift of God and who it is who says to you, give me a drink, you would have asked him and he would have given you living water."

The woman didn't understand that Jesus was pointing out her spiritual need and not so much the water. He used the water as a means to get her attention in order to probe her need."

Leah paused a moment from her story. Nadia's eyes were riveted to her every word. Leah continued.

"Jesus said to her" Whoever drinks the water from this well, will thirst again. But whoever drinks of the water I give him will never thirst. It will become a fountain of water springing up into eternal life."

So the woman finally breaks down and asks Jesus for the water.

Then Jesus politely confronts her. She has had five husbands and she's living with one right now. Notice Jesus confronts her gently and demonstrates her need for Salvation. Jesus is not soft on sin, rather respectful in approach. That's what I like about him," Leah said, her face glowing with gratitude.

"He is extravagant with His love, affection and respect. He wooed her with His gentleness and love and she ended up telling her whole village that she had found the Messiah. When I read this for the first time, I was so impressed with how Jesus treated women with such honor, respect and dignity."

Leah finished her story and then looked Nadia straight into her eyes.

"That reminds me how Jesus has treated and approached you in the dreams and visions you've had. He has conquered your heart with His love and not the sword, Nadia."

Nadia's heart was pierced by the portrait of Jesus that Leah had carefully painted. Leah sensed that fear, fear of offending Allah and fear of her family, was holding Nadia still captive, even though her heart had been genuinely touched by God's love. Leah reached over on the bench and gently held Nadia's hands.

"I am no stranger to what you've been feeling, Nadia, I once felt your torment and pain."

Nadia looked up from crying. She wiped the tears from her face and looked back at Leah.

Leah continued, speaking softly and respectfully.

"Jesus is calling you, pleading with you. He says," Nadia, come to me. When you're weary and overburdened and stressed. I will give you rest. Just come to me. This is the same Jesus that healed the sick and raised the dead. He spoke with divine authority. The wind and the waves obeyed His every word. The demons fled at His rebuke. He said to His disciples, "He who has seen me has seen the Father." He said, "All authority in heaven and earth belongs to me."

Leah paused and boldly emphasized her next point.

"Jesus is much more than a prophet. He is God."

Nadia's eyes grew wide. She had never heard that before.

Leah lifted up her Bible. It was a small and had a burgundy leather cover. Nadia had never seen a Bible before. Her curious eyes followed Leah's fingers as she flipped open the pages.

"Can I share some Scriptures from the Bible with you, Nadia?" Leah asked.

Nadia nodded her head.

"Yes, I'd like that."

Nadia scooted closer to Leah on the bench. Leah read down the page and pointed to a passage of Scripture.

John 6:35

Jesus said. "I am the bread of life. Whoever comes to me shall never hunger and whoever believes in me shall never thirst."

"You said when you were a little girl, that you had a desire, a longing as you put it, to know more about Isa. That longing pulling at your heart developed into a thirst. This is what Jesus is saying to you. "I will satisfy your hunger, I will satisfy your thirst." No mere prophet could ever claim to do that. Yet, Jesus did, Nadia. He claimed to fulfill the longings of your heart. Yet you know only God can do that."

Nadia was deep in thought, pondering what Leah was explaining.

Leah looked off to the side and took a deep breath as if she were remembering something very painful.

"Nadia, when I was a Muslim, I was constantly under pressure to be obedient, to live up to the standards set forth by the Quran."

Leah looked back at Nadia.

"I had no assurance that I would ever make it to paradise on Judgment Day. These verses from the Quran echoed in my mind."

Surah 33:3
Those who submit to God and accept the true faith. Who are devout, sincere, patient, humble, charitable and chaste, who fast and are ever mindful of God- on these, both men and women, God will bestow forgiveness and a rich recompense.

Surah 23:102
Those, whose good deeds weigh heavy in the scales, shall triumph, but those whose deeds are light shall forfeit their souls and abide in hell forever.

Leah looked at Nadia with an exasperated expression on her face.

"I grow weary just thinking of trying to measure up to that standard. I spent so much of my time in fear of not measuring up. I was in torment"

Leah then opened back up her Bible and turned the pages.

"Contrast that with what Jesus says in Matthew 11:28."

"Come to me, all who labor and are heavy laden and I will give you rest. Take my yoke upon you and learn from me, for I am gentle and lowly in heart and you will find rest for your souls. For my yoke is easy and my burden is light."

"What a contrast!" Leah shouted. "The Bible elsewhere says, the wages of sin is death but the gift of God is eternal life in Christ Jesus our Lord. We can never earn a gift, Nadia. Salvation is a gift. It is God's grace, his unmerited favor, freely given to us."

Nadia looked stunned at what Leah was saying. It was hard to accept Salvation as a gift when she had been taught all of her life that Allah would forgive her based solely on her good deeds.

Leah closed her Bible and looked at Nadia with compassion and love in her eyes.

"Nadia, I know what I'm saying is true. I now have peace and assurance of what Jesus has done.

"For God so loved the world that he gave His one and only Son that whoever believes on him shall not perish, but have everlasting life."

There was a moment of silence as Nadia sat quietly comprehending all that Leah had shared with her.

After a moment, Leah spoke up again.

"Nadia, God wants to lavish his undeserved favor upon you, his gift of grace. All you have to do is hold out your hands and receive his grace gift, Jesus Christ."

Leah peered intently into Nadia's eyes.

"Would you like to pray with me right now and ask Jesus to come into your heart and be your Savior?"

Leah watched as a tiny tear trickled down Nadia's face. Nadia nervously wiped it away and looked up at Leah. Her face shined with a penetrating look of longing.

"Yes, Leah," Nadia nervously replied. "Will Isa or Jesus as you call him, will He give me the same drink of living water like he did for the woman at the well?"

Nadia's question to Leah sent incredible feelings of joy radiating through her whole being. Leah fought back the tears.

"Oh yes, oh yes He will, Nadia!"

Darkness was beginning to fall as the sun set below the horizon. Leah and Nadia both held each others hands and bowed their heads together in prayer.

Chapter Twelve
Beyond The Veil

Nadia awoke early the next morning eager to begin reading her new found treasure, the Bible. This was her most priceless possession now. It held a special place in her heart since Leah had been kind and generous enough to give it to her. It was priceless because, this was Leah's first Bible when she became a Christian five years ago. All of the appropriate passages had been highlighted for Nadia to begin her first steps as a newborn Christian.

Nadia spent the entire afternoon reading about the life and ministry of Jesus in the four gospels. Despite being told as a Muslim that the Bible was not trustworthy and had been changed or corrupted, Nadia discovered instead the four gospels painted a beautiful and consistent portrait of Jesus. A tremendous weight of condemnation and guilt had been lifted off of Nadia's shoulders. As she read, Nadia felt a freedom that she had never experienced before. A freedom to learn, a freedom to experience, a freedom to worship and enjoy a new life without the dread and fear of punishment.

Many of the Bible passages Nadia read spoke so personally to her and brought healing to the very core of her being that had been held in bondage. Lying across the bed in Leah's sleep room, Nadia turned to Micah (one of the Minor Prophets) Chapter 7, verse 18. Her eyes were fixed on the words, "transgressions and anger." She began to read the passage out loud to herself.

Who Is a God like you, pardoning iniquity and passing over transgressions for the remnant of His inheritance?
He does not retain His anger forever, because He delights in steadfast love.
He will again have compassion on us.
He will tread our iniquities underfoot.
You will cast all our sins in the depths of the sea.

Nadia focused on the phrase, "steadfast love," and how God's steadfast love would forever cast her sins into the depths of the sea. The Scripture took Nadia's breath away as she pondered such love and such forgiveness. This was an entirely new concept for Nadia to digest. Fear and dread had been her daily diet as a Muslim. Now the Bible was telling her something entirely different. Nadia saw God now through the lens of Grace instead of dread. As she meditated on the Bible passage, she could only think of being grateful to God for His rich mercy.

Turning to the Psalms, Nadia followed Leah's highlighting down to Psalm 103: verse 18.

He does not deal with us according to our sins, nor repaid us according to our iniquities. For as high as the heavens are above the earth, so great is His steadfast love toward those who fear Him. As far as the east is from the west, so far does he remove our transgressions from us.

Nadia felt an exhilarating rush of gratitude flow through her body. Yet, she knew it would take time for God's Word to transform her mind from the constant threats of fear and punishment.

Thinking back to her dreams many months ago, Nadia remembered when Jesus appeared to her, how she felt a real sense of love and belonging. Jesus was like her warrior prince who rode in on his white horse to rescue her. Now she felt like a princess, a princess of God instead of a slave.

Turning to one more passage, Nadia gazed down at John 8: 31-32 in the New Testament. Jesus was speaking and this immediately got Nadia's attention.

If you abide in my Word, you are truly my disciples and you will know the truth and the truth will set you free.

The words, "truth and free" lept out of the pages into Nadia's heart. Was she really free, Nadia thought? Nadia sat up on the bed. Her mind was reeling from the new truths that had been deposited in her soul. She missed going to her secret prayer grove. Then, she remembered the courtyard cross. Nadia reached over to pick up a pen and a little journal that Leah had given her. She longed for the journal that Jason had given her. Tomorrow she would be returning home and then she would be reunited with both her parents and her journal.

Nadia looked at the clock on the wall. It was 7:15 pm. This would be the last time she could go to the courtyard. It was nearly sunset and Nadia had some personal issues to bring before God.

Nadia walked out the front door of the dormitory building and walked up the path to the old wooden bench a few feet behind the cross. Nadia gazed at the cross. Despite being taught all of her life by the Quran that Jesus was not crucified, Nadia was drawn to the pieces of wood that were before her eyes. As she continued gazing at the cross, the stillness and the silence spoke profoundly to her heart.

Inside, her whole being despaired with a sense of shame and unworthiness. Bowing her head, Nadia began wrestling with an intense feeling of guilt that tore at her soul.

When she could no longer bare the feelings of unworthiness and shame, Nadia slowly lifted her head back up and once again gazed intently at the cross. This time, however, her whole being radiated with a soothing and refreshing feeling of unconditional love and forgiveness. It was as if someone had slowly poured down fresh anointing oil over the top of her head. She felt cleansed of every wrong that she had ever committed.

Nadia sat completely still with her eyes closed basking in the mercy and grace of God, realizing that once and for all Jesus had removed all of her shame and disgrace.

At that moment, Nadia reached up behind her head and removed her hijab. Her thick, curly brown hair fell down across her forehead and over her eyes. The hijab lay wrinkled in a pile next to her on the bench. Years of tradition and religion suddenly melted away. For the first time in her life, Nadia felt completely fulfilled and utterly free.

Sitting all alone on the bench facing the wooden cross in front of her, God suddenly became more real and personal to her than ever before. Nadia remembered in her dream when Jesus reached down and gently touched her face. With tears of joy streaming down her face and her hijab lying next to her on the bench, for the very first time, Nadia could see the face of God beyond her veil. For far too long, the veil had masked and distorted the true face of God. Today, however, the veil was no longer blinding Nadia. As God's princess, she would no longer need it.

Nadia then closed her eyes. She had never uttered a prayer before spontaneously from her heart. It had always been a memorized recitation from the Quran. But this time, Nadia felt a rush of gratitude and affection bubbling up from the inside. She wanted to express her innermost thoughts and feelings to God. Feeling an overwhelming sense of intimacy, Nadia proceeded to utter her first, real, personal prayer to God.

"God," Nadia began.

True joy began to rise up from the inside. It felt almost like talking to her closest friend.

"Please hear my prayer, I," Nadia stuttered a bit. She felt a little awkward. She was used to being so formalistic. She remembered when she was a Muslim; approaching Allah in prayer was very uncomfortable for her. Allah always seemed so distant and far away. Now, Nadia had a different perspective. Praying was now a new and exciting adventure. She felt a real sense of intimacy and delight in approaching God. It was almost as if God desired and delighted in hearing the thoughts and intentions of Nadia's heart.

"I don't know what to say God, except thank you, thank you, "Nadia's voice intensified.

"Thank you, thank you for your love, thank you for forgiving me of all my sins and shame, God. Jesus I love you," Nadia cried out in gratitude. Her voice cracked with emotion. The revelation of God's love was still such a new reality to Nadia. It was still a struggle to really believe that God loved her.

Nadia finished her short prayer. Her heart was filled with joy and overflowing with gratitude. Nadia had never before experienced such feelings in prayer. She picked up her Bible and began reading Psalm 27. Looking over at her hijab lying on the bench next to her to her, suddenly her mind was captivated by this whole new experience. She picked up her journal and began to write a new poem reflecting on the events of the day. The words came powerfully to her like they used to back home whenever she was at her secret prayer grove. Nadia began writing:

There's only one thing that I desire
And one thing that I seek after
To gaze upon your beauty O' Lord
To see you face to face
I want to behold your glorious face
I want to see you face to face

You opened up the way
When your hands and feet were nailed
Now I can see your face beyond the veil
I want to touch your face
With these hands that are frail
I long to see your face beyond the veil
I want to see your glorious face
And be transformed by your infinite grace

Nadia laid down her pen and stared at the words that she had written. The words echoed the desire of her heart. Nadia yearned for a real intimacy with God. Intimacy with God had once been a foreign concept.

Now it was a reality.

Nadia closed her journal. Her first day as a Christian had been a rich and rewarding experience. Nadia rose up from the bench and headed back to the sleeping dormitory to meet Leah. She couldn't wait to share her new poem with her.

It was a cool and rainy Friday morning. The day had finally arrived for Nadia to return home to Dhaka and be reunited with her parents. It had been six days since her disappearance. Nadia had mixed emotions on how she was going to explain things to her parents. How would they react when she told them she had become a Christian? Nadia knew she would have to trust the Lord to take care of this delicate situation.

    Nadia joined Leah, Aisha, Fadwa and Abdullah for breakfast before leaving. They sat together laughing, joking and talking about how each of them adjusted to a new life after becoming a Christian. Abdullah reminisced about his family rejecting him and telling him to leave. He explained how he lived on the streets for a month before Pastor Ali found him in a homeless shelter in Dhaka. Abdullah's story encouraged Nadia as she sat listening and thinking about how her parents were going to react.

    Pastor Ali came over to the table and announced that he was going to warm up the old gray bus. Nadia glanced over to Leah. Leah's face looked sad. Abdullah and Fadwa followed Aisha in the kitchen to help with the dishes.

    Leah was not going to be able to make the trip back to Dhaka. She had to go to work today. She had a part time job at a clothing store in Rangpur. It would difficult to say good bye to Nadia today.

    After sitting quietly for a moment and collecting her thoughts, Leah got up from her chair as Nadia gathered together her belongings for the trip. Leah and Nadia stood face to face for a moment and then rushed into each other's arms. They both hugged each other tightly and then backed away, laughing and wiping away the tears.

    "Look at us," Leah laughed, wiping off her face with a napkin, "We're two grown up people, crying like babies."

    Nadia laughed back at Leah.

    "Nadia," Leah began. She had a serious look on her face.

    "We are here for you, if things don't work out. We're here. We're family now."

    Nadia smiled. Her face brightened up.

    "You know where to find us. We do a lot of street preaching in Dhaka. If you need us, we'll be there."

    Nadia nodded her head. Then she once again embraced Leah with a hug, breaking down in tears.

    "You're like the sister I never had," Nadia said, backing away from Leah.

"You are so much like Sarah was. I can tell you anything."

Leah was touched by what Nadia said. It was hard for her to hold back the tears.

"Please write," Leah said.

"I will," Nadia quickly said back.

Abdullah returned from the kitchen and carried Nadia's belongings for her. Nadia and Leah hugged once more and Nadia then followed Abdullah out to the gray bus.

Nadia found a seat by herself at the back of the bus where she could be alone. Pastor Ali put the bus in gear and drove away toward the highway. Nadia looked back at Leah standing in front of the Church. She smiled and waved as the bus turned off the gravel road onto the highway.

Abdullah led Fadwa and Aisha into songs of worship as the heavy raindrops beat against the windows of the bus. Nadia was in a reflective mood, listening and enjoying the songs that were being sung, but keeping to herself in the back of the bus. In less than two hours, she would be back in Dhaka and Nadia was still feeling apprehensive about telling her parents that she had become a Christian.

Nadia then remembered that it had been a week ago when Mr. Ridgeway had visited her. She remembered how kind and respectful he had been to her and how his whole being seemed to radiate the love of Christ. Nadia then remembered reading Mr. Ridgeway's letter at the secret prayer grove and how that letter had such an impact on her. Deep down inside, Nadia wished that Mr. Ridgeway was sitting right next to her so that she could tell him how her life dramatically had changed and she had discovered Jesus just as he told her to.

Nadia turned from looking out the window and being deep in thought and came back to reality. She reached across her seat and picked up her journal. Even though, obviously, Mr. Ridgeway was not here to celebrate her new life, Nadia decided to do the next best thing and tell him in writing. Nadia decided to keep a journal of her new Christian life and one day when she met Mr. Ridgeway once again, she would personally give it to him.

With the rain still beating heavily against the windows of the bus, Nadia turned her thoughts and affections toward the man who had been so instrumental in helping her discover who Jesus is.

Friday, November 30, 2004
Dear Mr. Ridgeway:
The most incredible thing has just happened to me! You said Jesus appeared to me in my dream because he wants me to discover who he is. I have discovered who he is, Mr. Ridgeway. He is more than a prophet to me. I am no longer a Muslim. I've become a Christian. I wish you were here now sitting next to me, so I could explain how all of this happened. It is unbelievable, but it happened to me. When I see you again, I will try to explain it all.

Thank you for telling me all about Jesus. You are a very special man, Mr. Ridgeway

Nadia laid down the pen and wiped the tears away from her eyes. She gazed out the rain-soaked window. It was still hard to believe all the things that had happened to her. She picked up her Bible and once again turned to Psalm 27. Her eyes fell upon verses 9-10:

Cast me not off, forsake me not,
O God of my salvation
For my Father and my mother have forsaken me. But the Lord will take me in.

Nadia quickly closed the Bible.
"Is God trying to prepare me, "Nadia quietly asked herself?
She opened up the Bible again and turned to Psalm 27, verse 10:

For my Father and Mother have forsaken me
But The Lord will take me in.

A Haunting feeling gripped Nadia's soul. Se picked up a pillow next to her on the seat and propped it up against the window and closed her eyes.

"Even if my parents forsake me, God, you will not," Nadia courageously whispered to herself. Then she peacefully drifted off to sleep.

Nadia was awakened by the bus abruptly stopping. She opened her eyes and rose up from the pillow. The rain had stopped and the sun was beaming through the hazy bus windows.

"We've arrived," Aisha told Nadia, standing in the front of her seat.

Nadia looked out the window and rubbed her eyes. The bus had pulled off to the side of the road and was parked in front of the entrance to the village project.

Nadia was finally home. She quickly gathered up her clothing bag, journal and Bible. By this time, Pastor Ali, Abdullah and Fadwa had gathered around where Nadia had been sitting at the rear of the bus. They had sad expressions on their faces. Nadia quietly sat in her seat, unable to find the words to say good-bye.

"We're going to miss you, Nadia," Pastor Ali said, sitting down next to her. Nadia struggled to fight back the tears.

"You all have been so kind to me," Nadia said tearfully.

"We loved having you," Aisha said, leaning over Nadia's seat from behind.

"You are very special to us," Abdullah said with a warm smile.

"Nadia," Pastor Ali said, "We are family. Now, if you have any problems, just remember, we are always in Dhaka, street preaching on the weekends. We will be there until Saturday afternoon. You know where to find us."

Nadia looked at them with gratitude. She felt so at ease and peaceful around her new Christian family.

"I'm scared. I have to be honest with all of you," Nadia admitted with her voice trembling. "But I know God is with me."

"Yes, yes, we agree," Everyone said, their voices echoing with encouragement.

"Let's pray before you go," Pastor Ali suggested. Everyone bowed their heads. Pastor Ali led a prayer of grace and encouragement for Nadia.

When the prayer ended, Nadia hugged everyone tightly and then stepped off the bus into the warm sunshine. Holding her Bible in one hand and her clothing in the other, she watched as the bus slowly drove away leaving a cloud of dust.

Nadia stared at the gravel road entrance. She took a deep breath and began walking. Walking past a grove of trees, she crossed the wooden bridge and in the distance saw the familiar playground that was only a few feet from the hut.

As she drew near the playground, suddenly the children stopped playing.

"It's Nadia!" they screamed, running towards her.

"Hi Nadia, where have you been?" little Sarah screamed excitedly.

Nadia reached down and hugged little Sarah and her two playmate friends.

"I'm home, I'm home!" Nadia cried out as she kneeled down to hug them.

Slowly getting up, Nadia looked directly in front of her. It was her hut! Gathering up courage, Nadia walked towards her hut with little Sarah and her playmates laughing and following close behind her.

Nadia laid down her clothing bag. She had arrived at the front door. Her body was shaking all over. She took another deep breath and looked up to God, whispering a quick prayer. She turned the latch. The door opened. Picking up her clothing bag, she walked into the hut.

"Mother, Father," Nadia nervously said, announcing her arrival.

Suddenly, Fatima's face emerged from around the corner. Their eyes met. Fatima shrieked and raced toward Nadia.

"Nadia, Nadia, you're home!" She screamed, holding onto Nadia with a tight grip.

Nadia hugged Fatima back, resting her head on her shoulder and weeping uncontrollably.

Rasheed came into the room and raced toward his daughter.

"Nadia!" he exclaimed, his face turning white with shock and surprise. He joined Fatima hugging Nadia.

"You're home, you're home!" Rasheed cried out with tears streaming down his face.

The hugging continued for another minute and Fatima finally released Nadia. Both of their faces were smeared with tears.

"What happened to you?" Fatima anxiously asked with desperation in her voice, wanting an answer.

Nadia calmed down trying to control her sobbing. Her voice trembled and her body was still shaking.

"It was horrible, horrible, mother. I was kidnapped!"

"Kidnapped?" Fatima shouted back.

"Yes, yes," Nadia said, brushing the strands of brown hair away from her eyes.

"Saturday, when I finished the fourth prayer at sunset, as I started to walk home, I felt a hand grab me-"

Nadia couldn't finish. She broke down in tears. Fatima tightly hugged her again.

"Who did this to you?" Rasheed demanded, his face radiating with anger.

"I don't know, father," Nadia answered.

"But, how did you escape?"

Nadia remained quiet for a moment.

"They took me to a vacant house and then there was an earthquake and-."

Nadia hesitated, afraid to tell the rest of the story. She noticed her mother going over to the dining room table. Then she saw her come back with her journal in her hand.

"My journal!" Nadia exclaimed with gladness.

The demeanor of Fatima's face suddenly changed from frantic fear to a sober, interrogating look.

"Nadia," Fatima began, with a serious tone in her voice. "I have some questions about your journal."

Nadia nervously stared down at her journal. Her mother's hand was firmly clutching the cover. She slowly looked up and made eye contact with Fatima.

"I don't know what you mean, mother?" Nadia said, her voice stuttering.

Fatima's voice intensified as she pounded her hand on the cover of the journal.

"You know exactly what I mean, Nadia!"

Nadia nervously gazed over at her Father. Rasheed slowly walked over closer to Fatima.

"Nadia, what exactly has Mr. Ridgeway been teaching you?" Rasheed asked with an interrogating tone in his voice.

Nadia felt desperately cornered wanting to escape.

"Nadia," Fatima's tone eased up a bit, "If you had doubts about Islam, why didn't you come to us?"

Nadia felt her heart racing in her chest. She nervously squinted and began to breathe heavier. Trying to compose herself, she looked down at the floor and then looked back up.

"Mother, Father, "Nadia began, her voice quivering with anxiety and fear.

"Nadia, I have to know!" Fatima, demanded, probing her.

"Tell us the truth, you weren't really kidnapped."

Nadia looked at Fatima shocked and insulted.

"I was, I swear, I!"

Fatima pressed herself up against Nadia's face.

"Isn't it true Nadia that you ran away with some Christians to their Church?" Fatima yelled, accusing her.

"No, No, I didn't!" Nadia screamed back defending herself.

"We were so worried. We called the police and then Jeremy found your journal," Fatima began shouting, tears of frustration and anger streaming down her face.

Rasheed moved closer to Nadia.

"Nadia, please tell us the truth," Rasheed asked, begging her.

"I am a Christian," Nadia announced, finally admitting it and surrendering to the pressure.

There was dead silence.

Fatima and Rasheed had horrified expressions on their faces.

Fatima stood completely still.

She stared at Nadia with a stunned expression on her face.

She couldn't believe what she had just heard Nadia admit to.

Then, Fatima broke into a hysterical and uncontrollable cry and stormed out of the room.

Rasheed remained behind, standing with arms folded; giving Nadia a grim and penetrating stare.

"Nadia, you have dishonored Allah with your Christian beliefs and have disgraced us."

Rasheed stood eye to eye with Nadia and sternly pointed his finger in her face.

"I want you to go to your room and seriously think about what you have done and we will talk about it again tomorrow morning."

Nadia walked into her dark and tiny bedroom, which was nothing more that a sectioned-off space in the hut that she shared with her brother Zak. Zak had not retuned home from school yet. How do I explain this to him? Nadia pondered to herself as she tossed her Bible and journal onto her bamboo cot. Nadia was emotionally devastated. She realized that she was already experiencing the high cost of being a Christian and following Christ.

Nadia sat down on the edge of her cot and wept.

"Dear God," she cried out, "Please help me, please strengthen me. I want to follow you Jesus. I will not deny you. I need your help."

Reaching for her Bible, Nadia needed a word from God to help her through this difficult trial. Feeling the pressure of being confronted by her parents was almost too overwhelming.

Nadia rose up, turned around and kneeled down, leaning her elbows across the cot. Her body was trembling with fear. She muttered some prayers out loud and poured her soul out before God.

Deep down inside, Nadia felt a calm and refreshing presence that began to bring comfort to her mind. She heard a voice that whispered encouragement to her.

"Nadia, do not be afraid, I am with you."

Nadia recognized the still, small voice and began to rejoice. She leaned forward, sitting on her knees and opened up the pages of her Bible.

She found Isaiah Chapter 49. Her eyes fell upon verse 10:

Can a woman forget her nursing child that she should

Have no compassion on the son of her womb?
Even these may forget, yet I will not forget you.
Behold I have engraved you on the palms of my hands.

This verse leaped out of the page to Nadia. God was telling her even if her parents forsake you, I will not. Nadia felt her whole being radiate with encouragement.

As she was rejoicing, she heard Zak walk into the room. Nadia turned around and looked at Zak.

"Nadia," Zak yelled, "You're back!"

Nadia rose up from kneeling and gave Zak a big hug.

"Where have you been?" Zak asked, his face flushed looking from surprise and excitement.

Before Nadia could answer, Zak interrupted.

"What's wrong with Mom and Dad? Why are they angry?"

Nadia's face dropped. She sat down on her cot. Zak took a seat on his cot and stared at Nadia, anxious for an answer.

Nadia composed herself. She looked seriously at Zak.

"They're upset of what they read in my journal."

Zak gave Nadia a puzzled look.

Nadia took a deep breath and looked at her brother. Her face brightened up with excitement.

"Zak, I know this will be hard to understand. But, I have become a Christian."

Zak gave Nadia a look of betrayal.

"What," He stuttered.

Nadia leaned forward from her cot closer to her brother.

"Zak, I have discovered the love and forgiveness of God that I never knew before. Can you understand?"

"But, you're a Muslim, Nadia!"

Zak's whole body tightened up. He looked astonished.

"Is this why you left?'

"No, no-."

Zak interrupted.

"Satan has lied to you!"

Nadia started to get up from the cot.

"Zak!"

Zak quickly rose up from his cot, angered and hurt.

"You're not my sister," He yelled as he stormed out of their room.

The room once again became quiet.

Nadia stood all alone.

She sat down on the cot and covered her face with her hands.

She knew what she had to do now.

Chapter Thirteen
Counting the Cost

Dawn was slowly breaking over the horizon. The first few rays of light peeked through the tiny window of Nadia's bedroom. Nadia slowly opened her eyes. She hadn't slept all night. She looked over at Zak. He was sound asleep on his cot. It was still dark outside just before sunrise as Nadia rose up from her cot and pulled back the sheet. She quietly sat up as to not disturb Zak. She walked over to her closet and pulled out a black tunic and a gray pair of pants. Quickly dressing, Nadia walked toward her mirror, combed back her hair and placed a hijab around her head. She would need to wear this today while she was in Dhaka and amongst the crowd of people.

As Nadia stood gazing at herself in the mirror, adjusting the hijab, the reality of what she was about to do began to tear at her soul. She knew she could never be at peace again at home. Her parents' ultimatum had forced her to an inevitable decision. She could recant and return to Islam or else follow the narrow road of Christ. For Nadia, the decision to keep following Christ compelled her to make a painful choice.

Turning away from the mirror, Nadia took one final look at Zak while he slept.

"I love you Zak," Nadia quietly whispered.

Her voice quivering and tears rolling down her cheeks, Nadia bent down and pulled out her Bible and journal from underneath the cot. Then picking up her bag of clothes, she slowly tiptoed in her sandals out of the bedroom.

Just around the corner was the family dining room with a table surrounded by pillows. Her eye caught the new brown pillows Jason had given her parents last week when he visited. Nadia looked above the pillows to the wooden wall. Lining the wall from one end was her colorful drawings and her poems. In the center of the wall was a photograph of her with Jason and Zak that Rochelle had taken. Nadia quietly walked over and removed the photograph from the wall and inserted it in her Bible.

She carefully observed all of her drawings and poems lining the wall, her eyes finally resting on a picture of Rasheed and Fatima. Tears rolled down her face. Nadia was feeling the intense pain and heartache of the decision that she had to make.

"I Love you, Mother and Father," Nadia sobbed, her lips quivering.

Quickly turning away, Nadia unhooked the latch from the front door and tiptoed outside. It was still dark with the first rays of sunrise illuminating the horizon.

Nadia stopped and stood completely still a few feet from the hut. This had been her home almost all of her life. Images of barely having enough food, flashbacks of struggling for money and clean water, raced through Nadia's mind. The enormous weight of what she was about to do was almost too much. Nadia felt broken and crushed inside.

"Lord, please be with me," Nadia asked, her voice trembling with anxiety and fear.

She turned and walked up the gravel pathway. There was the playground. The empty merry-go-round. She walked a few more feet. The empty soccer net, where she stood and played goalie for Zak.

"Goodbye," Nadia whispered, struggling to hold back the flow of tears. She dropped her clothing bag and Bible and sank to her knees.

"Lord, I'm scared! I don't know what else to do," Nadia cried out in desperation and prayer.

She remained kneeling for a few moments and then slowly got up. The long road to the wooden bridge and village entrance was just over the hill. Picking up her clothes bag and Bible, Nadia reached deep down inside herself, drawing on her faith and courage and began the long walk to the entrance of the village.

As Nadia reached the top of the hill and was looking down at the wooden bridge below, a voice shouted her name.

"Nadia!"

Nadia stopped and looked around.

The bright rays from the sunrise were glistening upon the leaves of the trees as daylight was fully breaking.

"Nadia." The voice shouted once again.

An eerie feeling rushed through Nadia's whole being. She had never heard this voice before. She nervously looked around expecting someone to come out from behind the trees.

Instead, it was strangely quiet.

Then, without warning, the voice to Nadia came for a third time.

"Nadia, why don't you go back home and give your parents another chance. Listen to them, Nadia. You're making a mistake."

The voice echoed through Nadia in a tempting and accusatory tone. Nadia stood all alone in the woods trembling with fear. For a moment, she entertained the advice the voice was giving her.

Then something deep down inside of her recognized what was happening. Nadia began to breathe nervously. She remembered as a Muslim the superstitious attachment she had placed on the teaching of the jinn. The jinn were an invisible life-form existing in another dimension that was responsible for deceiving or leading one astray from God. At this moment, Nadia was entertaining the impulse to return home and submit once again to what her parents had instructed her to do.

In the midst of her fear and frustration, Nadia, standing all alone in the middle of the woods, cried out to God with her whole being.

"Jesus, I know your voice. This voice is not your voice! Satan is trying to deceive me! Give me your strength and your authority!"

In the blink of an eye, Nadia felt a surge of faith rise up within her. Her body stopped trembling with fear and anxiety. She closed her eyes, lifted up her hands toward the heavens and began worshiping God with her whole being. An indescribable feeling of joy surged through her whole body. Nadia opened her yes and looked around her.

"You cannot have me Satan!" Nadia proclaimed in authoritative voice.

"I belong to Jesus!" Nadia boldly cried out.

She felt a tranquil peace flood her soul. There were no more voices. The fear had diminished and Nadia, determined to continue on her journey, confidently walked on.

Sunrise had fully come. The early morning darkness had disappeared. The sun was shining brightly as Nadia arrived at the entrance to the village. Nadia stared at the two lane highway in front of her. She had never walked outside of her village before. She didn't know what the world looked like. The world she knew and grew up in consisted of a tiny wooden shack and a playground. For the first time in her life, Nadia would be exposed to a totally different lifestyle. Yet, it was completely worth it to her. Nadia had promised Jesus that she would follow him and now the reality of that promise was about to be fulfilled.

Before journeying onto the highway toward Dhaka, Nadia took a moment to read a Scripture from the Bible. She gazed down at Mark, Chapter 10: verse 29. Her soul was comforted by what Jesus promised her.

Truly I say to you. There is no one who has left house or brother or sisters or Mother or Father or children or lands for my sake and for the Gospel, who will not receive a hundredfold now in this time, houses and brothers and sisters and Mothers and children and lands with persecution and in the age to come eternal life.

Nadia was filled with trust and confidence from Christ's promise as she finished reading the Scripture. She closed the Bible and gazed back out at the highway.

"Jesus, I believe your word!" Nadia boldly proclaimed.

Carrying her Bible and journal in one hand and her clothes bag in the other, Nadia set out on the long journey to Dhaka trusting in the promise of God.

The two-lane highway looked endless to Nadia. She slowly walked along the side of the road facing the sun. In the early morning hours a handful of cars passed her by. Already, Nadia was feeling weary. She had never walked this far since the time she ran through the woods fleeing her kidnappers. She began to get thirsty and hungry. Stopping for a moment to catch her breath, Nadia gazed down the stretch of highway. There was a thick haze beginning to loom over the sky above her. She smelt a strange odor coming from a distance away. Nadia was not familiar with this odor. The odor from the toxic waste began to burn underneath her nostrils. The brick manufacturing factories in Dhaka were largely responsible for the release of sulfur dioxide into the air, causing massive air pollution. Confined to a village all of her life, Nadia had never encountered anything like this before.

After adjusting to the offensive odor, Nadia began walking down the highway again. A few more cars passed by Nadia as she slowly continued walking. The weariness, hunger and thirst were really starting to take their toll. Once again Nadia stopped to rest.

Suddenly, she heard a noise behind her. Nadia turned and saw an unusual sight. It was a bicycle-driven carriage, a rickshaw. She had never seen one before.

"Hello young lady," The driver said, stopping next to Nadia.

"Hello sir, "Nadia replied, startled that the rickshaw had stopped right next to her.

The driver dropped his legs down from the bicycle to rest.

"You look like you could use a ride, "The driver said, smiling.

Nadia breathed a sigh of relief.

"Yes sir. I'm on the way to Dhaka."

"That's a long way to walk. Would you like a ride?"

"Yes sir!" Nadia excitedly said.

"Hop on," The driver offered her.

The driver parked the rickshaw and climbed off the bike and helped Nadia into the carriage.

"Thank you, sir," Nadia said.

At once, her body relaxed in the carriage. She placed her Bible and journal on the seat next to her.

"Nest stop, Dhaka." The driver enthusiastically said as he hopped back on his bicycle.

The rickshaw took off as Nadia leaned her head back into the carriage and began to enjoy the ride.

It was a welcome relief to be riding in a rickshaw. There was a cool, refreshing breeze blowing against her face as Nadia laughed and talked with the driver.

As they approached the city limits, Nadia saw in the distance a large golden dome with two towers or minarets. It was a mosque. After all, Dhaka was known as "the city of mosques." Lining the streets were rows of large, beautiful green trees. As they neared the city limits, the traffic began to get heavier. Buses and taxicabs and other rickshaws cluttered the streets. Nadia looked with eagerness and curiosity at the skyscrapers, high rise buildings and housing complexes.

The rickshaw made a turn off of the two lane highway onto Kamalapur road. Nadia looked with interest at the retail stores lining the streets. Then the rickshaw turned and entered a huge marketplace in Dhaka known as New Market. Nadia could not believe the enormous crowd of people she was seeing. Besides the rickshaws and taxicabs filling up the streets, Nadia saw numerous stores selling clothing, jewelry, fast food, books, purses, shoes and some vegetable and fruit stands. She smelt the delicious aroma of fish being grilled by the many vendors in the marketplace. Nadia marveled at the number of people that were gathered together in one place.

"We are here," the driver announced, looking back at Nadia.

"Thank you kind sir," Nadia said, getting up from her seat.

The driver smiled and hopped back on his rickshaw leaving Nadia in a sea of people.

Nadia stood still for a moment and gazed around her. There were women, wearing burqas, sifting through the many towels and rugs at one stand. She saw men and their children purchasing produce at the vegetable stands.

Nadia took a deep breath and stared in disbelief at the sea of people that she had been dropped into.

"Jesus is more than a prophet."

Nadia quickly turned and looked straight ahead. She recognized the voice. Filled with excitement, Nadia started to run toward the location of the voice. She recognized the voice belonging to Abdullah!

Pushing her way through the crowd of people, Nadia made her way toward a shoe stand sandwiched in between a vegetable and fruit stand.

"Abdullah" Nadia's face lit up with joy. Abdullah was standing on some boxes. There was a crowd of people gathered below him listening.

"Jesus is the way, the truth-"Abdullah suddenly hesitated. He caught a glimpse of Nadia out of the corner of his eye.

"Nadia!" he yelled, his face beaming with joy. He motioned with his hand for Nadia to come closer and then continued preaching.

As Nadia made her way closer to Abdullah, she stopped. Just a few feet away she recognized Aisha talking with a tall woman dressed in a black burqa. She was holding a pamphlet in one hand and staring up at the woman. It was an intense conversation. The woman appeared to be listening as Aisha spoke to her.

In the midst of the intense discussion, Aisha caught a glimpse of Nadia. She stopped talking and raced over toward Nadia and hugged her.

"Nadia, Nadia," she cried out, hugging her tightly.

"Oh, no!" Aisha abruptly stopped and looked into Nadia's eyes.

"Your parents?" Aisha gently inquired.

Tears flowed down Nadia's face. Aisha pressed herself up tightly against Nadia's chest. They once again hugged each other.

"I'm so happy that you came back to us!"

"I am too," Nadia said, her face filled with joy as she wiped away the tears.

"Here, I want you to meet someone," Aisha said as she escorted Nadia by the hand.

"This is Sakina."

Nadia looked up to Sakina. Sakina was a tall, slender woman dressed in an ankle-length long black burqa.

"Hello," Nadia nervously said looking up at Sakina.

Sakina managed a smile. Nadia noticed a profound sadness and loneliness in her beautiful brown eyes.

Aisha looked into Sakina's eyes smiling.

"I'm so glad that you came back to talk, Sakina."

Sakina nervously looked around the marketplace and then looked back at Aisha.

"My husband keeps track of where I go. I'm taking a risk being here. He would not like me talking to you."

Aisha drew closer to Sakina. She had an overwhelming feeling of compassion for her.

"It's alright, Sakina. I want you to feel comfortable talking to me."

Sakina put her hand up to her mouth and bowed her head in tears. Aisha placed her hand on her shoulder, comforting her.

"My husband talks terrible to me," Sakina admitted. "He verbally abuses me. I can never please him. That's why I'm depressed all of the time."

Sakina stopped for a moment to catch her breath.

"You are very courageous confiding in me Sakina. I admire you for that." Aisha said, encouraging Sakina.

Sakina tried to compose herself.

Aisha backed away from Sakina and opened up her Bible.

"Sakina, can I read a passage of Scripture from the Bible to you?"

Sakina wiped the tears away from her face and nodded her head in agreement.

"This is what God says about how husbands are supposed to treat their wives."

Aisha looked down at the Bible and began to slowly quote the passage to Sakina.

"Paul writes to The Ephesians in Chapter Five, verse 25,"

"Husbands, love your wives, as Christ loved the Church and gave himself up for her."

Aisha then looked back at Sakina.

"In the same way that Jesus died for his people, husbands are to love, to esteem, to value their wives with an unconditional, sacrificial love. The Bible tells us, Sakina, the value that God places on a woman."

Sakina listened intently to what Aisha was sharing. Her heart was warmed and attracted to what Aisha had explained to her.

Nadia had been listening carefully to what Aisha was sharing with Sakina. She moved up closer to Sakina. Nadia had to look up because Sakina was much taller than her. Sakina looked down at Nadia and saw tenderness and compassion in her eyes.

"Sakina, can I share something with you?" Nadia gently asked.

Sakina nodded her head.

Nadia looked back up and fixed her eyes on Sakina.

"When I lived at home, my Father only praised me when I did what was right. Yet, I didn't always do what was right or please him. My striving to earn his love brought the darkness of depression on me."

Sakina's eyes were riveted on Nadia. She felt as if someone was understanding and listening to her for the first time.

Nadia continued.

"Because my Father only praised my well doing, I was afraid to go to him when I failed. When I didn't measure up, I kept all of my problems inside me. I was empty and broken inside and when I prayed to Allah, he seemed so far away. Then one night, I had a dream and Isa appeared to me. He rescued me from a burning bridge in my dream. He came down to me as I was kneeling on the bridge and touched my face with his hands. He spoke to me and said, "Do not be afraid, Nadia. You belong to me.

Then He told me to stand up and he put a silver necklace around my neck."

Nadia paused and pointed to the shiny silver necklace that she was wearing. Sakina bent down and touched Nadia's necklace. She looked closely at the necklace, admiring it. She was fascinated by its shining beauty and the meaning behind it.

"Sakina, for the first time in my life, I felt loved. I felt like I belonged to someone. I felt valued and I didn't do anything to earn it. Isa reached down and loved me for who I was and not for what I could measure up to be."

A single tear slowly streamed down Sakina's face. Feeling embarrassed, she quickly wiped it away and continued listening.

"Sakina, depression, fear and loneliness is like a cancer that eats at our souls."

Nadia paused and pointed over to a pottery stand. Sakina's eyes followed Nadia's finger.

"We are like those beautiful pots, beautiful pieces of pottery. We are easily bruised and easily hurt. We're like a beautiful piece of pottery, broken and cracked by abuse, fear and depression. Jesus, the great Potter, takes the pieces of our broken pots and tenderly mends them back together, delicately with his marvelous hands of grace.

Sakina, you are precious to Jesus. He looks upon you as a person of value, a treasure, not a field to be tilled as the Quran teaches, but a beautiful flower pot in his eyes."

Sakina stood mesmerized at what Nadia had just shared with her. Suddenly, she burst into tears.

"I have to go," Sakina cried out and then she quickly disappeared into the crowd.

Nadia turned to Aisha.

"I'm sorry Aisha, did I upset her?"

Aisha's face was aglow with happiness.

"No Nadia, she's just afraid, she will be back."

Aisha stared intently into Nadia's eyes.

"You have a beautiful gift from God, Nadia. A beautiful way of sharing the love of God."

After Aisha finished encouraging Nadia, Pastor Ali and Abdullah came over. They embraced Nadia with hugs, overjoyed to see her. Nadia felt so close to them. It was like a new family to her. Even though the shock and sadness of her separation from her parents and her brother still haunted her, Nadia was determined to begin a new life. She had gained new friends who loved and understood her.

They departed the New Market Place in downtown Dhaka after an exhausting day of witnessing in the intense heat. Everyone was very hungry so Pastor Ali drove the bus further downtown to enjoy a relaxing and refreshing meal at the Club Mango. Nadia enjoyed her first chocolate milkshake and a blt. While there, Nadia shared some of her poetry and personal journal entries and the letter Jason had sent her about Jesus. Everyone was impressed with the passion and beauty that Nadia demonstrated in her writings.

Near the end of a long day, Nadia followed Aisha and Fadwa up the steps into the bus. Pastor Ali was at the wheel waiting for everyone to be seated. Nadia was laughing and having any enjoyable conversation with Aisha as they sat down next to each other across from Abdullah.

"Nadia," Pastor Ali said, as everyone became quiet on the bus. "It is so wonderful having you back with us again."

There was a chorus of amen's.

"We are so glad that you're part of the family and this time you're staying with us and not leaving."

Pastor Ali smiled and everyone clapped.

Nadia grinned and her face turned red from blushing, she was not used to so much attention.

Pastor Ali looked seriously into Nadia's eyes.

"All of us agree, Nadia, from the very beginning when we met you, that there was something special about you. It was no coincidence that God led us to the side of the road that day to find you."

There was a chorus of amen's.

"Nadia, all of us sense a very special call of God on your life."

Nadia was stunned and humbled. She was unable to say a word.

"When we return to Rangpur, we are going to have a very special service for you. All of us here, after we became Christians, were baptized, saying yes to following Jesus, demonstrating that our commitment is genuine. In baptism, Nadia, you are identifying with your Savior, Jesus Christ. You are dying to your old self and rising to new life in Christ."

Nadia looked puzzled at What Pastor Ali had explained.

"I don't understand. I've never heard of that before."

Pastor Ali smiled; realizing water baptism was a new concept for former Muslims.

"You will understand it more tomorrow, Nadia. It's a day you will never forget."

Nadia nodded her head. Tears began streaming down her face.

"I have never been as happy as I am now," Nadia exclaimed, turning her head to make sure that she made eye contact with everyone else on the bus.

"I have a new life now and I want to spend every moment of it with all of you. No one could ask for better friends than you."

Everyone on the bus was moved and touched by Nadia's sincerity and humbleness. Pastor Ali turned the key in the ignition and they were finally on their way. All the way home, Nadia joined in singing worship songs, laughing and enjoying the intimate fellowship of her new friends.

After driving for two hours, the bus pulled up to the entrance of Living Word Church outside the city limits of Rangpur. Nadia looked out the window and spotted Leah in her wavy blonde hair and gypsy dress standing a few feet away from the front door to the Church.

Grabbing her Bible and clothes bag, Nadia exited the bus and embraced Leah with a big sister hug.

They cried and hugged each other for a few moments.

"I knew you would come back," Leah shouted, tightly hugging Nadia.

"I couldn't live without my sister," Nadia answered back, laughing and smiling at Leah.

"C'mon," Leah told Nadia, taking her bag in her hand and heading toward the dormitory building.

They walked past the kitchen and dining room and turned right into Leah's bedroom.

"Close your eyes," Leah instructed Nadia.

Nadia grinned and closed her eyes, excited and anxious to know what Leah's big surprise was.

Leah opened the door leading Nadia by the hand and they both stood still.

"Okay, you can open them now."

Nadia slowly opened her eyes and stared into Leah's bedroom. In the corner and off to the side was another bed, neatly made with a pillow resting on top. To the right of the bed, up against the window was a small table and chair with a tiny lamp in the center. This was a special place Leah had created for Nadia to sit comfortably while she wrote in her journal. Right above the table on the wall was a scroll-like piece of paper inside of a glass frame. Nadia walked over and gazed up at the picture frame. It read, *To Nadia: Our little Warrior Princess, We love you*

Underneath was everyone's signature. Nadia was speechless and awestruck at Leah's kindness. She stood staring at the picture, reflecting on how blessed she was to have Leah as a very special sister in Christ. The emotion of the moment took its toll on Nadia in a very special way. She turned and hugged Leah with tears streaming down her face.

"I am so blessed to have you as a sister, Leah!" Nadia exclaimed.

"Met, too, "Leah replied," I knew you would probably be coming back."

They both sat down together on the edge of the bed.

"I've been there, too," Leah confessed, her eyes rolling back in her head as she reflected on a similar situation.

Nadia bowed her head in despair remembering the last time she had seen her parents.

"My father told me to go to my room and re-think what I believed and we'd talk about in the morning."

Leah could see the pain and hurt in Nadia's eyes. It reminded her of when her parents told her to leave when she confessed to being a Muslim.

"Did you read the Scripture at the bottom of the picture?" Leah asked.

Nadia got back up and looked closely at the picture. At the bottom of the picture was a verse from the Old Testament.

Joshua 1:9
Be strong and courageous. Do not be frightened and do not be dismayed, for the Lord your God is with you wherever you go.

"I could not have done this without knowing that God was with me," Nadia admitted as she turned back to Leah.

Leah got up off the bed and looked at Nadia seriously and intently in her eyes.

"Nadia, I am sorry about what happened with your parents. But, it's only the beginning."

Leah looked at Nadia. Her face had a cold and placid expression on it.

"Jesus warned his disciples that because the world, the Pharisees and Scribes hated him, that they would hate them as well, too."

Leah began to pace.

Nadia could see Leah was very burdened with something heavy on her heart.

"Jesus declared in Luke 9:23, Nadia, if anyone would come after me, let him deny himself and take up his cross daily and follow me. Whoever would save his life will lose it, but whoever loses his life for my sake will find it. For what does it profit a man if he gains the whole world and loses or forfeits his soul?"

Leah paused, deep in thought. Nadia's eyes were riveted on Leah.

"Muslims will not understand you. Some will hate you and persecute you and some might even try to kill you."

Nadia's face quivered thinking about the ramifications of being a Christian.

"But Jesus promised you and me that we are blessed when we're persecuted. The kingdom of heaven belongs to us!"

Leah finished and sat back down on the bed. Nadia remained standing, carefully watching Leah.

"Tomorrow, when you are baptized, you are publicly saying yes to Jesus, that you belong to him and that you will follow him for the rest of your life. Following him is not easy, Nadia. I'm telling you this sister, because I love you and want you to know that there is a cost to being a Christian."

Leah got up off the bed and kept her eyes focused on Nadia.

"Nadia, you are still very young and I don't want to frighten you my little sister, but you need to know what it means being a Christian, especially living here."

Leah didn't know what to expect from Nadia. Nadia remained completely quiet and didn't flinch her eyes, but had a confident and resolute expression on her face.

"Leah, all I know is this. Jesus loves me and he took away all of my sin and shame. I never knew love until I met him. No matter what, I want to follow him."

Leah looked back at Nadia overwhelmed with joy at her response. Nadia reached down in her journal and took out the picture of her standing with Jason and Zak. She walked over to the picture that Leah gave her and pasted it next to it on the wall. She stepped back smiling at the photograph.

"I can never repay Mr. Ridgeway. I'm so thankful that he told me about the love of Jesus."

The next morning, Nadia awoke early and stared out the window. It was a beautiful day for a baptism and the beginning of a new life for Nadia.

After a quiet breakfast in the kitchen and lounge area with Leah and Aisha, Nadia got dressed and attended her first real Church service. This time she wasn't tormented with fear and guilt like before when she ran out the front door. This time she sat next to Leah and raised her hands and voice in worship. The whole experience reminded Nadia of the dream she had months earlier. God was preparing Nadia for the most significant events in her life and at that time she was unaware of the glorious change that was about to take place.

After some songs of worship and praise, Nadia sat with her Bible open in her lap and listened intently as Pastor Ali exhorted everyone to put Christ first in every area of their life. Nadia was amazed at how the Bible spoke so personally and profoundly to her. It was not just a book of commands, laws and do's and don'ts. To Nadia, the Bible was a personal love letter and covenant from God to her. A book of life breathing truth and beauty to guide her in every aspect of her life. It was a book sealed in the precious blood of Christ full of promises from God to Nadia. When Nadia read the Bible, it was as if Jesus was sitting right next to her personally exhorting her to live a life of abundance and grace.

After the Church service, Nadia returned to Leah's room and changed into a grey and white robe. Then everyone boarded the bus for the short one mile trip to a quiet river that served as a baptismal for new members of Living Word Outreach Church.

Turning off to the side of the road, the bus parked on a small hill overlooking the river. Nadia followed Leah down the hill and waited on the river bank. Pastor Ali arrived, followed by Abdullah, Fadwa and Aisha. The rays of the bright sun quietly reflected off of the deep blue water of the Shahawnee River. The river was a small stream surrounded by a grove of trees and a gravel bank.

Pastor Ali, carrying his Bible in one hand, gently led Nadia by the hand from the bank and out into the river. They waded into the river until it reached their waists. Nadia grabbed her arms and started to laugh. The river was cold and she was shivering. Pastor Ali began to chuckle and everyone laughed. Suddenly, it became very quiet as the baptism was beginning. Ali turned and looked at everyone huddled together at the bank of the river.

"Today is a very special day!"

Nadia raised her head and looked at Pastor Ali with a huge smile on her face.

"God," Ali continued, "has blessed us with a beautiful little warrior princess." Ali turned and looked at Nadia.

"We are so glad that God brought you to us, Nadia."

Nadia blushed and bowed her head. She felt so honored to be a part of their family.

Ali turned back looking at Abdullah and Fadwa.

"Nadia has chosen to follow Jesus. In doing this, she is taking an important first step in obedience to Christ. Nadia has received Jesus as her Lord and Savior and today in baptism; she is making a public commitment declaring she is a member of his glorious Church. When Nadia is baptized, like each one of us was, she is dying to her old self and rising to new life in Jesus."

Pastor Ali faced Nadia and opened up his Bible.

"Nadia, I'm going to ask you a few questions. Don't be afraid. All of us have gone through this."

Nadia's face glowed with enthusiasm as she stood in waist-deep water facing Pastor Ali.

"Nadia, do you acknowledge yourself as a sinner?"

"Yes," Nadia answered without hesitation.

"Nadia, do you believe that Jesus Christ is the Son Of God who died on the cross to cleanse you from your sins and then rose again from the dead?"

"Yes"

"Nadia, do you believe that the Bible is God's Word teaching you and training you in all righteousness?"

"Yes"

Pastor Ali moved closer to Nadia. He instructed her to pinch her nose with her right hand. Nadia took her right hand and pinched closed her nose.

"Nadia, by the authority of Almighty God and his Son Jesus Christ, I baptize you in the Name of the Father and the Son and The Holy Spirit."

Pastor Ali tilted Nadia backwards until she was fully submerged under water. He then lifted her back up. Nadia stood up rejoicing and smiling wiping the water away from her face and hair.

There was a tremendous applause from everyone on the bank of the river. Pastor Ali tightly hugged Nadia and they together slowly walked back to the bank of the river.

Abdullah raced over and was the first to hug Nadia. Leah was next, followed by Fadwa and then Aisha.

The bright glare from the sun was blinding Nadia's eyes as she wiped off her hair and her body with a towel. Leah came over and began to comb Nadia's hair while she finished toweling down. Nadia was beaming with joy as she finished toweling off her face.

"Leah, I feel cleansed and whole. I feel like a new person!"

"You are Nadia. You're beautiful. I remember the day I was baptized and it's an experience you will never forget!"

"I wish Mr. Ridgeway could have been here," Nadia said with sadness in her voice."

"Why you don't tell him about it in your journal today, "Leah suggested.

"I will," Nadia said. Her face glowed with anticipation." I think I will spend the afternoon in the courtyard. I have a lot of things to talk with God about."

Leah nodded her head smiling as they walked back to the bus together.

Nadia couldn't wait to get back to the Church. She was anxious to go to the courtyard for some quality journal writing and prayer time. She missed her secret prayer grove in the woods back home, but she had discovered that sitting on the bench in the courtyard facing the wooden cross had become a very special place, too, to meet with God.

With the baptism experience fresh on her mind, Nadia changed into some new clothes, bid Leah good-bye for an hour and headed out to the courtyard all alone. She brought her journal and Bible along with her and a heavy heart ready to pour out to God.

Nadia looked up at the sky. The clouds looked a little dark and murky. It was going to rain soon. Nadia picked up her journal and her pen. She was anxious to tell Mr. Ridgeway all about her very special day.

Sunday, December 2, 2004

Dear Mr. Ridgeway

I am sitting here in the church courtyard outside of Rangpur at Living Word Outreach Church. This is a beautiful little place. It has a tall, wooden cross just a few feet away from the wooden bench that I'm sitting on.

I wish you could have been here today, Mr. Ridgeway. I was baptized in a river just a mile away by Pastor Ali. It was a very emotional and joyous experience. I have never experienced anything like that before. It is the beginning of a brand new life for me as Christian follower of Jesus.

When I think back to how all of this happened, I can only remember how much your letter meant to me. The way you described who Jesus was, Mr. Ridgeway, changed my whole life! Unfortunately, my parents did not rejoice in my new life. Yesterday morning, I packed up my clothes and left home to come here to be with my new Christian family. There are the most wonderful people I have ever met.

Mr. Ridgeway, I love my parents. I miss my brother Zak, but I have to follow Jesus. Jesus has given me a brand, new life through his love and forgiveness. Please pray for me, Mr. Ridgeway and pray for my parents and brother that they would come to know the love of Jesus like I have.

Your friend in Christ,
Nadia

Nadia put down the pen and bowed her head in tears. The pain of being separated from her family had crushed her spirit. Yet, deep down inside, Nadia knew shed had made the right decision. She knew Christ would never leave or forsake her and the knowledge of that brought healing to her sorrow and pain.

Nadia raised up her head and stared at the wooden cross. Thinking back to her Bible reading, Nadia remembered that during the agony of the crucifixion, Christ himself cried out to His Father," My God, my God, why have you forsaken me?"

The solemn reality of that penetrated her soul. Nadia's family had forsaken her as well.

"Jesus, what did that feel like to be forsaken?" Nadia whispered out loud wiping the tears from her eyes. Nadia could identify with Jesus. He too, had felt the awesome pain of being separated from His Father, while he was bearing the agonizing penalty for our sins. Knowing Jesus too had endured excruciating pain because he loved sinners and was willing to take their place, brought real comfort and perspective to Nadia. Jesus knew and understood the pain that she was enduring because he, too, had once been there.

Nadia reached over and picked up her Bible and bowed her head in prayer.

"Jesus, please help me to fathom and to understand your love that made you willing to die on a cross for my sins. When I was a

Muslim, I never believed this. Now, I want to understand your suffering as a Christian. Please show me what this means. Amen."

Nadia opened up her eyes and raised up her head. She opened up her Bible to 1 Corinthians, Chapter one and verse 18 and began reading.

> "For the word of the cross is folly to those who are perishing, but to us who are being saved, it is the power of God."

Reflecting on that verse, Nadia realized how foolish the cross was to anyone, including Muslims. It was foolish because it appeared as an utter failure and defeat. Why would anyone look to someone else to pay for their sins? Religion says, I am good enough on my own to merit my own acceptance and righteousness. It is my responsibility to accrue enough good deeds to balance the scales rather than to shirk my responsibility and expect someone else to pay for it. As a former Muslim, Nadia understood this kind of thinking far too well.

But now, the love and forgiveness of God had spoken a new and refreshing reality to her heart. Salvation was a gift that could not be earned, but was lavishly bestowed on her by a wonderful Savior.

Nadia closed her Bible and picked up her journal. She could feel the creative juices welling up in her heart. Gazing at the Scriptures and the lonely cross in front of her, Nadia began to write a new poem that captured her feelings about the cross.

Nadia paused and gazed once again at the cross in front of her. She began to write:

> *How beautiful are the nail prints in your hands.*
> *How beautiful are the scars on your feet and hands.*
> *How beautiful is the salvation that you planned,*
> *How beautiful!*
>
> *How beautiful are the wounds in your side.*
> *How beautiful is the cross on which you died.*
> *How beautiful are your arms held open wide,*

How beautiful!

How beautiful are the words that you spoke.
How beautiful is your gentle and easy yoke
How beautiful is your heart as it broke
How beautiful!

And you're so beautiful to me. Your holy blood has set me free.
You're the treasure I've been looking for. You're beautiful!

As Nadia finished writing the last verse, she was so deeply touched and moved that she laid down her journal and got up from the bench. She walked closer to the wooden cross and gently knelt down.

Kneeling in front of the cross in worship, Nadia heard a loud rumble in the distance. It began to rain.

Nadia closed her eyes as the raindrops splashed down her face.

"Jesus, I love you," Nadia whispered loudly above a gentle rumble of thunder in the distance.

Nadia felt humbled and exposed before the cross, realizing the depth of love and pain that Jesus endured while being suspended between heaven and earth.

Suddenly, a picture flashed before her eyes! The thunder and the raindrops seemed to vanish away as Nadia felt she had been transported body and soul to another dimension. Nadia saw a woman sitting on a cot in what appeared to be a prison cell. The woman was dressed in a blue jumpsuit. She was bent over, holding her head in her hands and quietly sobbing to herself in mental agony.

Then the scene abruptly disappeared and Nadia once again returned to kneeling in front of the cross with the rain pouring down upon her. Then, a soft, but authoritative voice spoke to her heart.

"Nadia, do not be afraid. The road ahead for you will be very painful, but I will not leave or forsake you. I am with you."

The voice then disappeared. Nadia listened to the quiet and relaxing raindrops gently splashing to the ground.

Nadia slowly opened up her eyes.

She stared at the cross quietly pondering what it had all meant.

Chapter Fourteen
Five Years Later

Jason gazed out of his bedroom window and watched the snowflakes gently drift down to the cold, winter ground. Winter had come a little early this year to the show me state. It seemed like time had swiftly passed Jason by.

Today was Thursday, November 27, 2009. It was exactly five years ago to the day that Jason traveled to Bangladesh to visit Nadia and her family. And then, she mysteriously disappeared.

Shortly after the death of his Mother, Jason had called Worldwide Compassion to inquire about Nadia. They informed him that Rochelle and Jeremy had been transferred to another village just after Nadia went missing. No word had been heard from Nadia. Her parents and brother were still living in the village, but Nadia seemed to disappear from off the face of the earth. Now Jason had to emotionally process not only the death of his mother, but also the sudden disappearance of a wonderful friend.

Jason felt like a father-figure to Nadia and although he had barely known her, he still grieved her disappearance as if she were his own child. Yet Jason knew that life had to move on. He would have to trust the Lord. Everyday he prayed for Nadia's safe return and thought about the prayer meeting the night of his mother's death. Both Pastor Willoughby and Jason truly had believed that Nadia was the girl that God had prophesied would shake the Muslim world as a warrior princess bringing many Muslims to a saving knowledge of Christ. Jason knew God could not lie and although the circumstances seemed to tell a different story, he would have to be patient and realize that God operated on a much different time table than his.

And timing was one of God's incredible attributes for Jason this year! Yesterday he received a phone call from an independent producer in Nashville. He had heard one of Jason's CDS and was impressed. Not only that, but he wanted Jason and his band to set up a time and come to Nashville for an audition for "Great Adventures Christian Production Company." Jason of course was thrilled and had a special meeting with the band. After a few tweaks to their schedule, they agreed to meet Friday afternoon for a special audition session. Today was Thursday and they had arranged to travel to Nashville on Friday.

Today, Jason was busy packing up his car. The band was going to take the rental truck, while Jason tagged behind them in his Mazda convertible. The only other appointment that Jason had to attend to today was a special meeting with Pastor Willoughby. Ever since the death of his mother and the disappearance of Nadia, Jason had once again been struggling with ongoing panic attacks. Pastor Willoughby had agreed to meet with him on a regular basis as they together sought counseling from the Scriptures.

Pastor Willoughby was quietly relaxing behind his desk reading his Bible as Jason stood in the open doorway to his office.

"Hi Jason," Pastor Willoughby said, smiling as he stood up to extend his hand. He was wearing a comfortable blue-jean colored flannel shirt and a pair of jeans on what he called "one of his non-formal work days."

"We've got a little snow," Pastor Willoughby observed, chuckling as he shook Jason's hand.

Jason grinned as he sat down opposite of the Pastor and reached into his pocket to put on his reading glasses.

"Thanks for squeezing me in on your busy schedule."

"No problem," Pastor Willoughby said as he relaxed back in his chair.

Jason became quiet, getting comfortable in his chair. He gazed around the office, pondering how to begin the conversation. After gazing a bit, Jason turned and looked intently into Pastor Willoughby's eyes.

"Sometimes I struggle with trusting God," Jason firmly said.

Pastor Willoughby had a blank expression on his face. He thought for a moment and then leaned forward closer to Jason.

"God's ways are not our ways, Jason" He emphatically replied, staring back at Jason with a look of compassion and understanding.

Pastor Willoughby realized that he too, even as a Pastor sometimes became anxious and impatient.

Jason had a look of frustration on his face. His heart was feeling heavy with guilt.

"I still struggle with panic attacks and then feel guilty for not trusting God, and-"

Jason began stuttering and then slammed his hand down on his knee in anger.

Pastor Willoughby remained quiet and focused on Jason's body language. He observed how his anger and frustration were keeping him paralyzed with fear.

Jason finally regained his composure and leaned forward in his chair.

"What about the prophecy?" Jason bluntly asked.

"You mean the prophecy about God bringing to us a warrior princess to be a missionary to Muslim countries?"

"Exactly!" Jason fired back.

"You're asking why in five years the promise has not yet been fulfilled, since Nadia disappeared."

"Yes."

"Well Jason," Pastor Willoughby leaned forward in his chair and rested his elbows on the desk.

"God didn't say when that would happen, but that we were to keep in prayer and readiness. Remember the night your mother died, the prayer meeting we had? You and I both were convinced that Nadia could be that person."

Jason eagerly nodded his head.

"It comes back to trusting God to fulfill that prophecy. Now if it never happens, then it was false, but I still believe it was valid and that God will do what He says, because he cannot lie."

Pastor Willoughby observed the sadness on Jason's face. He continued to press the issue with a sensitive question to Jason.

"Nadia means a great deal to you, Jason. Am I right about that?"

Jason kept silent and slowly nodded his head.

"I know it's tough to lose both your mother and a new friend both at the same time."

Jason looked down and nodded his head. He slowly rose up and looked straight at Pastor Willoughby.

"I feel so empty and sad a lot of the time. I can't write and yet I shouldn't be depressed. Tomorrow, I'm going to Nashville with the band and we could land a huge record deal!"

Pastor Willoughby opened up his Bible, turning to Isaiah Chapter 43.

"Jason, I'm sure you know this Scripture and yet you need to meditate on it tonight. God doesn't want you to be tormented with fear and uncertainty. Listen to what He tells us."

Jason moved over closer to the desk and leaned over as Pastor Willoughby read the Scripture:

Fear not, for I have redeemed you:
I have called you by name, you are mine.
When you pass through the waters, I will be with you:
And through the rivers, they shall not overwhelm you:
When you walk through fire, you shall not be burned, and the flame shall not consume you.

Pastor Willoughby closed the Bible and looked at Jason.

"Jason, you write beautiful songs of worship. The psalms are filled with praises to God, as you well know and words of comfort, penned by David, to run to God when we're afraid, because He's a refuge, strong tower-"

"That's why I'm frustrated," Jason loudly interrupted, "I know that and yet I struggle so much, I feel like a hypocrite!"

Jason put his hand over his forehead and stared down at the floor again in shame.

"Jason," Pastor Willoughby began, "I want your mind to be filled with God's peace and to do that you need to focus your mind on His character and His word and not your problems. Sometimes, we as Christians, develop an unhealthy selfish focus."

Pastor Willoughby's admonition cut through Jason like a knife. He rose up and looked emphatically at Pastor Willoughby.

"You're right. I am going home to finish packing and then I'm getting alone with God."

Jason stood up and leaned over to shake Pastor Willoughby's hand.

"My office is always open," Pastor Willoughby said giving Jason a hug.

"You just go up to Nashville tomorrow and bless their socks off with your music."

Jason cracked a smile.

"I will, thank you, thank you, again."

Jason returned home exhausted after pouring his heart out to Pastor Willoughby. It was almost dinner time and he had a lot of packing yet to do. Sitting down in front of the TV with some spaghetti, Jason began flipping through the channels. Just when he was about to turn it off because of lack of interest, Jason came upon the beginning of a program focusing on the persecuted Church around the world. There were scenes of men, women and children huddled around a tiny lamp reading the Bible in Iran. Taking a bite of spaghetti, Jason watched intently as the narrator described the hostile circumstances in Iran. Jason sat the plate of spaghetti down. His eyes were riveted to the story. There was the photograph of a 30 year-old girl named Lei Ming in the People's Republic of China. She was arrested for being part of an underground Christian newspaper who spoke out against the oppressive communist government and its no toleration policy of freedom of religion. Lei was beaten and tortured. The government officials tried to force her to sign a document revealing the names of her other Christian friends. When she refused, she was chained and put under house arrest.

Jason was astonished at how Lei refused to reveal the identity of her friend and would not compromise her faith in Christ.

Jason continued watching as the scene shifted to Pakistan spotlighting a 17 year-old girl named Safina. Safina lived in a small poverty-stricken village with her two sisters and her parents. She worked on a farm. One day, the woman found out she was a Christian and harassed her, trying to force her to convert back to

Islam. Safina refused and the other women workers severely beat her. Then they informed the local mosque what she had done and she was visibly humiliated and made to ride around the mosque on a donkey while bystanders insulted her and threw rocks at her.

Jason sat on the edge of his chair horrified at the brutal way Safina was treated and yet she refused to deny Christ.

The last segment of the program focused on Fernando. One day, Fernando and ten other workers who worked in the jungles of Columbia, were riding the bus to work, when they were stopped by a band of guerillas. Fernando knew what they were going to do and immediately he started praying. Everyone was forced to exit the bus in a single file. The guerillas then forced everyone to kneel on the ground and then they opened fire, executing everyone, but Fernando, who miraculously survived. Later, Fernando was interviewed recalling the horrible tragedy and said that he had forgiven the guerillas for what they did and was praying for their salvation.

Jason turned off the television and bowed his head in tears. He was humbled and amazed over the individual testimonies of the three Christians and how they refused to deny Christ and instead prayed for their attackers.

"Lord, forgive me of my selfishness," Jason cried out praying, "I'm so wrapped up in my little aches and pains and anxiety attacks that I have forgotten what it means to be a Christian. Lord I want to have the same faith and devotion of the Christians I just saw."

Jason continued weeping before God and praying while his plate of spaghetti got cold sitting on the table beside him. Wiping the tears away from his face, he picked up his Bible. His eyes fell on Romans Chapter Eight, verse eighteen:

"For I consider that the sufferings of this present time are not worth comparing with the glory that is to be revealed to us."

Jason closed the Bible and meditated on the passage he had just read. Suddenly his whole world began to get back into focus. He realized how self-centered he had become through all of the anxieties and worries over Nadia and the death of his mother. He sat in the chair quietly reflecting on the program he had just watched about the persecuted Church. Inside, he could feel a song flowing as a result of watching the suffering of his brothers and sisters around the world. Jason reached over and picked up his acoustic guitar. He always carried a pen and some paper with him since he was used to having the words to a song come to him through the mundane events of the day. Jason strummed a few chords on his guitar and reflecting on the faces he had just seen, he began to write.

> I see their faces staring back at me
> I see the tears that are in their eyes

Jason could see the facial expression of Safina as she told her story about being paraded around the mosque on a donkey.

> There's so many places where they are not free
> They're praying for us just to hear their cries.
> I hear their voices, they're crying to me in the night
> Saying, please let me live and please don't let me die

Jason paused, reflecting on the persecuted Christians meeting secretly at a house Church in Iran.

> I see their faith being tested in the fight
> They won't give in and they don't even ask why

Jason pictured Lei in China being chained to her bed under house arrest.

> They put them in prison; they torture them and tie them in chains

But they won't deny Jesus, no matter what the cost or the pain
They pray and forgive them and even all of their shame
They want to be like Jesus. They want to be worthy of his name.

Jason paused and thought about an appropriate chorus to the song that would sum up all of his thoughts and feelings about what he had just watched.

I see their faces and they've taught me how to live
I see the love that's in their eyes.
I see their faith and they're willing to forgive
I feel so ashamed. It makes me break down and I wanna cry
   When I see their faces
   `It makes me want to cry
   When I see their faces
   And the love that's in their eyes.

Jason stopped and put down the pen and fell to his knees in repentance. He asked God to forgive him of being so wrapped up in his own world and forgetting about the high cost of following Jesus in the hostile nations of the world. He put away his guitar and rejoiced that he had a powerful new song to teach the band tomorrow in Nashville.

Jason sped over the Kentucky line in his Mazda 6 on highway 24 on his way to Nashville. The sun was shining and it was a beautiful November day. Thanksgiving was just around the corner and yesterday's snow was slowly melting with temperatures soaring into the mid-forties! Today, Jason's focus was not on his anxieties and fears but on a bright future with a promising recording contract. God had opened up a very important door for Jason and the band. The opportunity to have a major label producing their worship music was the dream of a lifetime and Jason was pursuing it with all of his heart.

The Mazda 6 and the red van carrying the band members circled the busy traffic-filled Nashville loop and together they drove into the heart of the city.

After driving up and down the busy main street in the heart of Nashville, they arrived at Great Adventure Studios at 2:45 pm, just a half-hour before their audition. Jason and the band walked into the front doors and introduced themselves to Wes Collins, the local representative. Wes escorted them into the studio and the band quickly set up their equipment.

Wes Collins and his producer listened to Jason and the band perform, "reflections," a song that was written in Dhaka and also, "living sacrifice."

They were both well pleased with what they heard and offered Jason and the band a lucrative deal to begin production on a CD. They discussed and hammered out all of the contractual arrangements and agreed to return after the New Year for a two-week recording engagement.

Jason and the band departed Nashville praising God for the great accomplishments they had made with Great Adventure Productions. The five-hour trip home seemed to fly by as Jason turned his Mazda 6 into the driveway of his home.

Exhausted and yet exhilarated over the success of the day, Jason turned the key into the lock of the front door and closed it behind him.

"Yes!" he shouted out loud in triumph, carrying his clothes bag into the bedroom.

Jason sat down on the edge of his bed and took a deep breath. He began to mentally process all of the details of the day and thought about the upcoming New Year and the exciting things that lay just ahead for him.

"I think I'll write in my journal before turning in," Jason muttered to himself.

He rose up from the edge of the bed and was almost knocked over by an excruciating pain in his abdomen. Jason pressed both of his hands against his left side and hobbled back over to his bed. The pain was so intense that he couldn't stand up, but he managed to finally roll himself onto his bed. He lay motionless on his bed moaning in pain and staring up at the ceiling fan slowly rotating above him.

Chapter Fifteen
Persecution

"Surprise! Happy birthday, Nadia!"

Nadia couldn't believe her eyes as she stood in the doorway of the kitchen and lounge area. Now she understood why Leah had asked her to stay an extra hour after work at the Rainbow Clothing store.

Nadia had been working with Leah part time at the Rainbow Clothing Store in downtown Rangpur for the past three years. She enjoyed interacting with the local customers and helping them make the all important decisions on what to wear. This was Nadia's first job and it felt good and rewarding to succeed at earning a living. She felt like she was finally accomplishing something in life and although it was not a career job, it was definitely a beginning. Sometimes working made Nadia feel like she was going from rags to riches, from a humble peasantry beginning to a position of prestige.

"Former Muslims do indeed celebrate their friend's birthdays," Leah announced with a chuckle. Nadia remembered how she was taught as a Muslim that they only observed the Prophet Muhammad's birthday and not each others.

"We also celebrate Christmas and Easter, "Leah said.

Suddenly, the air was filled with noisemakers. Pastor Ali was blowing a kazoo and wearing a pointed birthday hat. Abdullah was blowing up balloons and Fadwa was playing some chords on the guitar.

Nadia was delighted and overwhelmed at what her friends had done for. Suddenly the lights went out and Aisha walked in with a chocolate-covered birthday cake with 21 candles burning on it.

Everyone began to sing happy birthday to Nadia. Nadia blushed and wiped away a few tears. Her face glowed with gratitude. Aisha gently sat the cake down on the table. Pastor Ali stepped up behind the cake and looked at Nadia.

"Today is a very special day. Our warrior princess has turned 21."

Everyone clapped as Nadia blushed.

"Nadia," Pastor Ali continued. The room grew quiet. "All of us want to wish you a blessed birthday and pray that our God would bless you many more and fulfill all of the dreams of your heart."

There was arousing applause and then it became quiet as everyone anticipated a speech from Nadia.

"I just want to say-"Nadia stuttered and stopped abruptly. All eyes were on her.

"I'm sorry." Nadia apologized and then rushed out the door.

There were shocked expressions on everyone's faces. Leah looked over to Pastor Ali. He looked stunned.

"Excuse me, "Leah said as she followed Nadia out of the front door.

Nadia stood all alone on the sidewalk sobbing.

"What's wrong?" Leah asked, walking up to her.

"I'm sorry I've ruined your surprise, Leah."

Nadia was embarrassed and ashamed as she lowered her head to her chest.

"No, no, of course you didn't," Leah said trying to reassure her.

Nadia remained quiet for a moment and then looked seriously into Leah's eyes.

"A man came into the clothing store today. As I finished with one customer and looked up at him, I became very frightened."

Leah looked surprised and listened intently.

"He said nothing," Nadia continued. "But just stared at me. He had a tattoo on his arm and-."

Nadia broke down in tears. Her whole body was shaking.

"What! Go on!" Leah urged her.

Nadia took a deep breath and looked intently at Leah.

"I think it was him, the tattoo. He was one of the kidnappers that-."

Nadia gasped for breath as if she were having a seizure. Leah grabbed her by the arm and shook her.

"Nadia, are you alright?"

He's the one who raped me!" Nadia screamed.

Leah backed away from Nadia with a stunned expression on her face.

"What! Oh, no!" Leah shrieked. Her eyes grew wide. She was shocked and unable to speak. Nadia began to cry uncontrollably while Leah hugged her.

"He raped me!" Nadia screamed once again.

Leah held Nadia as they both cried together and comforted each other. Then Leah backed away and looked Nadia straight into her eyes.

"Are you sure he recognized you, Nadia?"

Nadia composed herself and thought for a moment.

"I'm not sure. It's been five years, but I recognized him because of the tattoo on his left arm."

"We need to tell the police!" Leah insisted.

"No! " Nadia protested.

Leah could see the terror in Nadia's eyes.

"It's just my word against his," Nadia said, realizing her dilemma.

"How can I prove it?"

"Nadia, "Leah said grabbing her by the arms. "I want you to be safe."

Nadia quieted down and composed herself once again.

Leah looked seriously into her eyes.

"He may not have recognized you since he didn't say anything. Since you won't go to the police, we need to pray and pray hard for your safety."

Nadia nodded her head and agreed.

"Nadia, "Leah asked.

Nadia saw the compassion in Leah's eyes.

"Can you forgive him? You can put an end to the torment and fear by forgiving and praying for him."

Nadia had a perplexed look on her face. She remained silent and seriously considered Leah's challenge. Then she stared back at Leah with a look of calmness and resoluteness on her face.

"You're right, Leah. God has forgiven me so much. So I too must forgive him. Jesus said to love your enemies and pray for them."

Nadia's lip began trembling as a tear streamed down her face.

"I will forgive him, Leah and pray for him."

Leah's face beamed with joy. She embraced Nadia.

"Happy birthday sister," Leah said with tears in her eyes.

"You're the best sister that God could have given me."

The next day at the Rainbow Clothing Store, Leah and Nadia waited on customers and watched to see if the man would return. Nadia was still apprehensive but Leah stayed right by her side and comforted her.

At 6:00 pm, the long day finally ended and Leah and Nadia bid the manager good-bye and walked out the door together. As they turned to walk down the sidewalk and begin the long walk back to the Church, they were suddenly greeted by a crowd of people blocking their pathway along the sidewalk.

A young, teenage Muslim walked boldly up to both Leah and Nadia. Leah and Nadia stood still as the young man approached them out of the crowd behind him.

"Don't you both go to that Church about a mile from here?"

Leah and Nadia glanced at each other and then looked back at the man. Leah composed herself, realizing what was coming next.

"Yes, we are Christians that belong to that Church."

"Blasphemers, idolaters, and traitors!" the crowd angrily shouted back at them.

Nadia tensed up inside and nervously swallowed. Leah boldly stepped closer toward the young teenager.

"You have dishonored Allah," the teenager accused her, pointing his finger in Leah's face.

"You are both infidels, believing in that trinity and every false doctrine from your so-called Bible that is filled with so many errors. It is corrupt and has been changed as you well know!" The teenager declared, shouting into their faces with the crowd roaring its approval behind him.

Leah looked down at the ground for a moment, whispering a quick prayer and then inched forward, closer to the teenager and fixed her eyes intently on his.

"Do you really believe the Quran?" Leah challenged him.

The teenager chuckled, looking back to the crowd.

"What kind of question is that?"

Leah looked up to sky and then quickly back down into the teenager's eyes.

"I asked, do you believe your own Quran?"

The crowd jeered and laughed at Leah's question.

Leah, filled with the spirit of boldness, stepped aside from the teenager and gave a piercing look toward the hecklers in the crowd.

"You claim that the Bible is corrupt and has been changed. How can that be?" Leah sarcastically asked, mocking their accusations.

"The Quran says, now I'm quoting," Leah declared, her voice filled with a holy boldness.

"In Surah 63:4, none can change the decrees of God. Surah 6:115 declares," Perfected are the words of your Lord in truth and justice. None can change His words."

Leah paused, letting her point sink in. The crowd grew quiet. There was one young Muslim with his arms folded and listening intently to Leah.

"If no one can change the words of Allah, if His decrees cannot be altered, then how can you say and claim that The Bible has been changed or corrupted?"

"Furthermore," Leah continued. She began to pace while she made her presentation and then stopped giving the crowd a defiant look.

"If the Bible is corrupt, why would Muhammad instruct his listeners to pay attention to it?"

The crowd remained ominously still.

"Listen to what Surah 10:95 says and I'm quoting. "If you doubt what we revealed to you, ask those who have read the Scriptures before you. The truth," Leah cried out, quoting from the Quran, she struck her hand against her palm emphasizing her point.

"The truth has come to you from your Lord, therefore do not doubt it."

Leah finished quoting and paused. The hostile crowd was strangely quiet. They had been silenced and left speechless by their own book.

"The Bible came 700 years before the Quran. The Gospels are written by the eyewitnesses and Apostles who were with Jesus day and night for over three and one half years.

My point is this. You cannot make the claim that the Bible has been changed or corrupted. The Quran says it's impossible. God has sovereignly preserved His Holy Word and what does the word point to?

Jesus says, the law and prophets, the Scriptures point to and are fulfilled in him. He is the Messiah, just as the Quran says.

What does Jesus say about the Holy Scriptures that as I have shown, have not been changed or corrupted?

Jesus says in John's Gospel, Chapter five, verses 39-40:

"You search the Scriptures, because you think that in them you have eternal life, and it is they that bear witness about me. Yet you refuse to come to me that you may have life."

The young man that had been intently listening to Leah had a stunned and convicting expression on his face.

Leah filled with compassion and a heart broken over unbelief, fought back the tears. She desperately wanted the crowd to believe the truth and come to Christ.

"I plead with you today," Leah cried out.

She looked over the faces in the crowd. Nadia stood behind her with her eyes closed and in an attitude of prayer.

"Come to Jesus, He will give you life, He will-"

Suddenly a young child yelled. "Mr. Policeman, Mr. Police man, that girl has thrown my Quran down on the ground and ripped out its pages!"

Instantly, the crowd became enraged and began picking up rocks and threw them at Nadia and Leah. Leah backed away covering her face as the rocks struck her in the chest and hands. As

Nadia raced up to save Leah, she was struck by a glass bottle. Screaming, Nadia fell to the ground as Leah dove on top of her to protect her from the hostile crowd.

Just then, two Policemen intervened, blowing their whistles and escorting both Leah and Nadia off to the side of the building.

The Police officer grabbed Leah by the arm and confronted her in a harsh tone.

"Both of you must immediately leave. You're disrupting the peace and inciting a riot. If you don't leave now, both of you will be arrested!"

With crowd screaming threats in the background and hurling rocks and bottles at them, Leah grabbed Nadia by the arm and together they both ran down an alleyway that intersected the main street.

"Quickly! Let's go! Keep running sister," Leah urged Nadia as she gasped for breath.

Panting and filled with anxiety and fear, Nadia ran for her life keeping close behind Leah as they reached the side street and headed toward the main highway out of Rangpur.

After an agonizing hour of walking, Leah and Nadia finally returned to Church. They were both exhausted and out of breath and sore from their cuts and bruises. They shared with Pastor Ali how the crowd became hostile and nearly got them both arrested.

After hearing about their ordeal, Pastor Ali called everyone into the kitchen and lounge area for an informal Church service. Sensing that the persecution was increasing and becoming more violent, Pastor Ali thought it best to have a time of intense prayer and intercession.

Abdullah and Fadwa, followed by Aisha, Hakeem and Jubbar all assemble together in the lounge area. They brought with them some chairs and formed a circle.

Nadia and Leah leaned forward in their chairs. They had exasperating and exhausting looks on their faces. Pastor Ali picked up his Bible and everyone in the circle became quiet. Pastor Ali noticed the apprehension in everyone's eyes.

"Today, "Ali began, "Our sisters, Nadia and Leah were almost arrested after confronting an angry crowd. Yet, they boldly preached to the crowd about Christ."

Everyone said amen. Nadia had a frightened expression on her face, still trying to mentally process all that had happened to her.

"We all know," Ali continued," That we are engaged in a spiritual warfare. We love Muslims. We don't hate them. We desire for them to know the forgiveness and mercy of Christ. It is important for us to remember that our struggle is not against flesh and blood, that is, our struggle is not directly with Muslims, but our struggle is against the principalities and powers of darkness that Satan controls. That's why we need to keep our hearts cleansed before God so that we don't become angry or bitter, but rather walk in Christ's love to our Muslim friends."

There was an echo of amen's from everyone in the circle.

Pastor Ali paused and turned the page in his Bible.

"This evening I want to encourage us and remind us that the battle is not ours, but the Lord's. I want us to focus on the love of God in our trials and confrontations. Hear what the Apostle Paul writes in Romans 8:35-39:

> Who shall separate us from the love of Christ?
> Shall tribulation or distress or persecution or famine
> Or nakedness or danger or sword?
> As it is written, for your sake we are being killed all the
> Day long. We are regarded as sheep to be slaughtered

Pastor Ali paused and his face beamed with joy.

"Listen to what Paul says about all of that."

He looked back down at the Bible and his voice grew louder with excitement.

"No, but in all of these things, we are more than conquerors through Him who loved us.

Nadia's tired face became aglow with joy after hearing what God's word said about their persecution.

Pastor Ali looked back down at the Bible and began quoting again from verse 38:

For I am persuaded that neither death, nor life, nor angels, nor rulers, nor things present, nor things to come, nor powers, nor height, nor depth nor anything else in all creation will be able to separate us from the love of God in Christ Jesus our Lord.

After Pastor Ali finished quoting, everyone rose up from their chairs as Abdullah began playing a worship song on his guitar. The power of God's Word had energized and comforted them. They began rejoicing and praising the Lord in the midst of their persecution.

Nadia and Leah held hands and everyone else followed as the music became softer. Everyone closed their eyes to begin praying.

"Lord," Pastor Ali began. "We praise you in the midst of persecution. Thank you for protecting Nadia and Leah from serious harm. Lord, we cry out for strength and boldness so that we may preach Christ to our Muslim friends. We cry out to you to save them and bring them to a saving knowledge of Christ. You told us to love our enemies and pray for them who persecute you. We forgive them for attacking us and pray for them."

After a chorus of "amen's", it became quiet with Abdullah softly playing in the background. From deep down inside, Nadia could feel a warmth and a peaceful sensation grasping her soul. She thought about how God had miraculously protected them. She could feel the words to a poem stirring within her. Usually Nadia was very shy about sharing her poems. But at this moment, she was filled with the Spirit and was grateful that God had protected them.

For the first time, Nadia opened her mouth and began to sing as the Spirit of God prompted her.

> *I will be your comfort and I will be your peace*
> *I will be your refuge where the raging winds cease*

The way the words flowed out of Nadia's mouth startled her. She wasn't used to anything like this. Nadia began to tremble, but continued singing.

> *I will be your stillness and I will be your calm*
> *I will be your shelter through the raging storm*
> *And when you walk through the valley of death*
> *And when you take your very last breath*
> *I am with you, I am with you, I am with you*
> *Do not fear, cause I'm right here, I am with you*
> *I am with you. I'll be your shelter in the storm*
> *Don't be afraid of what they do*
> *I will carry you in my arms*
> *I am with you*

At that moment, everyone cried out with "amen's" and rejoiced responding to the comfort that God had given them through Nadia's song.

Nadia opened her eyes. She observed Aisha and Fadwa raising their hands in praise with tears streaming down their faces. Pastor Ali's face beamed with joy. The Spirit of God had visited the small band of Christians in a beautiful way showering them with great comfort and encouragement.

There was a chorus of enthusiastic cheering at the conclusion of Nadia's prophetic song.

Suddenly, the sound of breaking glass interrupted their quiet time of worship and praise. A large, heavy rock landed only a few feet from the circle of the chairs. Pastor Ali ran over to the rock and then raced over to the broken window. He saw four young men dressed in gray muscle shirts and wearing black bandanas on their foreheads.

Leah ran over to the window as Ali was heading toward the side door to the courtyard.

"No! Don't go out there!" Leah pleaded with Ali, placing her hand on his shoulder.

"I have to," Pastor Ali replied turning around to face Leah. "I have to try and reason with them."

Leah gave Ali a frightened and worried look. Then Pastor Ali opened the door to the courtyard. As he walked out to the angry crowd, he noticed three other young men in the prayer courtyard tearing down the wooden cross.

"No!" Pastor Ali shouted.

Three of the four men walked slowly up to Ali, while the fourth one remained behind clutching a wooden bat in his hands. One of the young men, apparently the spokesman, stepped up and stared straight into Ali's eyes with his chin lining up with his just inches away.

Meanwhile, Leah had slipped out close behind Ali and Nadia remained behind standing in the doorway.

"You must stop poisoning Muslim's minds with your blasphemous Christian doctrines!" The young man demanded as he stood face to face with Ali.

Pastor Ali remained calm and kept his eyes fastened on the young man's eyes.

"It's not poison that we're telling Muslims. It's God's love."

The young man's face tightened and grew red. Ali could see the blind rage growing in his eyes. He braced himself as he stood face to face with him. The Muslim man backed up a few inches and then pressed his finger against his chest.

"Anyone who tries to convert Muslims to another religion is worthy of death!"

After finishing his statement he spit in his face. Humiliated, Ali reached down to get a handkerchief to wipe off his face, when suddenly he found himself on the ground after being punched in the jaw.

Withering in pain, Ali tried to get up, but the two other men pounced on him and began severely beating him. The remaining young man dropped the wooden bat and joined in on the beating.

"Stop! Stop!" Leah yelled and raced toward the brawl.

"Leah!" Nadia shouted in fear.

Abdullah tried to run out to help Ali, but Nadia grabbed him and held him back.

When Leah could take no more, she sprinted out to help Pastor Ali.

"Leah!" Nadia screamed.

Leah grabbed one of the attackers by his shirt yelling at him to stop. When he felt her hands on his shirt, he spun around and with both of his hands pushed Leah backwards. Unable to keep her balance, Leah tripped over the wooden bat and fell hard onto the ground striking her head. She rolled over and moaned out loud in pain.

Something inside Nadia snapped when she witnessed her best friend fall to the ground. Suddenly, all of the fear and anxiety seemed to melt away and all she could think about was protecting her friends.

As the mob continued pounding their fists on Ali who was hopelessly pinned to the ground, Nadia slowly walked out into the center of the courtyard and picked up the wooden bat lying on the ground. She raised the bat in the air and slammed it back down on the ground. The attackers, hearing the sound, momentarily stopped their beating and stared back at Nadia. Nadia released the bat from her hands and let it drop to the ground. She wiped the beads of sweat from off of her face and brushed back her hair. Filled with anger and righteous indignation, she stared adamantly at the four men who attacked Ali. She pointed her finger at them.

"I've had enough of your beating and attacking and killing in the name of God!" Nadia shouted.

The attackers looked at each other perplexed and astonished that Nadia would have the courage to stand up to them. One of the young men turned from beating Ali and slowly walked toward Nadia.

Bleeding and writhering in pain, Pastor Ali tried to slowly get up from the ground. Abdullah watched on in amazement. Leah, dizzy and unaware what was happening, stayed lying on the ground and watched with astonishment at Nadia's boldness.

Pointing to Ali and Leah on the ground, Nadia boldly walked closer toward the attackers.

"These are my friends and I will not allow you to lay another hand on them!"

The attackers stared at each other in astonishment. Nadia kept her eyes riveted on them.

"The Quran tells you that there is no compulsion in religion, yet you are forcing your beliefs on us! You are in disobedience to your own holy book!"

Nadia reached down and picked up the bat once again. The attacker watched on in disbelief and shock.

"Go ahead and beat us with your weapons," Nadia challenged them.

"Force us to believe and what have you accomplished? We've become unwilling slaves of blind obedience."

Nadia banged the bat down on the ground to emphasize her point.

"Tell me, is that what God desires for us to be? To be beaten in submission or does God desire that we come freely in response to his love?"

The attackers remained silent. Nadia continued.

"My God did not come conquering me with the sword, as you have done. My God drew me to Him by His love and mercy."

The four attackers angrily brushed off their clothes. They did not know how to deal with the situation presented before them. Nadia bent down over Leah with tears in her eyes worried over her injuries. Then she looked back over to the attackers. She slowly rose up.

"Until you learn what love and mercy is, stay away from us!" Nadia sternly rebuked them.

"When you want to know what true love and mercy is, then you can come back and we will gladly share that with you."

Humiliated and in shock, the four Muslim men dusted off their clothes and left the courtyard. Nadia bent back down over Leah. Leah slowly tried to sit up, her head pounding with pain and her face smeared with dirt and dust.

"Leah," Nadia said weeping, "Are you alright?"

Leah, half-dazed, sat up completely. Nadia helped her to a sitting position as Leah grabbed her head in pain.

Abdullah and Aisha rushed over to Pastor Ali. His face was smeared in blood. He sat up and bent his head down over his knees. He was in excruciating pain. Leah was now standing up. She brushed off her clothes and together they walked over to Pastor Ali.

In the midst of his pain, Ali looked up to both Nadia and Leah. He shook his head and managed a smile, wiping away the blood from his nose.

"Nadia. You saved our lives!"

"That's my sister!" Leah chuckled, patting Nadia on the shoulder.

Nadia blushed. She was very happy that everyone was going to be alright.

"Now you know why we call you our warrior princess," Ali pointed out with a huge smile on his bruised and beaten face.

"You are my friends. You are family now and I love each one of you," Nadia declared, giving each of them an intense hug.

"I will not allow anyone to ever treat you the way that they did."

Ali and Leah's face broke into smiles of gratitude as they affectionately hugged each other.

Near the end of what was a faith challenging day, Nadia retreated to her favorite place in the courtyard as the sun was beginning to set. Fiery orange, majestic blue and brilliant yellow colors seemed to collide with each other in a beautiful artistic display. Nadia was awestruck at the beautiful sunset. She whispered a prayer to God, gazing up at heaven.

"God, you are beautiful and you have really put yourself on display tonight!"

Nadia turned from gazing upward and then looked down at the ground. She was saddened to see pieces of the wooden cross scattered all over the courtyard. The attackers in their religious rage and hatred had mangled the cross to pieces with their weapons. Nadia's heart was saddened seeing that they attacked the most important and precious symbol of the Christian faith.

Looking at the pieces of the cross on the ground, Nadia realized just how much they hated Christ. She sat down on the bench and placed her Bible beside her. Compassion and love, instead of bitterness and anger, began to flood her soul. Nadia had known for a long time and today's event confirmed it, that God had chosen her to be a missionary to Muslims. She was driven with an overwhelming desire to love and labor among Muslims, to do everything she could by the grace of God to reach them for Christ.

Nadia picked up her Bible and turned to the book of Esther. She had been fascinated by the story of Esther. Esther and the Jewish people were in exile in Persia, which today is modern Iran, since the invasion of King Nebuchadnezzar in 597 b.c.

Esther had become Queen through God's providential favor. Mordecai had told Esther "And who knows but that you have come to royal position for such a time as this."

It was evident that God had providentially placed Queen Esther in this position so that she could be instrumental in saving her Jewish people from extermination. Nadia was fascinated by Queen Esther's courage and willingness to risk her own life for the safety of her people.

Over the past five years, Leah had taught Nadia English and other languages, so that she would be able to communicate with Muslims wherever God placed her. Nadia's hearts desire was to be a missionary to Muslims. Pondering over Mordecai's statement to Esther, Nadia laid down her Bible and wondered if she too was here for such a time as this. Like Esther, Nadia too had a deep desire to risk her life for her people.

"God," Nadia quietly prayed, gazing at the beautiful sunset, "You have given me a beautiful love and burden for my people. Please show me what I can do to reach them so that they can know the love of Christ."

Nadia bowed her head and closed her eyes, overwhelmed by the peace that was flooding her soul. At that moment, Nadia surrendered her plans and purposes into God's sovereign hands.

Satisfied that she had gotten her answer, Nadia started to get up and was suddenly seized by an overwhelming sense of danger. Slowly sitting back down on the bench, Jason's face flashed before her in her minds eye. Nothing like that had ever happened to her before. Then she remembered that it was five years ago, almost to the day, when Jason had visited her.

"Mr. Ridgeway," Nadia quietly whispered to herself, "What's wrong?"

There was an intense tug on her heart that wouldn't let her go. Nadia began to cry out to God in prayer and lost track of the time as the sun disappeared behind the horizon of Rangpur.

Chapter Sixteen
Broken Wings

Jason stared up at the steel ring directly over his head. He lay completely still on his back, slowly inching closer toward the center of the ring. The ring made clicking noises and began rotating from the inside taking photographs of his body from the chest down. In a few minutes, the scan was complete. Jason rose up from the table and quickly dressed. He thanked the technician and headed out the front door of the hospital.

Just a few days earlier, Jason and the band had a successful audition in Nashville. Their dreams of contracting with a top Christian label had been rudely interrupted! Now Jason feared the return of cancer.

"Why God?" Jason thought. His mind was filled with anxiety and fear as he turned his car onto highway 70. It seemed so cruel for a door of opportunity to be opened and then the future to now be in question.

"I don't understand," Jason confessed out loud trying to keep his mind on his driving. He had tried to rationalize and reason through every angle of his dilemma and ended up being more confused and perplexed.

Jason took the Riverview Boulevard exit and drove up the hill to Bethlehem Cemetery. He slowly drove up an isolated roadway. There were trees lining the road on both sides. Jason looked up at the twisted tree limbs. There were barren without leaves. They looked cold and lifeless. Jason identified with the tree limbs. He felt cold, abandoned and deprived of life. He was anxiously awaiting the bright sunshine and the new life of spring to return, just like the tree limbs. But for now, it was cold and miserable in the middle of winter, just three weeks before Christmas.

Jason pulled over to the side of the road and parked the car. As soon as he opened the car door, the bitter cold wind blew across his face. Jason quickly crossed the road to the other side and walked across a row of tombstones until he came to his Mother's grave. The tombstone read:

> Helen L. Ridgeway
> Born: Sept. 28, 1918
> Died: Nov.28, 2004

Jason stood quietly in front of his mother's grave. He was rapidly puffing cold air out from his mouth. Both of his hands were stuffed warmly in his pockets. Like the tree limbs, his mother's grave looked cold, impersonal and devoid of life.

"Mom," Jason whispered out loud. His cheeks were red from the cold and his eyes were filled with tears.

"Mom, I love you. I miss you." Jason said.

The only sound that he heard was the rustling of a few leaves and the howling of the cold wind. That's what life seemed like right now to Jason. Cold, meaningless and without purpose. There were no answers. Where was God?

Jason felt cold, numb and oppressed and looking down at his mother's grave, he felt abandoned and lonely.

"Why won't you answer me, God?" Jason asked with a depressed tone in his voice.

"Why?" Jason repeated the question. His voice growing louder and sterner.

Anger and bitterness filled his heart, as he continued staring down at his mother's grave. His face and body were trembling from the cold weather and the stone-coldness of his angry heart.

"Why did you do this God?" Jason demanded, staring angrily at his mother's tombstone.

There was no answer. Wiping tears away from his wind-chapped face, Jason turned and walked away. He was weary from the cold and dreary day and needed to find a place to hide.

Still dripping wet from the shower, Jason raced to the bed to answer the phone. The voice on the other end told him it was Dr. Mason's office. The results from the cat scan were in and the doctor wanted to see him right away.

Jason quickly hung up the phone and sat on the edge of the bed trembling. Drops of water dripped down from his body and onto the floor.

Please God, give me some good news," Jason pleaded with his head bowed and whole body trembling from anxiety and fear.

He got up from the bed and hurriedly put on some clothes. Grabbing his car keys, he ran out the front door and quickly got in his car. He put in one of his worship cds and cranked up the volume all the way to the doctor's office.

Dr. Mason was a short and stocky distinguished looking man with a shiny bald head and a gray beard.

He shook Jason's hand and asked him to sit down.

Jason studied Dr. Mason's face. It looked serious and sober. Jason slowly sat down in the chair in front of Dr. Mason's desk. He nervously gulped and took a deep breath.

"You wanted to see me?" Jason squeamishly asked.

Dr. Mason sat down and rested his elbows on his desk and leaned forward looking intently in Jason's eyes.

"Jason, I'm afraid I don't have good news."

Dr. Mason's words thundered through Jason's whole being. Tears began to well up in his eyes. Jason shifted in his chair and tried to hide his fear.

"The ct scans show that the cancer has returned in your colon. It's a very aggressive cancer that is already beginning to spread."

Jason was hoping that this was just a bad dream and that someone would punch him and he would wake up. He sat speechless for a moment and then finally spoke up, stuttering.

"I-I –don't understand."

Dr. Mason nodded his head, sympathizing with Jason's reaction.

"You were cancer free for over five years and unfortunately an aggressive cancer has returned."

Dr. Mason leaned forward in his chair.

"We can try to stop the spread with an aggressive round of chemo and radiation."

Jason remembered back to how he felt going through chemo before and how exhausted he was for so long.

Dr. Mason continued.

"Jason, I'm not sure we'll be able to stop the spreading, but we can try. We can try aggressive treatment if you can tolerate it."

Jason's whole world had just come crumbling down. He sat speechless once again in shock.

"Jason" Dr, Mason said trying to get his attention.

Jason shook his head and once again focused his attention on Dr. Mason.

"Sorry," Jason replied, stuttering. He nervously adjusted his body in the chair.

"Okay. Okay Dr. Mason, let's try."

Dr. Mason was silent and thought for a moment. The he leaned forward in his chair.

"If after two weeks, there is no progress and you body is unable to withstand it, we may have to discontinue the treatment."

Jason knew what that meant and at this moment he didn't want to have to cross that bridge.

Dr. Mason stood up and Jason quickly rose up out of his chair. Dr. Mason extended his hand toward Jason.

"We will do our best, Jason,"Dr. Mason said reassuringly.

Jason reached forward shaking Dr. Mason's hand and then quickly departed from his office walking past his secretary. He wiped the tears away from his face and walked out into the hall. Jason's heart was racing. He leaned up against the wall, trying to catch his breath. Two young children ran past him, laughing and having fun playing with each other. Jason closed his eyes for a moment trying to emotionally come to terms with the news he had just received. He was crushed in spirit and feeling completely helpless and trapped with no where to run.

Jason climbed into his car and put the key into the ignition. It was a cold and dreary day with rain-threatening clouds swirling overhead.

Jason sat quiet for a moment pondering what to do. He needed to go somewhere to be alone and think. His mind was filled with anxious, racing thoughts.

The image of the old Chain of Rocks Bridge flashed through his mind. The bridge had been a favorite place for him to go walking across in the summer. Yet, today, in the dead of winter, Jason needed a secluded getaway, a place where he could be alone and think deeply about life.

Putting the car into gear, Jason drove out of the hospital parking lot and exited onto the highway. When he was a young boy, Jason used to sneak away and go tot the old bridge to play. The old chain of Rocks Bridge was a historic landmark in St. Louis. Built in 1929, the bridge joined Missouri to Illinois stretching across the mighty Mississippi River. The bridge spanned 5,353 feet across the river and ended at Chateau Island in Madison, Illinois.

The steel truss bridge had a famous 22 degree bend in the middle, unlike any other bridge in the world. In 1975, Hollywood descended onto the old bridge to film a cult-classic movie, "Escape from New York."

In 1991, the bridge was the sight of a gruesome murder. After that, it became a tourist attraction closed to normal traffic and only allowing hiking and bicycle riding.

Turning off I-270, Jason exited onto Riverview Boulevard and found a parking spot a few hundred feet from the bridge. It was quiet and peaceful as Jason exited the car. The wind wasn't blowing hard. Jason bundled up inside his hooded sweatshirt coat and walked onto the entrance of the bridge. There was no one else around. He was completely alone.

Jason began slowly walking across the steel edifice. He gazed down from the bridge at the mighty Mississippi River below. The river looked calm and peaceful on the surface, but underneath she was like a madman or a monster possessed by a mighty torrential current that was ready to sweep you underneath its watery vortex.

Jason felt a lot like the river. On the outside he appeared peaceful, but underneath he was possessed by a torrential current of anger, rage, frustration and sorrow.

A Slight breeze blew Jason's hair away from his forehead as he continued to gaze down. He looked intently at the water intake tower in the middle of the river.

"Do you really want to suffer through all of that pain?"

Jason turned and looked to see who had asked him that question. There was no one else on the bridge. A few drops of rain splashed across his face. He bundled up tight in his jacket and then leaned back over the railing of the bridge.

"You don't want to go through all that pain."

This time the voice came deep from within. Jason was shaken by how real the voice sounded. He thought about the question posed to him.

"No, I don't," Jason answered back.

There was an ominous moment of silence. The rain began to come down heavier. The drops streamed down Jason's face and the air turned colder.

"Do you really believe God loves you now? He's taken away your career and this is what you get for serving him?"

The question that was posed to him shot like a bullet through his body. Jason was stunned by the voice asking him the question. Yet at this moment, he was crushed in spirit. He felt abandoned and unloved. He didn't want to go through suffering and pain.

Jason tightened his grip on the railing. He continued to look down at the river. The rain was coming down harder.

"What is left to do? God doesn't love you anymore. You have no career. You're going to die-."

"No! No!" Jason shouted back.

His hands were shaking. He lost his grip on the railing and fell to his knees in the pouring rain. He began crying uncontrollably.

"God help me! God help me!" Jason shouted to the top of his lungs.

He was kneeling on the floor of the bridge, just a foot away from the railing and looking down at a hundred-foot descent into the river. Humiliated and frightened to death, Jason let go of everything and cried out to God from the depth of being. His whole world had been shattered. He didn't care if anyone else was around.

It was just him and God on the bridge all alone and he had descended into a pit of darkness that seemed inescapable.

The cold rain poured down on his body and Jason continued to cry out to God in the most desperate moment of his life, hoping that in his agony somehow he would be heard.

It was nearly 5:00 pm before Jason finally pulled his car into the driveway of his home. He was drenched from the rain, utterly despaired and broken inside. He felt ashamed and humiliated at his reaction to the bitter news.

"Where is my faith?" Jason asked himself as he sat quietly in the car with raindrops dripping down from his nose.

"Aren't you the musician," Jason asked himself sarcastically, "writing all of those worship songs about how great God is and when the darkness comes, this is how you react?"

Jason pounded the steering wheel with his fists. He was angry at himself and thoroughly ashamed. The guilt of how he acted was much too suffocating for him to bear. He needed room to breathe again.

Slamming the car door behind him, Jason walked in the front door and headed for his bedroom. He changed out of his wet clothes and into a nice warm housecoat. He wasn't in the mood to eat or watch television. He wanted to write in his journal.

Now was the time to sort out and collect his thoughts. His journal was the most intimate and priceless possession that he owned. Talking to God through his journal brought Jason peace and assurance. Journaling was the way he found intimacy with God even beyond playing his guitar.

Jason sat at the table and turned on the small lamp. He opened up his Bible to get God's perspective on the day. He fingered through the Psalms and his eyes fell upon Psalm 34:18:

The Lord is near to the broken hearted and saves the crushed in spirit.

Then he flipped the pages ahead to Psalm 40.

I waited patiently for the Lord
He inclined to me and heard my cry.
He drew me up from the pit of destruction
Out of the miry bog and set my feet upon a rock, making my steps secure.
He put a new song in my mouth
A song of praise to our God.

The Psalms spoke profoundly to Jason's dilemma. He felt a peace and a reassurance after reading and meditating on them. Then he picked up his pen and began writing in his journal.

Thursday, December 5, 2009
Dear God:
Forgive me for being such a poor Christian today. I don't know what happened to my faith. Yet, I don't understand God. I thought you opened up the door for the recording contract. I'm confused! Why this, why this now? I Know you have your reasons, but why God? I know you can heal me. Maybe you're going to show your power to Dr. Mason and heal me. Maybe that's your plan. What a witness that would be to him. Please come and heal these broken wings. I want to fly high. I want to soar again.

Jason put down the pen. He felt faith rise up within him. In his darkest hour, he felt God was going to meet him at his greatest need and heal him.

"What a testimony that would be!" Jason reasoned within himself. He would share it at every concert that he played at.

Jason rose up from the table full of life once again. He began singing. "Please come and heal these broken wings. I want to fly high. I want to soar again."

Chapter Seventeen
Providence

Nadia and Leah walked out together after a busy day at the clothing store. Turning the corner to begin the long walk home, they stopped in the middle of the sidewalk as a tall, thin young man dressed in shorts and a muscle shirt stepped in front of them. Both Nadia and Leah braced themselves for another hostile confrontation.

"No, no, relax," the young man assured them, holding up both of his hands, "I am not here to argue."

Both Nadia and Leah relaxed and gave each other a look of relief.

"You look familiar," Leah pointed out, "Weren't you in the crowd of people that attacked us a few days ago?"

"Yes, yes, I was. My name is Ahmed," Ahmed said, introducing himself.

Ahmed looked down at the ground with a look of shame and guilt on his face. He then looked back up at both Leah and Nadia.

"I wanted to say to you that, I don't believe violence is the way to treat anyone, just because they believe differently than you."

Both Nadia and Leah nodded their heads in agreement.

Ahmed stared at them with a passionate look on his face.

"While I don't agree with what you believe, I believe respectful dialogue is much more appropriate than violence."

"That is all we're asking," Leah broke in saying with a look of relief on her face. "Just listen to what we have to say."

Ahmed looked toward Nadia and smiled at her.

"What is your name?" Ahmed asked.

Leah looked embarrassed.

"I'm sorry Ahmed, I'm Leah and this is Nadia," Leah answered pointing at Nadia.

Ahmed's face broke into a warm smile.

"I'm very glad to meet you, Nadia."

Nadia smiled back, blushing.

"Ahmed, how would you like to join us for tea at that outdoor café?" Leah asked pointing down the street.

"It would be my pleasure," Ahmed answered approvingly.

Nadia gazed intently at Ahmed's deep brown eyes. He was six feet tall, thin and very handsome with short black hair and olive-colored facial skin.

Together, they walked a few more feet down the street and sat down at a table outside and ordered three cups of tea.

After taking a sip, Ahmed put down his cup of tea and adjusted himself in his chair, preparing for a good conversation.

"I took up you challenge, Leah," Ahmed said folding his hands. He leaned forward in his chair and rested his elbows on the table.

"You said, in defending the Bible, that the Quran says that there's no changing of God's Word, so the Muslim claim that the Bible has been changed, is false one."

Leah nodded her head approvingly at Ahmed. Ahmed seemed intelligent and well versed in the way he articulated himself by restating Leah's point.

"Very good, Ahmed. That's exactly what I meant," Leah affirmed.

"Alright," Ahmed replied. He paused for a moment, collecting his thoughts and then asked the next question.

"If the Bible hasn't been changed, then where did the pagan doctrines about Christ come from?"

Leah thought for a moment and then leaned forward looking intently at Ahmed.

"First of all, there are no pagan doctrines about Christ in the Bible. It wasn't until one hundred years, in the second century, after the death of all the Apostles that you begin to see the Gnostic false gospels beginning to circulate. These were heretical views denying the deity of Christ that were allegedly written by Peter and Thomas. The problem is that these were not real gospels, but forgeries of the true gospel, written long after the death of the Apostles. They bear no resemblance to the first century eyewitnesses who spent over three years with Jesus."

Ahmed shook his head listening carefully to Leah's point.

"The Gospels and the Epistles were written just before the destruction of Jerusalem in ad 70. This is over six centuries before the Quran. There are over 5,000 Greek New Testament manuscripts, Ahmed and over the centuries, scribes have copied and recopied these manuscripts. You can see these manuscripts in museums all over the world. The early Church Fathers wrote books quoting verbatim from these manuscripts. In all of these years of copying and recopying, you have no corruption or essential change in doctrine. The Muslim claim that the Bible has been changed is just not true."

Ahmed put his hand on his chin and nodded his head, thinking deeply about what Leah had said.

"On top of that, The Bible itself says something powerful about the integrity of Scripture," Leah said with a look of certainty in her eyes.

"I Peter Chapter two, verse 24 declares, "The grass withers and the flowers fade, but the Word of our Lord remains forever.""

As soon as Leah was finished, Nadia looked over to Ahmed, anxious to add her thoughts to the discussion.

"Ahmed, in addition to that, don't you believe as a Muslim, that God is sovereign?"

"Yes, of course. Whatever Allah wills, will happen."

Nadia looked into Ahmed's eyes with compassion and conviction.

"Don't you agree, if God is sovereign, then He would be able to preserve His Word?"

Ahmed looked down at the table and took a sip of his tea.

"Of course," Ahmed admitted, wiping his mouth off with a napkin.

Nadia reached into her purse and pulled out her Bible.

"Ahmed, would you mind if I shared a verse from the Bible with you?"

"Sure," Ahmed answered approvingly.

Nadia thumbed through some pages and then looked down at her Bible lying on the table.

"Isaiah Chapter 46, verse 9, says," and this is God himself speaking," Nadia pointed out as she briefly looked up at Ahmed.

I Am God and there is none like me, declaring the end from the beginning and from ancient times things not yet done, saying, " My counsel shall stand and I will accomplish my purpose.

Verse 11: I have spoken and I will bring it to pass. I have purposed and I will do it.

Nadia finished quoting and gently closed her Bible. She stared back at Ahmed. His face was riveted on hers.

"Ahmed, do you believe that God always accomplishes his purposes?"

Ahmed shrugged his shoulders and shifted a little in his chair.

"Of course," he replied with a grin on his face.

Nadia remained silent for a moment allowing Ahmed to think through the implications of his answer.

"This is the God who revealed His Word to and through His Apostles over the centuries, through Isa and also His Apostles. If you claim that the Bible became corrupted and was changed, are you not also admitting that God was not able to accomplish his purposes?"

Nadia's point took Ahmed by surprise. He felt as though he had been intellectually cornered. Ahmed realized that he hadn't seriously thought through the ramifications of his objection.

Nadia could see the stunned expression on Ahmed's face. She waited quietly and respectfully for his response.

"Well," Ahmed began, nervously swallowing. "Of course, Allah does what pleases him and no one or nothing can stop Him from doing that."

Leah looked over at Nadia realizing the dilemma Ahmed had created for himself.

"Ahmed," Leah said gently. "We're not trying to humiliate you. We apologize if we have."

Leah reached down in her purse and pulled out a small paperback copy of the injeel. She held it in her hand in front of Ahmed.

"I believe the Bible is true, Ahmed and it is life-changing. Would you take this copy home with you and do what I did ten years ago? I read the Gospel of Luke. It answered a lot of my questions."

Ahmed cautiously reached over and took the injeel from Leah's hand and nervously stared down at it.

Then he gazed back into Leah's eyes with a determined look on his face.

"Alright. I will. But that doesn't mean that I will come to the same conclusions as you did."

"I understand," Leah said approvingly.

Ahmed stood up. He smiled back down at Nadia.

"It has been a pleasure talking with you," Ahmed said respectfully.

He turned and walked away back down the sidewalk.

Leah giggled and stared back at Nadia.

"Nadia, I believe you have an admirer."

Nadia giggled also and her face turned red from blushing.

"C'mon. We need to get back." Leah announced.

Leash and Nadia both got up and broke into laughter as they headed back through the alleyway to the Church.

Leah and Nadia arrived back at the Church anxious to tell everyone about their exploits of the day. Nadia strolled in behind Leah, excited and laughing and out of breath. She flopped down at the table and took a deep breath and began to relax.

Over in the corner, Nadia spotted Abdullah out of the corner of her eye. He was seated in a chair wearing headphones and enjoying some music on his CD.

Nadia got up and walked over to Abdullah. She tried to talk with him, but Abdullah was too absorbed in his music to hear her.

Stepping in front of him, Nadia reached down and pulled off his headphones.

"Hey!" Abdullah jumped up.

Nadia burst into laughter and gave him a hug.

"You're always full of jokes and surprises, warrior princess." Abdullah exclaimed as he hugged Nadia back.

"What are you listening to?" Nadia asked as she grabbed the CD out of Abdullah's hands.

"Great worship music," Abdullah answered back, his eyes sparkling with delight.

"That's Mr. Ridgeway!" Nadia shouted in surprise, holding the CD up to her eyes.

"Yes, oh, that's right. He's was your friend." Abdullah replied. He reflected back on his encounter with Jason five years earlier.

"I was busy street preaching and this American Musician came up to me and we talked for awhile and before he left he handed me this CD.

Nadia kept gazing at the CD and looked closely at Jason's picture. She slowly sat down in the lounge chair and opened up the CD case to look at the lyrics.

"Here, Nadia," Abdullah said as he carefully placed the headphones on Nadia's head.

"You've got to hear these songs. You'll be incredibly blessed!"

Nadia relaxed back into the chair and pressed the buttons to begin track one.

Nadia listened carefully to the first song entitled," Living Sacrifice." She was immediately drawn into the beautiful guitar melody and the lyrics. As the song progressed, Nadia reminisced back to Jason's visit five years ago. In her mind, she recalled when Jason entertained them after dinner playing his acoustic guitar. Nadia's heart was challenged by the haunting chorus of the song describing the Christian life as a total surrender and commitment to Jesus.

I want to be a Living Sacrifice
I'm bowing at your altar. I'm laying down my life.
I offer up my plans and dreams to you.
I lay down all my Isaacs and I give them back to you.

And I live to worship you.
Yes I live to worship you.

As the song came to a conclusion, Nadia took off the headphones. With tears streaming down her face, she excused herself from everyone and walked out to her favorite place of solitude in the courtyard.

The sun was shining brightly and the air was quiet and still with the faint distant sound of chirping birds.

Sitting down on the bench, Nadia bowed her head into her hands and began to cry. For the past week, she had been specifically burdened to pray for Jason. Now, after listening to Jason's song, she had been taken back to when she lived at home with Zak and her parents. Remembering all of this was very painful. Nadia desired so much for her parents to know Jesus. Today had been the day when her deepest longings were finally surfacing.

"Lord, I cry out to you. Please hear my prayer! Open my Father and Mother's eyes to you. Open their eyes to see your love, your beauty and your forgiveness. Please touch my little brother Zak's heart, too. Save them God, save them!"

Nadia's heart was broken in sorrow and sadness as she wrestled with God in prayer. It was almost too much for Nadia to bear, realizing that they were completely lost without Jesus.

Composing herself, Nadia lifted her head back up and glanced at the CD that was still in her hand. On the back side of the CD, she noticed an e-mail address for Spirit and Word Outreach Church.

Suddenly, she realized that she might be able to actually talk with Jason. Pastor Ali had just obtained an old, refurbished computer. Nadia sprang up from the bench and headed back into the Church. Nadia sensed that something was terribly wrong with Jason and she was determined to find out what it was.

Nadia laid down her pen. She was finished writing a morning devotional in her journal. Standing up from the lounge chair, Nadia stretched and glanced at the clock on the wall. It was 9:15 am and it was time for some breakfast.

As Nadia began to walk into the kitchen, there was a sharp knock at the front door. That's strange, Nadia thought, who would be coming to the Church at this time in the morning?

Nadia walked a few feet from the kitchen-lounge area and opened up the door. Standing in the doorway with a pleasant smile on his face and a small Bible in his hand was Ahmed.

"Good morning Nadia," Ahmed said.

Nadia was taken by surprise and didn't know quite what to say. There stood Ahmed, dressed in a formal striped-shirt and a pair of brown dockers.

"I'm sorry," Nadia replied, stuttering a bit, "Leah is not here today. She had to work-."

"That's alright," Ahmed explained, interrupting. "Actually, I came to see you, Nadia. I was hoping, if you don't mind, that you would answer some questions that I have."

"Sure," Nadia answered nervously.

Nadia stepped to one side and pushed open the door letting Ahmed walk in.

Ahmed gazed around and looked into the lounge area. Then he looked at Nadia.

"You will have to excuse me Nadia, but I've never been in a Church before."

"I understand," Nadia answered reassuringly. "Would you like to sit in the lounge?" Nadia said pointing toward a table and chairs in the lounge area.

"That would be fine," Ahmed agreed.

Nadia led the way as they walked into the lounge area and found a table. Ahmed walked over to the chair and pulled it out for Nadia.

Ahmed was such a gentleman and Nadia was impressed and speechless from his politeness.

"I promise not to take up a lot of your time, Nadia. So I will get right to the point."

Nadia looked into Ahmed's eyes intently. He had a persuasive and passionate way of articulating himself that put Nadia at ease with talking with him.

"Leah said I should read the gospel of Luke. I spent all of last night reading it. Then I came to the part of the story where Jesus was crucified."

Nadia could see the frustration building up in Ahmed's eyes.

"Of course, you know that The Quran teaches us that Jesus was not crucified. As a prophet, Allah would not allow for him to be humiliated like that, so instead He raised him up to heaven. Do you understand, Nadia?"

Nadia nodded her head and listened carefully to what Ahmed was saying. She sat relaxed with her hands folded together on the table. She looked compassionately and patiently into Ahmed's eyes, fully understanding his objection.

"Yes, I do understand, Ahmed. I too had the same objection at one time. Now as a Christian, I really understand why it was necessary for Jesus to die on the cross for our sins. Ahmed, do you remember the story of Abraham in Surah 37:102 in the Quran?"

"Yes," Ahmed answered immediately.

"Remember, Abraham's son was ransomed by the death of an animal?"

"Yes."

"Well, the Quran uses the words," sacrifice" and "ransom" in this chapter."

Nadia paused from her illustration and opened up her Bible.

"The Bible uses the same words to describe Jesus' death on the cross," Nadia pointed out.

"Therefore, the sacrificial death of Jesus is not really anti-Quranic, since the Quran itself uses the same words to describe what happened to Abraham's son."

Ahmed thought for a moment and nodded his head.

"Well, alright," Ahmed began. He shifted in his seat and leaned forward closer to Nadia at the table.

"But, the Quran teaches that on Judgment day, Allah will evaluate our good and bad deeds on the scale. We will go to Paradise based on our good deeds outweighing our bad deeds. So, it's up to us to pray, fast and be obedient and be ready. We are never to look to anyone else to do this for us. We are to look to Allah only."

Nadia remained patient with Ahmed's objection. She understood his feelings and objections very well since she too had been exactly where he was five years ago.

"Ahmed, do you believe that God speaks to us in dreams and visions?"

"Sure. He spoke that way to all the prophets. The angel Gabriel appeared in a vision to the Prophet Muhammad, peace be upon him and that is why we have the Quran."

Nadia waited patiently for a moment.

"While I was praying one day, over five years ago. I had a lot of fears, frustrations and questions. I cried out to Allah, asking Him to show me the straight path. Instantly before my eyes, Jesus appeared to me in a vision and looked deeply into my eyes. I was overwhelmed with both fear and joy! He said," Nadia I am the straight way. I am the way, the truth and the life."

Ahmed sat motionless and quiet after hearing Nadia's testimony. He made no reply and looked down at the table with a dejected look on his face. Then he looked back up and quickly stood up away from the table.

"I appreciate you taking the time to talk with me Nadia but I need to go."

Nadia stood up and smiled compassionately at Ahmed.

"I hope I haven't offended you Ahmed."

"Not at all, Nadia," Ahmed said, smiling graciously back at Nadia. Then he headed toward the front door.

As Nadia turned to go back into the lounge, she saw Pastor Ali hurrying out from his office.

"Who was that?" Ali asked suspiciously

Nadia grinned.

"A friend," she answered with a guilty smirk on her face. "He had some questions about the Bible and-."

"Nadia!" Ali hastily interrupted her. "You've got a reply from your e-mail to Jason."

Nadia felt an adrenaline rush through her body.

"Really!" she snapped back in excitement.

Nadia and Pastor Ali rushed back into his office. She quickly sat down in the chair in front of the computer and clicked on the e-mail.

Pastor Ali stood behind Nadia peering over her shoulder.

Suddenly, Nadia's excited expression on her face melted in shock. She clasped both of her hands onto her face in astonishment. She was not prepared for what she was now reading on the computer screen.

Chapter Eighteen
Reunited

Jason peered through the curtains looking down from the fourth floor to some children playing in the snow. The window pane was laden with frost and blurring with the cold, yet there was enough light to gaze outside into the frozen world below.

He could almost hear their laughter as they gathered up the cold snow in their hands and hurled icy snowballs at each other. They were having fun amidst the cold barren landscape and the dreary sky hanging over them from above. Jason remembered as a child hurrying out the door after breakfast and laying on his back in the cold snow to make a snow angel. His mother would get so upset when he came in soaked from head to toe. Yet Jason loved the winter and would always bring in some snow and hide it in the refrigerator for some juicy snow ice cream later on.

Those were the days of innocent childhood fun and pranks and snow angels and ice cream. Mr. Ridgeway would always come home and scold Jason for not shoveling the sidewalks and instead be busy building snowmen in the yard or sneaking off with his friends to go sledding down the big hill in Bangert Park.

As Jason watched the children below, a tall slender woman appeared on the scene and stopped them from having fun and scolded them. The children laughed as the woman pulled them away from the snowman they were building.

Jason pushed back the curtain and stared at the wall. He sat motionless in his wheelchair. The lights in the hospital room were dim. Once again, he felt the darkness all around him beginning to close in. He felt the despair begin to choke away the little bit of amusement that he had just experienced watching the children playing in the snow.

He looked over at the table by the bedside. There lay his journal and glasses. He wasn't in the writing mood anymore. Alongside his journal was his iPod. He didn't care about listening to music either. He didn't care anymore. His world had been shattered. Jason was broken inside. Not more than an hour earlier, Dr. Mason had come in with grim news.

"We have to discontinue the treatments Jason. I'm sorry Jason, but the cancer is spreading. It's getting out of control. You have less than three months to live. I'm sorry."

The news had crushed Jason. He had expected that God was going to heal him. His hopes had been so high. Now this!

This was not the news he had anticipated hearing. There would be no recording contract. There would be no more concerts where he could share his testimony. His time had suddenly become very limited.

Jason sat quietly in his wheelchair in the nearly dark room. The curtains behind him were drawn. He thought back almost three weeks ago when he stood all alone on the old Chain of Rocks Bridge and looked down at the Mississippi River below. The question now was, why didn't he jump then? If he had, none of this would have ever happened.

There was a soft tapping knock at the door. Jason sat quietly and didn't answer. Pastor Willoughby poked his head in and saw Jason sitting in front of the window. The curtains were drawn and the room was dimly lit. He could see the dejected expression on Jason's face.

"Okay if I come in?" Pastor Willoughby meekly asked.

There was no reply from Jason.

Pastor Willoughby slowly pushed open the door.

"Jason." Pastor Willoughby struggled to find the words of comfort to say to Jason. He turned around and pushed the door so that it was slightly ajar, just enough to let some light come through the crack.

Pastor Willoughby slowly walked over toward Jason and sat on the edge of the bed. He sat quietly and stared at Jason. Jason sat with his hands folded and his head down. After a few moments, Jason lifted up his head and stared at Pastor Willoughby. His face and complexion was twisted in bitterness and anger.

"I guess I'm supposed to say something."

There was a moment of silence.

"No, you don't have to."

"I guess, I'm supposed to be strong."

Jason's speech was filled with anger and sarcasm. Pastor Willoughby bowed his head in frustration and then looked up at Jason.

"Being angry will only make it more painful." Pastor Willoughby replied in a sympathetic and corrective tone.

"What do you expect me to be like?" Jason fired back with his voice cracking and tears streaming down his face.

"Why didn't God answer my prayer? Why didn't he heal me?" Jason demanded.

"Jason," Pastor Willoughby said, "God has your best interests at heart. He would never do anything to hurt you. He would never leave or forsake you. I can assure you. He heard your prayers. He is a good and loving God. He is working out His plan for your good Jason and for His glory."

Pastor Willoughby waited. There was another moment of silence. He purposely waited for Jason to think about what he had just said.

"When I said He heard your prayers, Jason, I think-."

Pastor Willoughby stuttered and looked amazed. His eyes began to well up with tears. Jason looked back at him curiously wondering what he meant. Pastor Willoughby composed himself and continued.

"Like I said, Jason, I think I can show you now, why I know God has truly answered your prayers. There is someone here who can't wait to see you!"

Jason shook his head in protest.

"I'm in no mood to see anyone, Pastor."

Pastor Willoughby stared back at Jason intently and then rose up from the bed.

"I think you will want to see this person," Pastor Willoughby said.

He walked over to the door and stuck out his head. He then gently pushed it shut except for a few inches.

Jason's eyes were fixed upon the door. He felt a cold chill rush through his body. The door to his room creaked as it opened. A tiny shaft of light streaked across the cold, barren hospital floor.

Just a few feet in front of Jason's wheelchair stood a beautiful young girl dressed in a light blue blouse and brown slacks. She had thick, curly brown hair and dazzling blue eyes that penetrated through Jason's whole being. Jason gazed at the silver necklace adorned around her neck. It looked so familiar to him. Slowly lifting up his eyes, he looked up and stared.

Their eyes met.
He couldn't believe what he was seeing.
It was Nadia!
Jason sat spellbound in his wheelchair.
For the first time in a very long time, Jason's world shifted back into focus. It was if God had just pulled back the curtain for him to see and comprehend the reason and purpose for his suffering. The chains of despair and brokenness that had held Jason captive finally fell powerless to the floor in this incredible moment. He felt free once again! Jason wanted to jump up out of his wheelchair and run and hug Nadia.

Nadia walked over to Jason and threw her arms around him as he sat spellbound in his wheelchair. Jason responded by pulling Nadia's head toward his chest. Nadia dropped to her knees and gently laid her head against his chest.

They both cried together. Tears of joy streamed down both of their faces. Pastor Willoughby looked on unable to hold back his tears. Neither Jason nor Nadia could utter a word to each other. They held each other tightly, crying for joy. God had brought them back together and at this very moment nothing else really mattered to them.

"I missed you so much!" Nadia cried out.

Jason stopped for a moment, composing himself and gave Nadia puzzled look.

"Hey, you can speak English!" he said half-chuckling as he wiped away the tears from his face.

Nadia chuckled, wiping the tears off of her face.

"Yes, Mr. Ridgeway, my best friend Leah taught me."

"Please, call me Jason, Nadia," Jason politely insisted.

Nadia stood up and gave Jason a look of respect and nodded her head.

"Yes, Mr. Ridgeway," Nadia paused feeling awkward and chuckled a bit.

"I will call you Jason."

Pastor Willoughby managed a smile and walked over. Nadia ran to him and hugged him tightly.

"I can never repay you, Pastor Willoughby."

"My pleasure," Pastor Willoughby replied holding onto Nadia.

Jason stared at Nadia. He still couldn't believe that she had come so far to see him. He was mesmerized and overwhelmed with joy.

Nadia once again bent down beside Jason in his wheelchair. Jason continued to wipe the tears away from his eyes. They both laughed and cried together and rejoiced that God had brought them back together again.

Nadia stood up and sat down on the bed facing Jason. They were both quiet for a moment. Nadia could see the agonizing look in Jason's face. The joy of their reunion had suddenly become interrupted with the cruel facts of reality.

"I don't want to put a damper-," Jason began.

Nadia observed the pain in Jason's eyes. She wanted so much to take the pain away from him. She knew what he was trying to tell her.

"I-I-," Jason stuttered with tears flooding his eyes. "I don't have much longer," Jason blurted out in pain. Nadia rose up from the bed and once again wrapped her arms around Jason.

"That's why I came," Nadia said as she held Jason.

Nadia then backed away from Jason and looked up at Pastor Willoughby.

"I don't know what to say," Nadia said with a grateful tone in her voice. Then she looked back at Jason. Jason had a puzzled look on his face.

"Jason. Your wonderful Pastor insisted on paying for my plane flight."

Jason stared back at Pastor Willoughby with tears in his eyes.

"Thank you, thank you. Thank you so much, Pastor. I can't tell you how happy you've made me," Jason admitted.

Nadia walked back over and hugged Jason, her face glowing with joy and gratitude.

After a few moments, Nadia sat back on the bed and leaned forward staring at Jason with an anxious look on her face.

"I have so much to tell you Jason," Nadia paused. Her face radiated with joy as she thought about what she was going to tell Jason.

"I did exactly at you told me to do."

Jason stared at Nadia wearing a blank expression on his face, not knowing what to expect.

"You told me in your letter that the reason Jesus was appearing to me in my dreams was because he wanted me to discover who He was."

Jason nodded his head nervously with a look of curiosity on his face.

Nadia paused. Her face glowed.

She could hardly wait to tell Jason her story.

"I discovered who Jesus is, Jason. He is the treasure of my life. Your letter spoke so beautifully to my heart. Now, I'm Christian."

Nadia's testimony of becoming a Christian overwhelmed Jason as he sat weeping in his wheelchair for joy.

"That's so beautiful, Nadia. I am so thrilled that you now know Jesus as your Lord and Savior!"

Jason could hardly speak. Tears of joy once more filled his eyes. More than anything, he wanted to have the strength to stand up and hug Nadia.

After composing himself once again, Jason looked back at Nadia. She looked so serious.

"What's wrong Nadia?" Jason tenderly asked.

Nadia took a deep breath and searched for the right words.

"As long as I live, I can never thank you enough for what you did for me and my family."

Nadia's voice began to crack. Jason observed the intense pain in Nadia's eyes. From Nadia's reaction, Jason knew inside that her parents had been devastated when they learned that she had become a Christian.

"Your parents were upset when they found out that you had become a Christian."

Nadia shook her head in agreement. Jason could sense how painful this was for Nadia to talk about.

"I haven't seen them in over five years." Nadia explained with a blank stare on her face. She shook herself back to reality and then looked seriously at Jason.

"I was so honored and humbled that you were my sponsor, Jason. Now I have the opportunity to do something for you."

Nadia stopped. She looked afraid to continue. She composed herself and then began again.

"I want to take care of you Jason. Would you please let me help you? Would you please let me be there for you?"

Jason was stunned. He didn't know what to say or how to answer Nadia. Pastor Willoughby stood quietly by and listened intently.

"Do you mean stay with me?"

"Yes." Nadia answered meekly and tenderly.

"I don't know what to say, Nadia." Jason stuttered.

"I don't want to be a burden for you. I mean, well. There will be Hospice nurses there from time to time. You're so young and beautiful and I don't want-."

"You're not a burden!" Nadia sternly said, interrupting Jason.

Jason was speechless.

"We will set our boundaries," Nadia spoke up saying.

"Of course." Jason agreed.

Nadia rose up from the bed and placed her hands on the arms of Jason's wheelchair. She leaned closer, staring into Jason's eyes.

"You were there for me, Jason. Now I want to be there for you."

Jason was touched. Deep inside, he felt humbled and honored to be presented with such an offer. Jason cracked a smile and looked back at Nadia.

"Miss Mustafa, I would be honored to accept your offer," Jason said grinning. Nadia chuckled back at him.

"Mr. Ridgeway, "Nadia said with a grin on her face. "Thank you for giving me the privilege of being your special nurse."

Nadia and Jason broke out in laughter at each other. Pastor Willoughby laughed along with them.

In the midst of their laughter, Jason suddenly became serious. His face changed from joy to a look of despair.

"What's wrong Jason?" Nadia inquired.

"God has brought you to me for a very special purpose and-"Jason once again began to emotionally break down.

"I just want God to give me some time to be with you." Jason pleaded.

Pastor Willoughby walked over.

"Let's pray for that, shall we?" Pastor Willoughby said.

Pastor Willoughby, Jason and Nadia joined hands together forming a circle.

"Lord, you are so good. You have reunited Jason and Nadia. We are so thrilled and so thankful to you. At this time, Lord, we ask that you please give Jason and Nadia time together. Please give Jason strength and healing so that they may enjoy each other's friendship. We ask and pray these things in your Son's name and for His glory. Amen."

Jason turned and looked out the window. Snowflakes began to fall as the evening sunset approached. He chuckled under his breath and looked back at Nadia.

"This is your very first Christmas in St. Louis and by God's grace, I want to show you the town and celebrate with you."

Nadia's face glowed with anticipation.

"Mr. Ridgeway. I am your guest and you must show me the great city that you call St. Louis."

Nadia and Jason laughed together once again. Jason pushed his wheelchair closer to the window. He thrust open the curtains and gazed out at the snowfall. Nadia stood behind Jason and watched in awe at the first snowfall she had ever seen.

Chapter Nineteen
A very special Christmas

From the very beginning when Jason and Nadia first met, God had blessed them with a unique and intimate friendship. God sovereignly used Jason's desire to financially sponsor Nadia to bring her to faith in Christ.

All of his life, Jason carried a burning passion within himself to share the love of Christ with everyone he met. God blessed Jason with powerful worship songs to reach those who normally would never enter a Church building. Because of Jason's love to communicate Christ, it was a privilege for him to travel halfway around the world to bring the good news of the gospel to a young Muslim girl and her family.

As a result of his love and passion for Christ, Nadia came back into his life to bring hope and healing into his darkest hour.

For two days, she remained at Jason's bedside praying and watching him regain his strength. Their friendship had weathered some difficult storms and now at last they were enjoying a wonderful time together.

Once again, God had blessed their friendship. He was answering their prayers in a marvelous way. Jason's appetite had returned. His demeanor had improved and he was able to walk without his wheelchair for the first time.

However, when Dr. Mason came by on his rounds, he cautioned Jason not to take for granted his present condition. He explained to Jason that terminal cancer patients can rebound, but only for a short while. He pointed out to Jason that he still had terminal cancer and would still need hospice care. Yet Dr. Mason rejoiced with Nadia and Jason for the sudden rebound and counseled them to enjoy the temporary reprieve.

Early Tuesday morning, December 22, 2009, just three days before Christmas, Dr. Mason dismissed Jason to go home. Jason was overjoyed. He would even be able at this point to drive Nadia home in his car. He was so excited to be well enough to show Nadia St. Louis and enjoy Christmas with her.

Jason pulled his car into the driveway. He shut off the engine and turned to look at Nadia. She was admiring the size of Jason's home.

"You have a big house!" Nadia exclaimed with a smile.

"It's an improvement on your hut," Jason said with a smile.

Jason opened up the trunk and carried Nadia's luggage to the front door. He opened up the door and let Nadia walk in first. She stood in the hallway gazing into the living room. She saw the couch, a couple of lounge chairs, a television and a stereo. This moment was a culture shock for Nadia. Her eyes grew wider as she gazed around the room.

"This is very beautiful!" Nadia said in awe.

"I'll give you the tour," Jason said, sitting down Nadia's luggage on the floor.

He took Nadia into the kitchen. She stared at the microwave, the dishwasher and the refrigerator. Jason took her to the sink and she turned on the faucet.

"I can't believe what I'm seeing!" Nadia exclaimed as she marveled at all of the modern conveniences.

Jason escorted Nadia down the hallway and sat down her luggage in a small bedroom. The bedroom had a single bed, a closet and a small table and lamp. Jason held out his hand and pointed into the room.

"Miss Mustafa, this is your room."

Nadia slowly walked into the bedroom and then sat down on the bed. Her eyes were still absorbing the comfort and beauty of the room.

"This is so comfortable," Nadia said, pressing down on the mattress. Her eyes sparkled with delight at all that she was seeing. Jason smiled back at Nadia.

"No more bamboo cots, young lady."

Nadia got up from the bed and opened the closet. She spun around and looked at Jason.

"Back at Living Word Church in Rangpur, I had a picture of you and Zak on the wall."

"Living Sword Church?" Jason said curiously.

Nadia grinned realizing Jason had not yet heard her story.

"Sorry. Yes. Living Word Church. I will explain all of that to you later."

Jason placed both of hands on his legs and bowed toward Nadia.

"Miss Mustafa, would you care to join me in the kitchen for some tea and biscuits?"

"Yes sir, Mr. Ridgeway," Nadia answered with a grin on her face.

Nadia and Jason retired to the kitchen. Jason heated up a kettle on the stove and made some tea for the both of them. They sat down at the kitchen table. Nadia kept gazing at the walls and appliances in disbelief. She was not accustomed to such modern conveniences, even when shed lived at The Living Word Church in Rangpur.

Jason took a sip of tea and looked seriously at Nadia.

"You mentioned Living Word Church. Tell me all about it, Nadia."

Nadia sat down her cup of tea. Her eyes sparkled with joy as she thought about the church and all of her friends.

"It was the day that you left to fly back to St. Louis. I was in my prayer grove reading your letter-."

Nadia paused, remembering that fateful moment. Tears welled up in her eyes. Jason laid his hand on top of Nadia's hand.

"Sorry," Nadia said half-laughing, embarrassed by her crying.

"Go on." Jason said, encouraging her to continue.

Nadia stared intently into Jason's eyes with a look of extreme gratitude.

"Your letter, Jason, it – it," Nadia said stuttering. "Opened my eyes to the beauty of Christ. It was at that moment, I was desperate, so I cried out in prayer, "Allah, show me the straight path!"

Nadia paused. Jason's eyes were glued to Nadia's.

"Then I heard a voice say to me, I am the straight path. I am the way, the truth and the life. Jesus reached down in this vision I had and touched my face."

"That's amazing!" Jason shouted back.

While Nadia looked excited sharing her testimony, her facial complexion suddenly changed from delight to fear.

"What's wrong?" Jason asked.

Nadia reached down and took a sip of tea. She began to shake. Jason became upset and worried, but Nadia insisted on continuing.

"I remember as I left the prayer grove, suddenly out of nowhere a hand grabbed me. After that, all I remember was looking up in the dark and being terribly afraid."

Jason was shaken. Then suddenly, he burst into the conversation full of excitement.

"I remember the night my mom died. We had a prayer meeting at the Church and the Pastor began praying and it was powerful. Also I remember having a dream that day and in the dream you were crying out for help."

Nadia's eyes grew wide.

"Don't you see Nadia?" Jason shouted. "God knew you were in trouble and he made that known to me in a dream so that I could pray for you!"

Nadia leaned back into her chair, shaking in awe and amazement.

"Our God is so good!" Nadia finally said.

They took a moment to rejoice together and then Nadia continued.

"They took me to a deserted house. I was so afraid Jason. I found out later that these men were part of a human trafficking ring."

Jason shook his head in disgust.

"But," Nadia exclaimed, recalling her deliverance. "God sent an angel to me. There was an earthquake and he led me to a path in the woods and helped me escape."

Jason looked stunned. He couldn't believe what he was hearing.

"As I ran into the woods, I could hear these men in the distance pursuing me. So I ran faster and faster until all at once I collapsed. When I woke up, I saw the face of a girl helping me get up off the ground. He name is Leah, Jason. She is Jewish. She witnessed to me about Jesus. One day, when the fear was so great, we prayed and I became a Christian. The amazing thing is, God sent me through the woods to escape from my kidnappers and I ended up being found by a busload of former Muslims. They are the most precious friends in the world to me."

"Wow!" Jason exclaimed. He sat for a moment trying to digest the incredible story Nadia had just told him.

"I am so grateful that God answered our prayers and saved you and gave you a group of incredible friends."

"I can't wait for you to meet Leah, J-." Nadia abruptly stopped, realizing what she had just said.

"I'm sorry, Jason," Nadia said putting her hand up to her mouth and feeling ashamed.

Jason bowed his head in despair and looked back at Nadia. He took a hold of Nadia's hand.

"That's okay, Nadia. I'm just thankful to God that He's given me this short time to be with you."

Nadia put her other hand on Jason's hand and fought back the tears. They both finished their tea and retreated into the living room. Jason sat in one chair and Nadia sat in the other instead of sitting together on the couch. They did this in order to respect each others boundaries and be pleasing to God.

As Jason surfed through the channels, Nadia was fascinated that she could see Jerusalem on one channel, London on another and the local news on the other. She had never been exposed to such technology before.

Jason continued flipping through the channels and finally came upon a historical perspective on the immigrants coming to America from Italy and Germany. The perspective showed the immigrants riding the ferry toward Ellis Island and gazing up at The Statue of Liberty. Nadia was drawn to the amazing architecture and the story behind the Statue of Liberty. The narrator read the famous slogan that encapsulated the meaning behind the Statue of Liberty.

"Give me your tired, your poor, your huddled masses yearning to be free, the wretched refuse of your teaming shore. Send these. The homeless, the tempest tossed to me. Lift my lamp beside the golden door."

Jason glanced over and noticed Nadia's face looked sad and grief stricken after hearing the narrator recite the Statue of Liberty slogan.

"You look sad Nadia," Jason stated.

Nadia shook her head in agreement.

"This is my first visit to America, Jason and I am afraid to say it, but I believe your country has taken its freedom for granted. Freedom is so precious, Jason."

Jason immediately agreed with Nadia.

"Yes. We have forgotten that our country was founded on religious principles, Life, liberty and the pursuit of happiness. In Pakistan, in Saudia Arabia, in Iran, if you're a Muslim that has converted to Christianity, you are marked and you don't have the freedom to worship Christ. Instead, you could go to jail or even worse be put to death."

Nadia had a look of despair on her face.

"Just two days ago, when I was on the computer before I came to see you. I read about the story of Miriam in Tehran, the capital of Iran. She and her two sisters were arrested on Christmas Eve right in their own apartment. The secret police confiscated their Bibles, their music and their radios and carted them off to Evin Prison. Their crimes? Converting from Islam to Christianity. In Iran, that is the sin of Apostatsy. They could receive a lengthy prison sentence or be put to death."

"The young people in Iran," Jason pointed out, "are hungry and thirsty for the truth. They are tired of governmental control and the oppression of Islam. That's why they have formed a secret underground church movement. Many of them are turning to Christ and going on the internet to print out verses from the Bible. They are hungry for Christ and The word of God."

As Jason finished, he notice Nadia was strangely quiet and seemed to be in a daze.

"Jason," Nadia said, finally speaking up. "Right before I found out about your illness, I was studying about Queen Esther in the Bible."

Nadia stopped. Her face lighted up with joy.

"Jason. I want to bring the good news of the gospel to my Muslim people. Esther and the Jewish people were in captivity in Persia, which today is Iran. Esther was faithful to God in preserving the Jewish people from harm."

"Are you sensing God's call on your life?" Jason asked, interrupting Nadia.

Nadia though carefully for a moment.

"Yes. The story of Miriam in Iran has really stayed with me. My heart goes out to her. All she wants is the freedom to worship Christ. I want to help her and people like her in Iran, just like Esther did for her people when they were exiled in Persia."

"That's fantastic," Jason said, encouraging Nadia. He glanced down at his watch as Nadia yawned and stretched.

"I believe you are very tired, Miss Mustafa, after a long plane flight," Jason said as he stood up.

"Yes. Yes, I am," Nadia agreed.

"Tomorrow will be a busy day. We're going Christmas shopping at the mall. Then, we're putting up the Christmas tree and having an intimate candlelight service. Plus, I'll give you a tour of my studio."

Nadia smiled back at Jason while walking to her guest room. She stopped and looked intently in his eyes.

"You have made me the happiest person in the world today, Mr. Ridgeway. Good night."

The next day was Christmas Eve. Jason and Nadia met with Jennifer his hospice nurse. Jennifer explained to Jason that his temporary reprieve would not last forever and counseled him that one day soon he would probably be confined to his bed. Both Nadia and Jason listened intently and understood the reality of his condition. Jennifer was glad to know Nadia would be with Jason to help him with his oxygen and applying pain patches on him on a daily basis. Although Jason was still able to move about, he understood it was only for a short time. In light of that, Jason and Nadia both agreed to celebrate and enjoy the time together that God had graciously blessed them with.

After Jennifer left, Jason invited Nadia to take a tour of his recording studio. Nadia was fascinated by all of the computers, guitars and microphones that filled the little basement room. Jason picked up his acoustic guitar and began to play and sing Nadia's favorite worship song, "living sacrifice." Nadia watched with excitement and joy as Jason ministered to her. As Jason played, Nadia remembered the poems God had given her while she sat in the Church courtyard gazing at the wooden cross. She was anxious to share them with Jason in the hopes that he would compose some appropriate music and turn them into worship songs.

Jason and Nadia went back upstairs and got dressed to go shopping at the mall. They headed out the front door together. It was a cold and windy day with the sunlight glistening brightly and reflecting off the snow.

As Nadia walked toward the car, Jason reached down and made a snowball from a clump of wet snow. Then when Nadia turned her back, Jason hurled the snowball at Nadia, striking her in the shoulder.

"Hey!" Nadia exclaimed, wiping the cold snow off of her back. She gave Jason a dirty look, putting her hands on her hips.

"So, Mr. Ridgeway. You want to play rough!" Nadia shouted back, jokingly.

Jason stood staring at Nadia, holding onto his belly and laughing. Nadia quickly reached down and made a snow ball.

"No! no!" Jason pleaded with Nadia, covering his face in his hands. As he backed up, Nadia charged toward him with a large clump of snow in her hand and slammed it down on the top of his wool cap.

"Hey, hey," Jason shouted out, laughing.

Nadia grabbed some more snow in her hand and began plastering it all over his body. Jason slipped and fell backwards in the snow. Nadia laughed hysterically. Jason laid there for a moment and then proceeded to make a snow angel with his body motion. Nadia continued to stare at Jason and laughed hysterically once again.

Out of breath and panting, Jason sat up in the snow.

"There. I did it!" Jason said.

Nadia had never seen a snow angel before. Jason sat in the snow very proud of his artistic work. Nadia held out her hands, chuckling and making fun of his snow angel. Jason grabbed onto

Nadia's hands. He slowly got up and then suddenly grabbed his abdomen.

"What's wrong?" Nadia cried out in a panic.

Jason stood still for a moment trying to collect his breath.

"I guess I'm getting too old for this," Jason admitted, smiling.

"You need to be careful," Nadia answered swallowing nervously as she helped Jason to the car. Jason's pain was a rude reminder to Nadia that in all of their frolic and fun that the cancer was still there and slowly taking its toll on his life.

Jason and Nadia drove onto highway 270 and headed toward the West County Outlet Mall. The sun was shining brightly and although the temperature was below freezing, they determined to make every second count for the time they had been given together.

Parking the car, Jason and Nadia walked into the mall entrance. "It came upon a midnight clear," was playing on the overhead speaker system. Nadia was fascinated by all of the colored Christmas lights, trees and nativity scenes spread out all over the mall. She watched as some young boys and girls waited patiently in line to sit on Santa Claus's lap.

"I'll be right back," Jason told Nadia as he walked into a bookstore.

Nadia waited outside taking in all of the Christmas sights.

"They're all terrorists!"

Nadia turned her head and saw a group of teenage boys standing in front of a nativity scene. They were having a heated discussion. One teenager shook his finger at the other screaming loudly above the Christmas music.

"We need to put an end to all of them. I say that we bomb 'em all today and get this war over."

The teenager took a deep breath finishing his point. His eyes were bulging with anger and fear.

Nadia was very distressed at what she had heard. She slowly walked up to the group of teenagers. They saw her coming and stood still, surprised that she had walked up to them.

"Excuse me," Nadia said.

The bold teenager that had been doing all of the talking looked sheepish and a little stunned as Nadia stared into his eyes.

"Did I hear you say that all Muslims are terrorists?" Nadia inquired.

The teenager looked stunned. He didn't expect to have to defend his point.

"Ah-," he replied with a stutter. "I guess that's what I said."

He nervously looked around at the other teenagers. They didn't say a word but remained quiet.

Nadia continued to stare at the young teenager.

"I used to be a Muslim sir, but now I am a Christian. Do you know why I am a Christian?"

The teenager nervously shook his head.

"No."

"I became a Christian because I discovered how much God loved me."

The teenager looked ashamed, bowing his head.

"Jesus told us to love our enemies," Nadia pointed out. She looked at the teenager. Her eyes were filled with grace and compassion for him.

"Sir. Don't you think we should love Muslims instead of hating them? Maybe some of them will discover the love of Jesus like I did."

Nadia waited as the young teenager looked remorseful.

"Mam," he began. I'm truly sorry for what I said."

Nadia nodded her head and smiled back at him. At that moment Jason returned with a package in his hand.

"Are you alright?" Jason asked.

"Yes." Nadia replied. "We were just having a nice, little talk."

Jason and Nadia walked away. The teenagers stood completely still with their hands in their pockets not knowing what more to say.

After a short drive, Jason and Nadia arrived back home after an eye-opening shopping experience at the mall. It was 6:15 pm when Jason laid the bag of groceries down on the kitchen table.

"Now," Jason said, catching his breath. "Tonight, Miss Mustafa, stove 101 class is in session and you have Christmas cookie duty."

Jason handed Nadia an apron. He had a smirked look on his face. Nadia stood in the corner of the kitchen with her arms folded together giving Jason a nasty look.

"Very funny, Mr. Ridgeway." Nadia shot back, grinning sarcastically at Jason.

"Then you trust me not to burn down the house?" Jason laughed.

"Well, it's very expensive for the fire department to come to your house on Christmas Eve."

They both laughed together as Nadia fitted the apron around her waist. Jason ran downstairs to get the Christmas tree while Nadia heated up the oven.

A few minutes later as Jason was busy putting up the tree, he could smell the delicious aroma of cookies baking in the oven.

"Mmmm, something smells good," Jason said.

Nadia poked her head around the corner while adjusting her apron.

"They are done." Nadia announced.

As Jason finished putting the artificial limbs on the tree, Nadia emerged from the kitchen with a plate of fresh baked Christmas cookies.

"Mr. Ridgeway, would you like a Christmas cookie?" Nadia offered holding the tray in front of Jason.

"Yes, I would." Jason replied, reaching for a cookie.

"Delicious!" Jason said, munching on a cookie.

When Jason finished eating the cookie, he reached down and opened up a box of candy canes.

"Would you assist me in putting the ornaments on the tree?"

"I'd love to." Nadia answered. Her eyes sparkled with wonder as she held the candy cane in one hand and looked up at the Christmas tree.

"I remember as a Muslim. We of course never celebrated Christmas. We were taught it was nothing more than a Christian pagan festival. We only celebrated the Prophet Mohammed's Birthday."

"I understand," Jason said. He held the candy cane in front of Nadia's eyes.

"Did you know, Nadia that the gospel message is on this candy cane?"

"No. "Nadia answered, gazing up at the candy cane that Jason was holding.

"The color white symbolizes the purity of Jesus that he is our pure and sinless savior born on Christmas day to save us from our sins."

Nadia listened carefully. Her eyes were fixed on the candy cane.

"The color red," Jason explained, "is the precious blood of Jesus shed on the cross to wash away our sins. The color green symbolizes the new life that Jesus gives us because he rose again from the dead defeating Satan on our behalf."

Nadia had a look of fascination on her face.

"That is so beautiful, Jason. It's so simple, yet so profound that God became a human being for us. He came to us, because we couldn't come to him."

"That's right." Jason agreed.

Nadia helped Jason put the last strand of lights on the tree and then they both sat down exhausted from all of the hard work.

Nadia leaned forward in her chair and gazed up at the Christmas tree. Then she looked back at Jason.

"It's so beautiful, Jason. I can't believe that I'm actually sitting here with you on Christmas Eve!"

Nadia bit her lip and brushed a tear away from her eye.

"I'll never forget sitting in the courtyard and suddenly I felt an enormous burden to pray for you. Now I know why and I'm so glad that I did!"

Jason nodded his head feeling humble and grateful inside.

"Thank you, Nadia, "Jason said with a look of gratitude on his face.

"Now," Jason said, reaching for his Bible. "It's time for our special candlelight service."

Jason stood up and turned the knob on the wall dimming the lights. Then he reached over lighting a single candle in the middle of the coffee table.

"I will read first." Jason said.

Nadia reached down and picked up her Bible.

"In the beginning was the Word and the Word was with God and the Word was God. He was in the beginning with God. All things were made through Him and without Him was not anything made that was made. In Him was life and the life was the light of men. The light shines in darkness and the darkness has not overcome it.

Verse 14 — And the Word became flesh and dwelt among us and we have seen His glory, glory as of the only Son from the Father full of grace and truth.

There was a moment of silence as Jason finished his reading. Then Nadia reached over, lit her candle and began reading.

<u>Isaiah 9:6</u>
*For to us a child is born. To us a son is given
And the government shall be upon his shoulder.
And his name shall be called Wonderful Counselor,
Mighty God, Everlasting Father, Prince of peace.*

As soon as Nadia had finished reading, Jason put down his Bible and folded his hands.

"Let's pray for the persecuted Church in the middle east tonight, Nadia. I'll begin and then you can follow."

Nadia nodded her head in agreement. They both became silent and bowed their heads.

"Lord, we marvel at your glorious incarnation. You stooped down so low and took on human flesh to rescue us from the chains of our sins.

Tonight, we direct our thoughts and prayers toward the suffering Church in Pakistan. We ask that you give our brothers and sisters boldness and courage to proclaim Christ in the midst of their oppression. Give them endurance and steadfastness to be strong in

Jesus as they demonstrate your love to every Muslim that they meet."

Jason finished praying. There was a moment of silence and then Nadia began to pray.

"Dear Jesus. Tonight we celebrate your birth. We worship and praise you! Jesus, you are our life, our love, our salvation, our only hope. I ask that you shine your love and light into the darkness of Iran. Open hearts and minds and set Muslims free. Dear Jesus, I pray that you would appear to Muslims in their prayer time as you did to me. And I pray that they would experience your love and forgiveness and realize that you are a gift that cannot be earned. Jesus, you are my treasure and I want Muslims in Iran to know you in that very same way. Amen."

As soon as Nadia finished praying and Jason opened his eyes, they both heard voices outside their window singing a Christmas carol. Jason and Nadia both stared at each other in awe and wonder. They got up from their chairs. Jason kneeled on the couch and pulled back the curtain. Nadia kneeled down next to Jason and they gazed out the living room window together.

Standing outside in the front yard was a group of young men and women holding sheet music in their hands and singing, "O come all ye faithful." Their voices harmonized beautifully together and the quiet Christmas Eve night suddenly burst forth with praise and adoration to Christ.

Kneeling next to Jason on the couch, Nadia stared at the carolers. She was mesmerized by the beauty and magic of the night and what it all meant.

"That is so beautiful," Nadia said with tears of joy flooding her eyes. Jason watched alongside with Nadia and began to sing. "O come let us adore Him, Christ the Lord." Nadia looked back at Jason smiling and followed along singing.

The quiet Christmas Eve night was bursting forth with praise to God. Nadia looked back over to Jason. His eyes were closed and his voice soared in worship to Jesus. Nadia looked back at the carolers. Her heart was wonderfully warmed by the beauty of the moment. Nadia realized that this was a very special Christmas that she would remember for the rest of her life.

Chapter Twenty
A Prophecy Fulfilled

"Good morning, Nadia. Merry Christmas!" Jason enthusiastically proclaimed.

He stood outside Nadia's room in his bare feet. Nadia quickly thrust open the door and emerged in her bare feet wearing a blue housecoat. She quickly brushed back her curly, brown hair away from her forehead.

"Merry Christmas, Jason!" Nadia said smiling.

"I guess we should go open our presents." Jason announced.

"I think that's a good idea," Nadia agreed.

They both bumped into each other in the narrow hallway and laughed as they made their way into the living room. Nadia reached the Christmas tree first before Jason and picked up a white envelope.

"Merry Christmas, Jason." Nadia said with her eyes beaming with joy, holding the envelope up to Jason's face.

"Thank you, Nadia," Jason said, sitting down on the floor.

Nadia plopped down on the floor next to Jason wearing a silly, girlish grin on her face, anxious for Jason to open up his present. Jason carefully tore open the envelope and pulled out a folded white piece of paper. At the top of the page it read:

Reunited
A poem by Nadia

"I wrote that for you on the way over on the plane." Nadia explained.

Jason smiled and began top read Nadia's poem.

Today has been the happiest day of my life.
It's been such a long, long time, since I've seen your face.
You are the answer to my prayer.
I've been searching for you everywhere.
Let me wipe away the tears from your eyes.
I am here with you. You don't have to cry.
God has brought us back together. This time its forever.
No more separation, no more.
We're reunited, no more divided. And I'm so excited
Just to see your face again.
We've been invited. To be reunited and you have ignited
My faith once again.
Through all the pain and all the tears.
Through all the sleepless nights and through all the Lonely years.
We are here. We are here. We are finally here.

Jason put down the poem. His face glowed with admiration.

"Nadia. This is beautiful," Jason said peering into Nadia's eyes. "I hardly know what to say. You write so well and I am humbled by your kindness."

Nadia smiled, brushing back her hair from her forehead. She reached underneath the tree and handed Jason another present.

"For me? Another present?' Jason asked. Nadia smiled and nodded her head.

Jason took the package from Nadia's hand. He had a look of unbelief on his face as he slowly untied the ribbon. Nadia grinned and watched Jason slowly unwrap the package.

Suddenly, Jason gave Nadia a look of astonishment.

"This is your journal, Nadia." Jason said with a perplexed look on his face.

Nadia reached over and turned some pages in the journal and pointed her finger to the top of the page. Jason gazed down at the page.

"It's addressed to me?" Jason said shrugging his shoulders.

"Yes," Nadia answered as she leaned closer to Jason to explain. "This was written the morning after I prayed with Leah to receive Christ. After I became a Christian, I started out every entry addressed to you."

Jason's face turned white. He felt amazed and humbled at the same time.

"You see, Jason, your letter that you wrote me to tell me why Jesus was appearing to me in my dreams. That letter changed my life forever. That's why after I prayed with Leah, I wanted to dedicate my journal to you."

Jason's eyes began to well up with tears. Nadia reached over and turned the page.

"I wrote this on the day I was baptized saying how I wish you could have been there with me."

Jason brushed away the tears from his eyes.

"For the next five years, I wrote to you as if you could read what I was saying. I never forgot for one second about you and I prayed every day that God would somehow bring us back together. Jason, your friendship to me has been one of the most important gifts that God has ever given me."

Jason reached over and hugged Nadia tightly.

"Nadia, you are the greatest friend that I've ever had. I will never forget you."

Jason let go of Nadia, laughing and wiping away the tears from his face. He composed himself and reached under the tree to give Nadia her present.

"For you Nadia. Merry Christmas!"

"Thank you." Nadia replied.

She quickly tore open the wrapping, anxious to see her present. Her eyes widened as she held a new Bible in her hands with her name engraved on the front cover.

"Thank you, Jason! Thank you!" Nadia excitedly said as she flipped through the pages.

Jason reached over and picked up Nadia's poem once again.

"Nadia," Jason said, interrupting Nadia as she browsed through her new Bible.

"I would like to write the music to your poems as my final project."

Nadia suddenly stopped. Her face turned ashen white. For a moment, all of the joy had suddenly evaporated. She looked back at Jason, giving him a serious and sober look.

"I would be honored."

"I want to do this Nadia."

Nadia understood the reason Jason wanted to write the music as his final project.

"Together, we will tell the whole world about Jesus." Nadia said.

"Yes, we will," Jason firmly agreed.

After finishing breakfast, Jason and Nadia retreated to their individual rooms to get dressed for the Christmas Day service at the Church. Nadia emerged wearing a dark blue skirt and a light-colored blouse with the shiny silver necklace draped overtop that Jason had given her over five years ago. Jason was dressed in a brown shirt and tie and light-colored cacki pants.

"Well, Miss Mustafa. You look delightful." Jason said observing Nadia as she stood in the hallway.

"Well, thank you, Mr. Ridgeway. " Nadia replied taking Jason's arm.

They both laughed out loud and headed out the front door.

The parking lot at the Church was packed with cars. Droves of people walked through the front door of the Church.

Nadia stood still. She was awestruck as she looked around the vast auditorium of the main sanctuary of the Church. She gazed at rows and rows of padded pews and the magnificent blue-colored carpeting that stretched from one end of the auditorium to the other. All the way at the end of the sanctuary was a stage filled with Christmas trees, presents, and a large stairway section for the choir.

There were television cameras, large screen monitors and several light grids that rose above the main stage. The pulpit stood in the center of the stage surrounded by two padded chairs.

As Nadia gazed around the auditorium, she thought back five years earlier to the dream that she had and suddenly everything began to take focus. Almost everything she had dreamt had taken place according to God's providence. Today, one more piece of the puzzle was being fitted into the big picture.

"Hello. My name is Robbie."

Nadia suddenly snapped back into reality from her daydreaming and looked down at a teenage boy in a wheelchair.

"Nadia" Jason spoke up," This is my good friend Robbie."

Robbie smiled, extending his hand.

"I've heard a lot about you, Nadia."

Nadia smiled back and knelt down beside Robbie's wheelchair.

"I'm so glad to meet you Robbie. I hear that you're becoming quite a guitarist."

Both Robbie and Jason looked at each other and chuckled.

"He's a very good teacher," Robbie admitted.

For the next few minutes, Jason introduced Nadia to several of the Church families. Then as the lights grew dim, they found an empty pew at the front just in time as the service began.

Nadia had never seen such a large Church compared to the tiny one she attended in Rangpur. She was thrilled and amazed at the wonderful choir voices as they went through a medley of Christmas songs. Nadia listened intently to Pastor Willoughby's Christmas sermon about how Christ came as light in the darkness to rescue the sinful human race.

As the service began to wind down and Pastor Willoughby concluded his sermon, he paused a moment and stared directly at Nadia.

"Today. We have a very special person in our midst."

Nadia was startled and looked over to Jason hoping he could explain what was happening. Jason was also taken by surprise as he stared back at Nadia.

"Five years ago. If you can remember," Pastor Willoughby explained. "Jason had a special evening to encourage sponsorship for Worldwide Compassion. Just before his presentation, a young lady came up to the stage and gave an amazing prophecy that God was soon going to shake the Muslim world in Iran, Saudia Arabia and Bangladesh."

Suddenly, Nadia felt cold chills all over her body. She began to tremble as Pastor Willoughby's eyes met hers.

"God said he would send us a special warrior princess that we would receive, train and send out as a missionary. Tonight, that prophecy, after five long years, has been fulfilled."

The sound of murmuring could be heard all over the Church for a moment and then it became still once again.

"God is faithful. He has kept his promise. That young warrior princess is among us. Jason and Nadia. Could you both please come up here?"

Nadia shrieked. She could not move. She shot a nervous stare toward Jason as he slowly rose up. Shaking and trembling, Nadia rose up from the pew. All eyes in the auditorium were focused on her. Jason carefully escorted Nadia up the stairs and onto the stage.

Nadia was extremely nervous as Pastor Willoughby reached over to greet her with a handshake. Suddenly, the Church erupted in applause as they all stood to their feet in recognition of Nadia.

Pastor Willoughby stood in between Jason and Nadia as the Church finished their applause. Nadia nervously gazed out at the sea of people. She was spellbound and unable to speak.

"I would ask that you all please bow your heads. We are going to pray and recognize God's sovereign hand in bringing Nadia to us."

The Church became silent as all heads were bowed.

"Almighty God. We praise you for your faithfulness and your providence today in sending Nadia to us. We ask you now God to anoint and send out Nadia in the power of your Spirit to be a mighty missionary to the Muslim world. You have declared that she will have the fire of Esther and the boldness of David. Fill her God with your Spirit. Teach and train her O Lord and equip her with boldness and passion to preach your holy gospel, that through her, you will bring multitudes of Muslims to a saving knowledge of Jesus Christ. Give Nadia your compassion and love, Jesus that she will shine brightly in every area of darkness and break down religious strongholds for your glory and your name sake we pray. Amen."

Nadia stood transfixed and astounded after hearing the powerful prayer that Pastor Willoughby had given. Pastor Willoughby glanced over at Nadia. Tears were streaming down the cheeks of her face. Jason stood next to her unable to control his tears as well. Pastor Willoughby gently pinned the lavalier microphone on the neckline of Nadia's dress. Wiping away the tears from her eyes, Nadia cleared her throat and struggled to compose herself. There was utter silence in the auditorium as she began to speak.

"I am humbled and I don't know what to say," Nadia began. She paused and gazed out into the sea of faces hidden in the darkness across the auditorium.

Jason stood a few feet away near the pulpit. His eyes were riveted on Nadia. Nadia turned to look at Jason. Beads of sweat began to trickle down her face. Taking a deep breath, Nadia turned once again toward the audience and continued speaking.

"Five years ago, during my prayer time as a Muslim, I saw Jesus as if he were standing right in front of me."

Nadia swallowed nervously.

"He told me. Nadia, I am the straight path. I am the way, the truth, and the life. I told Jesus. I will follow you."

The emotion of the moment brought tears to Nadia's eyes once again. She struggled to maintain her composure.

"Two weeks later, I met some former Muslims who had become Christians. Leah, a wonderful Jewish Christian, who once was a Muslim, prayed with me one evening and I committed my life to Jesus. My life has never been the same since then. As I look out at each of you from this stage, I tell you the truth, you too are chosen by God. You, you, you," Nadia said with boldness, pointing her finger out toward the audience.

"You are chosen, just as I am, to be a light in the darkness of where you live. Jesus wants you to shine your light, to shine your light of God's truth to everyone that you meet. You have the treasure, the treasure of the gospel. The treasure is Christ. He brings hope, healing and salvation to every broken heart, every lost person, to every one who thirsts. Jesus quenched my thirst and satisfied my hunger over five years ago."

Nadia paused for a moment. Tears continued to stream down her face. She turned her gaze from the audience and looked up at the ceiling.

"Jesus. I will go to the ends of the earth for you. I surrender to your will tonight."

The auditorium remained quiet. No one moved or spoke a word. Nadia turned and looked back at the audience. Pastor Willoughby stood next to Jason. Jason had his arms raised in the air in worship as he quietly prayed with his eyes closed.

"There is a beautiful song of worship written by Jason."

Nadia turned and smiled at Jason.

"Jason is the most wonderful Christian friend that I will ever have. His song, "living sacrifice," defines what it means to me to follow Christ and be a missionary to the Muslim world. The chorus of the song declares:

> I want to be a living sacrifice.
> I'm bowing at your altar. I'm laying down my life.
> I surrender all my plans and dreams to you.
> I lay down all my Isaacs. I give them back to you.

"These words, when I first heard them, spoke profoundly to my heart. God said to me, Nadia I am going to make you light in the darkness and I will cause many people to find their hope and purpose in Jesus. I have not forgotten that promise God made to me. As I stand here before you, I ask for your prayers that I will be faithful to go to the ends of the earth for Jesus. That is my heart's desire."

Nadia concluded and walked back over to Jason. Pastor Willoughby's face beamed with joy as he began to clap. Suddenly, everyone in the auditorium rose to their feet and loudly applauded in response to Nadia's speech. There were shouts of praise as the momentum of the applause grew louder. Pastor Willoughby walked over to Nadia. Nadia broke away from Jason and threw her arms around Pastor Willoughby, embracing him. Jason stood to the side clapping loudly.

The special Christmas service had finally come to a close. Nadia and Jason stood at the front entrance of the Church chatting with everyone and shaking hands.

Filled with plenty emotion and joy, Nadia and Jason managed to break away from everyone long enough to say their goodbyes and return home.

Jason turned to lock the door behind him. Exhausted, Nadia hung up her gray coat and collapsed in the living room chair.

"Nadia," Jason said taking a deep breath, "You stay right there and relax. I have a surprise for you."

Nadia sat up anxiously in the chair, taken by surprise.

"A surprise!" Nadia exclaimed. "I'm exhausted from the first one." She said laughing.

Jason returned to the living room wearing a kitchen cooking apron.

"Today is your very special day, Miss Mustafa. I am going to cook for you a very special turkey dinner."

Nadia fell back into the chair with a stunned expression on her face. "Why Mr. Ridgeway, men do not cook for their wives where I come from."

Jason looked at Nadia grinning.

"In this house, they do."

Jason and Nadia broke into laughter together. Nadia settled down in the living room with her new Bible while Jason busily prepared their special Christmas dinner. The lights had been dimmed and there was some instrumental worship music playing softly on the stereo.

It had been an incredible worship service! As Nadia relaxed in her chair, she thought back to what had taken place today. She was still awestruck and amazed at the incredible story that Pastor Willoughby had shared. Nadia was humbled and mesmerized that God had called her to be a missionary to the Muslim world. Yet this had been her heart's desire. She had studied the story of Queen

Esther and was drawn to the amazing courage she demonstrated in protecting her people from harm.

In spite of Nadia's overwhelming desire to be a missionary, she still felt inadequate for the task. At that moment, Nadia opened up her Bible to find strength and grace for the task ahead. Her eyes fell upon 2 Corinthians Chapter 12 and verse 9. Paul had pleaded with God three times to remove an affliction from him. Nadia looked down to verse 9 for God's response to Paul's prayer.

"My grace is sufficient for you, for my power is made perfect in weakness."

Paul then declared:

"Therefore, I will boast all the more gladly of my weaknesses so that the power of Christ may rest upon me.

For the sake of Christ, then, I am content with weaknesses, insults, hardship, persecution and calamities. For when I am weak, than I am strong."

Nadia looked up from the Bible and rested her head back against the chair. She had found her answer. Regardless of her fears, weaknesses or inadequacies, God was saying, "Nadia, my grace is sufficient for you. I didn't call you because of your strength, wisdom or experience. I called you to embrace my will in spite of everything and trust me. My power and grace will give you everything you need."

Reflecting on the meaning of Scripture, Nadia released all of her fears and anxieties and began to take refuge in the grace of God.

It seemed like only a moment that Nadia had closed her eyes, when she began to smell a delicious turkey baking in the oven and heard Jason setting dishes on the dining room table.

"Are you hungry, Miss Mustafa?" Jason asked as he stood in front of her wearing an apron.

"Oh!" Nadia said, looking startled. She quickly sat up in the chair.

"It's okay," Jason said smiling, "You've been napping."

"I'm sorry." Nadia said, blushing with embarrassment.

"That's alright," Jason reassured her. "You needed the nap."

"Can I help?" Nadia asked, getting up from her chair.

"You don't have to. Dinner is served." Jason said, pointing toward the dining room.

Nadia looked and saw two candles slowly burning in the center of the table. The lights had been dimmed and there was beautiful, expensive china neatly placed on the table for the two of them. There was instrumental worship music softly playing in the background. Jason walked ahead of Nadia and pulled the chair out from the table.

"Thank you Mr. Ridgeway." Nadia said smiling as Jason gently pushed the chair back underneath the table. He then walked to the other side of the table and sat down across from Nadia.

"Everything looks delicious." Nadia said, her eyes sparkling with delight as she gazed at all of the food on the table. There was a small basted turkey, green beans, stuffing, cranberries and a salad. Jason said a quick blessing and then looked at Nadia.

"I have thought about our special little dinner together all day. So, don't be shy. Please eat to your heart's delight."

Nadia could see the joy in Jason's eyes. He looked satisfied and delighted to sit down to dinner with his best friend. The two candles flickered and burned brightly in the dimly-lit room. The atmosphere was tranquil and peaceful complimented by the soft worship music playing in the background. Nadia felt like a princess dining in the banquet hall of a great noble king.

Nadia wiped her mouth with her napkin and stared intently at Jason. Jason could see Nadia was deep in thought.

"Is something wrong?" Jason asked.

Nadia looked a little hesitant to respond. She slowly put down her fork and rested fully back in her chair.

"Jason. Can I ask you something?"

"Sure."

"Why are you so good to me?"

Nadia's question took Jason by surprise. He dobbed his mouth with his napkin and swallowed nervously. He thought for a moment.

"When you wrote me that letter asking me why I thought Jesus was appearing to you in your dreams. Something inside of me was so moved with compassion and I knew beyond any doubt that God had placed you in my life. I knew then that we were meant to be great friends. When I met you for the first time, I just wanted to pick you up in my arms and tell you how much Jesus loved you."

Nadia had a look of humility in her eyes. She had that feeling of belonging once again that she felt when Jesus reached down and touched her face in her dream.

"You make me feel so special, Jason. I don't know what to say."

Jason took a drink of water. Putting his glass down, he leaned forward closer to Nadia.

"I can't exactly explain it, Nadia, but I know God has blessed us with a very special friendship. That's why I want to be good to you."

Jason reached across the table and gently gripped Nadia's hand. Nadia looked down and softly gripped Jason's hand back. Jason then suddenly pulled his hand back, giving Nadia a more serious look.

"Nadia. Do you mind if I ask you a personal question?"

Nadia looked surprised and bit her lip.

"No. Not at all."

Jason remained quiet for a moment.

"Why don't you talk about your parents?"

Jason's question pierced through Nadia's heart. She felt convicted and taken off guard. Jason saw the uncomfortable expression on Nadia's face.

"I'm sorry." Jason said.

"They hurt you, didn't they, Nadia?"

Nadia nodded her head and slowly looked up at Jason.

"Can you forgive them?" Jason asked with a tone of pleading in his voice.

"My Father gave me an ultimatum. That's why I ran away. I would not deny Christ and return to Islam," Nadia admitted. Her voice filled was filled with despair.

Jason slowly reached over and took Nadia's hand once again.

"Please promise me that when you return back home, that you will go to them."

A single tear trickled down Nadia's cheek. She nervously wiped it away with her napkin.

"They don't understand God's love and I know that He will give me the grace to explain that."

Nadia's face broke into a smile. She looked relieved.

"I think about them all of the time. I miss Zak and my mother and father," Nadia said stuttering as she leaned back in her chair chuckling.

"Look at me Jason. God has called me to be a missionary to Muslims and here I am struggling to talk to my parents."

Jason grinned and nodded his head.

"He's called you," Jason said confidently, "He knows how much you miss your parents and your brother. Go to them, Nadia and don't be afraid. Look at it this way. This is your first step in being a missionary.

Nadia broke into laughter and wiped her mouth with her napkin.

"As always, you are right. What would I do without you?"

Nadia suddenly hesitated, realizing what she had just said.

"Oh. I'm sorry Jason."

Jason cracked a smile and leaned back in his chair chuckling.

"That's my Nadia."

Chapter Twenty One
Saying Goodbye

    Ever since the day Jason picked up a guitar and learned how to play, it had been his passion to write songs telling the world about Christ. Now, a lot older and much wiser, in his final days, Jason's desire was to put God on display through his worship songs. Reading through the journal Nadia had given him for Christmas, Jason's eyes fell upon the extraordinary poem that she had written while gazing at the wooden cross in the Church courtyard. Jason was drawn to the beautiful words that described Nadia's vision of Jesus. He also was intrigued by the poem that she wrote a few days later that described the "beauty" of Christ's death on the cross and how beyond the outward horror of the crucifixion, what took place was "beautiful" in the salvation of sinners.

    It was the last day of 2009, Thursday, December 31. Jason was hard at work downstairs in the studio composing music to Nadia's poems, "beyond the veil" and "how beautiful." Nadia was upstairs outstretched on the couch reading her Bible. The sun beaming through the living room window illuminated the page Nadia was reading. She paused to watch a squirrel climbing down from a tree limb in search for food. Anxious to see how it progressed, Nadia closed her Bible and sat up on the couch intrigued by the squirrel's hunt for food. The squirrel came upon a piece of bread and clenched it between its tiny hands. Nadia laughed, watching the squirrel dart back up the tree.

    "Nadia, Nadia!" Jason yelled from the basement. "Come down. I've got a surprise for you."

    "Coming." Nadia replied. She sat her Bible down and hurried down the basement stairs.

    As she turned the corner, she saw Jason standing in front of the microphone holding his acoustic guitar.

"I absolutely loved your poem "beyond the veil." Jason said his voice vibrant with excitement.

Nadia stood in front of him with her arms folded and blushing at his compliment.

"Would you like to hear it?" Jason asked.

"I can't wait," Nadia replied, anxiously looking at him in the eyes.

Nadia stood and watched intently as Jason poured out his soul in worship. She was captivated by the haunting melody of beyond the veil and was transported into the presence of God. Nadia remembered back to the day she wrote the poem while gazing at the wooden cross in the courtyard. The way Jason structured and played the chorus penetrated her heart.

You opened up the way when your hands and feet were nailed
Now I can see your face beyond the veil
I want to touch your face with these hands that are frail
I long to see your face beyond the veil.

Nadia could once again see the beauty and glory of Christ just like that day. She reflected on when she removed her hijab that day and for the first time could see by the eye of faith, the true glory and beauty of Christ.

"That is incredible!" Nadia said, her face glowing with excitement as she clapped he hands in approval.

Jason stopped playing.

"I hope you don't mind that I added a second verse."

Nadia nodded her head in approval.

"Of course not. Please sing it."

Jason began playing his acoustic guitar once again.

Your beauty is indescribable
Your wisdom is unfathomable

Your love is undeniable
You're so trustworthy and reliable
You're so desirable to me
You're so desirable to me

The words and music flowed through Nadia's mind and heart. It was soothing and beautiful and quickly turned her heart toward worship. For a few moments, they were lost in awe and worship together.

Suddenly, their intimate time of worship was rudely interrupted by the phone ringing.

"I'll get that," Nadia said, running back up the stairs.

She hurried to the phone and picked it up. It was one of Jason's band member friends calling to see how he was doing.

"I was just in the studio with Jason," Nadia began.

"Nadia! Nadia! Help!"

It was Jason.

Something was terribly wrong. The scream of desperation from Jason pierced through Nadia's heart. She erupted in fear.

"I have to go!" Nadia yelled. She quickly slammed down the phone and raced back down the basement stairs.

Jason was leaning up against the wall with both of his hands grabbing his abdomen. His face was contorted from the excruciating pain.

"Jason! Jason!" Nadia screamed. She ran over to him and helped him sit down in a chair. Jason pointed to his cell phone. Nadia nervously picked it up. She tried to remain calm.

"Jennifer." Jason murmured, unable to speak because of the pain. Nadia scrolled down and found Jennifer's name and clicked on it.

After a few seconds there was a "hello." Nadia took a deep breath.

"Jennifer." Nadia said in a panicky voice.

"What's wrong?" Jennifer asked.

"Jason is sick." Nadia nervously answered.

"I'll be right there. I'm just a few blocks away finishing up with another patient."

There was a click and the conversation ended.

Nadia stuffed the cell phone in her pocket and reached down to help Jason stand up.

"Can you walk?"

Jason flinched in pain, struggling to stand up. He took a few steps with Nadia's help. Together, they slowly ascended the stairs, step by step and walked through the kitchen and into Jason's bedroom. Nadia helped him sit down on the edge of the bed and removed his shoes.

"Just lay back and try to relax." Nadia said.

Suddenly, there was a loud knock at the front door.

"I'll be right back. " Nadia said.

She looked back at Jason as she left the room and raced to answer the front door.

"Where is he?" Jennifer asked.

"In his room." Nadia answered, pointing around the corner.

With her stesiscope draped around her neck, Jennifer hurried into Jason's room and closed the door behind her.

Nadia sat down in the living room chair and bowed her head in tears. Panic and anxiety gripped Nadia as she began to pray intensely.

"Why? Why?" Nadia asked in anguish with her head bowed. Everything had been so tranquil and peaceful for the last few days. Yet Nadia knew that eventually this was going to happen and being strong for Jason was the most important thing she could do.

Nadia heard the bedroom door open and close. She stood up as Jennifer walked into the living room and sat down across from her. Jennifer had a troubled expression on her face. Nadia sensed that it was not good news.

"Here's where we're at." Jennifer said with a serious tone in her voice.

"The cancer has spread into Jason's liver."

The impact of Jennifer's assessment pierced through Nadia's heart. The reality of the words were numbing to her soul.

"Have you noticed the yellow discoloration in Jason's face and around his eyes?" Jennifer asked.

Nadia nervously shook her head.

"Nadia," Jennifer asked bluntly. "Are you going to be able to take care of Jason? If not, it's alright. I understand."

Nadia took a deep breath.

"Yes. Yes, I can. That's why I came."

Jennifer nodded her head.

"I'm going to show you where to put the pain patches on him. I will instruct you on putting the oxygen tubing in his nostrils and turning on and off the tank. Can you do this?"

Jennifer wanted to make sure that Nadia was mentally and emotionally capable of the task ahead of her.

"Yes, Jennifer. Yes I can." Nadia reassured her.

Jennifer leaned closer in the chair toward Nadia.

"Nadia," Jennifer began. She paused and stared intently into Nadia's eyes. "He doesn't have too much longer."

Nadia's lips began to tremble. Tears streamed down her face. Jennifer stood up and then leaned down putting her arm around Nadia.

"I will be here two three times this week to evaluate, bath and administer pain meds to Jason. I want you to call me anytime on my cell phone."

Nadia nodded her head and then stood up. Jennifer could see the pain and brokenness in Nadia's eyes.

"Call me," Jennifer instructed her. She smiled as she flung her stesiscope into her medical bag and quickly walked out the front door.

Nadia gazed up toward the ceiling and uttered a short prayer to God for strength. She then slowly walked to Jason's room and carefully opened the door, poking her head in.

Jason was sitting up in bed with his head leaning up against a pillow.

"Is it alright if I come in?" Nadia asked.

Jason turned his head and looked at Nadia. Nadia didn't know what to expect. Less than an hour ago, Jason was withering in excruciating pain. Now he looked more relaxed. He managed to smile seeing Nadia as she poked her head in the room.

"Sure. Come in," Jason answered.

Nadia walked in and shut the door behind her. In the corner of the room propped up in the corner was the oxygen tank. On the table beside Jason's bed was a box containing pain patches, a towel, a glass of cold water and a small plastic tub for sponge bathing.

As Nadia drew closer, she noticed the yellow jaundice coloring in Jason's face. Yet his face was no longer contorted with pain. He had a contented and accepting look in his eyes.

"How do you feel Jason?" Nadia cautiously asked. She felt apprehensive and at a loss for words, afraid of saying the wrong thing.

"Well," Jason grinned, leaning his head back against the pillow. "I guess this means, no more snow angels or snow ball fights or long shopping trips to the mall."

Nadia's face broke into a smile. She nodded her head and chuckled a bit.

"Well, Jason. If I remember well," Nadia said with a grin, sitting down at the foot of Jason's bed. "I won all of the snowball fights anyway."

Jason bit his lip and thought carefully about what Nadia said. He rolled his eyes up in his head.

"If you say so, Miss Mustafa."

Nadia laughed. Their eyes met. They stared at each other intently as the reality of the moment weighed heavily on their hearts. Tears began to well up in Nadia's eyes. She leaned over closer to Jason and threw her arms around him sobbing. For a brief moment they held each other tightly amidst their tears.

Nadia finally lifted her head off of Jason's shoulder. She brushed away the tears from her eyes and began to softly stroke Jason's blonde hair. Jason leaned back against his pillow wiping the tears away from his eyes.

"Nadia. I want to tell you something."

Nadia composed herself and gave Jason her full attention. Jason looked intently at Nadia.

"There is no one else in the world that I would want to spend my final days with but you."

Jason took his right hand and began to gently stroke Nadia's curly brown hair. The tears once again began to well up in Nadia's eyes.

"I've made up my mind, Nadia, that we will not be depressed together. This will not be a time for mourning or morbidness, Nadia, but a time of celebration and worship."

Nadia was taken back by the force of Jason's words. She had never heard him talk as seriously as he was at this time.

"Worship and celebration?" Nadia said with a puzzled look on her face.

Jason slowly nodded his head.

"I want you to bring up my CD player and the songs I just wrote. The atmosphere in this room is always going to be filled with the presence of God."

Nadia could see the determination and acceptance written all over Jason's face. He had come to the place of full surrender and acceptance of God's will.

"The Bible says, "to live is Christ and to die is gain," Jason said as he stared up at the ceiling. "Therefore," Jason continued, "We have a great future to look forward to. You said it well in the poem that you gave me. "God has brought us back together and this time it's forever, no more separation. No more."

Nadia smiled amidst her tears and nodded her head in agreement.

"One day, you will be with me in heaven, where there will be no more sorrow, sickness or pain and then we will be together forever," Jason said with face beaming with joy and expectation.

Nadia broke away from staring at Jason and gazed out the bedroom window.

"When I was a Muslim, I never had the certainty of Paradise. I always lived with the fear that on Judgment Day, my good deeds would never outweigh my bad deeds. And even if they did, Allah could still change His mind."

Nadia turned from gazing out the window and looked back into Jason's eyes.

"You're right! We will be together forever, because Jesus will never change His mind. He is a faithful savior."

Jason and Nadia grasped each others hands tightly. Their faces were aglow with joy as they talked together about the glory of heaven.

"Do you know what I am hungry for?" Jason said, changing the subject. Nadia let go of Jason's hand and gave him a perplexed look.

"What?"

Jason leaned his head back against the pillow.

"Your delicious sweet rice cakes."

"Sweet rice cakes?"

"Yes, my favorite," Jason said.

Nadia rose up from the foot of the bed.

"Looks like its going to be a lot of work being your nurse," Nadia said chuckling as she walked out of the room.

As Nadia closed the door behind her, Jason lay back against his pillow and began to cry.

"Thank you God for Nadia. Thank you God for giving me your peace in accepting your will."

As Jason finished his prayer, he was filled with a joy and a peace that he had not felt in a long time.

The sweet smell of fresh sweet rice cakes began to fill Jason's nostrils. He had once again regained his appetite. The pain medication patches Jason was now wearing had done their job.

The door creaked open and Nadia walked in wearing a huge smile on her face.

"Dinner is served, Mr. Ridgeway."

Nadia was holding a plate of three delicious sweet rice cakes. The cake in the center had a single birthday candle burning on it.

"Wow!" Jason exclaimed, surprised and delighted.

Nadia carefully walked over to the bed and handed the plate to Jason. Jason looked like a little boy standing all alone in the finest candy shop in the world. Nadia sat down at the foot of the bed and watched with delight. She was happy and relieved that Jason was out of pain for the moment and hungry again.

"M-mm-m," Jason groaned as he bit into a sweet rice cake.

"I'll never forget," Jason said with his mouth half-full, "The first time I ever ate these."

Jason leaned his head back on the pillow enjoying the last bite of the first cake.

"And I'll never forget," Nadia said, reaching for a napkin out of her pocket, "when you ate these for the first time, how you got crumbs all over your mouth."

Nadia laughed as she gently dobbed around Jason's mouth with the napkin. Jason began to laugh hysterically and almost dropped the plate of cakes. Nadia laughed, reaching over to quickly steady the plate. Jason finally put the plate down and rested his head back up against his pillow. He became strangely quiet and then stared back intently into Nadia's eyes.

"Nadia" Jason said nervously stuttering. His eyes became misty.

"You're incredible and you're going to make an incredible missionary."

Nadia remained completely still with a look of humility and gratitude on her face.

"You've got a sweet and gentle spirit and yet you're a true survivor. You've got a holy boldness when you need it. I know this to be true. Look what you survived! You ran through a dark and dangerous woods all night. You're a survivor Nadia and I know how you will treat the people that you will minister to. You will treat them with love and respect and they will listen to you."

Nadia remained quiet. She was speechless. Then she looked up at Jason. Her eyes beamed with gratitude.

"Jason. I am who I am because of God's great love and mercy and yet I also am who I am because of you. You have been such a godly teacher to me. You were my sponsor, my example. You helped me and my family financially and sacrificed your hard-earned money for me so that I would have a chance to live. I will never forget your love and sacrifice and kindness for the rest of my life."

Nadia reached down and gently clasped Jason's hand into hers. Jason reached up and softly wiped away the tears that were rolling down her cheeks.

"I love you Jason," Nadia whispered out loud. She dropped her head down against Jason's chest and began to let go of all of the hurt and pain. Jason didn't say a word, but gently stroked her soft brown hair with his right hand.

For the rest of the week, Nadia demonstrated true courage and grace under pressure as she excelled in taking care of Jason. She learned how to give Jason oxygen as his breathing became more difficult. She stayed up late at night right by his bedside reading the Bible to him and playing worship music. Jennifer would come by to bathe him and check his vitals.

As the next week began, Jason required a higher dosage of pain medication. His appetite was steadily deteriorating along with his physical body. Jason began to rapidly lose weight and sleep for longer periods of time. Nadia realized that his time to leave was drawing nearer.

The sun peeked through the blinds on Saturday morning, January 10, 2010. The rays of sunlight streamed through the blinds and flashed across Nadia's face. Startled, she opened up her eyes and looked down at Jason. He had been asleep all night. His breathing was beginning to sound labored and congested.

Nadia had been awake most of the night camped out by Jason's bedside. She got up and rubbed her eyes. She was exhausted and hungry and feeling despaired as Jason continued to rapidly deteriorate.

Suddenly, the phone rang. Nadia quickly answered it. It was Jennifer. She was calling to inform her that Kathy would be by very soon to give her a much needed break. Nadia thanked Jennifer and hung up the phone. She looked back down at Jason. He lay completely still, looking weary and tired and struggling to live.

Nadia knew she needed a break. Today, she was taking the bus and going to spend some time alone at Jason's Church.

As soon as Kathy arrived, Nadia updated her on Jason's condition and then instructed her to call her on the cell phone if there was any change. Kathy agreed and Nadia threw on her coat and walked out into the frigid cold winter morning.

It was a very quiet bus ride to Spirit and Word Outreach Church. There were only two other riders beside Nadia on the bus. The bus pulled up to the front entrance of the Church and Nadia stepped off, bundling up in the freezing weather. She quickly hurried through the front entrance and walked into the sanctuary.

Nadia looked all round the vast sanctuary. She gazed at the blue-colored empty pews. The lights were dimmed and there was an eerie, empty quiet inside the sanctuary. Nadia gazed up at the vaulted ceiling above her and then down toward the stage where the pastor's pulpit was located. It was so vast, so empty and so quiet and peaceful. Nadia was immediately captivated by the quiet solitude that engulfed her whole being. This was the break that she had been so desperately needing.

Nadia slowly walked down the carpeted aisle and sat down in one of the pews a long distance from the stage. She removed her coat and laid her Bible down beside her and sunk completely into the pew with her whole aching body. Nadia leaned her head back, closed her eyes and took a long, deep breath. The quietness of the sanctuary was like a soothing, warm bath to her aching body and soul. Nadia sat completely still and kept her eyes closed. Deep down inside, she longed for home and to be back at her sacred prayer spot in the woods.

"Dear God, please take me home," Nadia pleaded in a soft whisper.

Immediately, her mind drifted back home to the trail in the woods. She could smell the pleasant aroma of the flowers along the trail and see the groves of trees just ahead. Nadia found her sacred spot and carefully laid down her prayer rug. Just a few feet away was the creek. She could hear the gentle sound of the flowing water splashing over the rocks. She looked up and saw the bright sun peeking through the tree limbs above her head. She was back home in the most special place in the world. She had her Bible and her journal with her. The sweet and relaxing sound of chirping birds quietly interrupted her prayer time. Nadia raised her hands in worship. She looked up at the deep blue sky and-."

Suddenly, her dream was jolted by a mysterious hand tugging at her shoulder. Nadia jumped up, her whole body jerking.

"I'm sorry."

Nadia opened up her eyes. Pastor Willoughby stood next to her.

"Pastor Willoughby!" Nadia said, excited and startled back into reality.

Pastor Willoughby smiled and sat down beside her in the pew.

"Do you mind?" Pastor Willoughby asked.

"No. Not at all."

"How are you?" Pastor Willoughby asked.

Nadia could see the care and concern in Pastor Willoughby's eyes. He always had a gentle way of approaching people and Nadia felt very comfortable around him.

Nadia bowed her head and was unable to restrain herself. She felt broken and crushed inside and the despair of what was happening had finally caught up with her.

"I'm sorry Pastor Willoughby. I'm afraid. I'm really afraid. I'm trying to be strong for Jason."

Pastor Willoughby put his arm around Nadia. Nadia leaned up against his chest as he held her tightly trying to bring comfort and reassurance to her.

"Don't apologize Nadia. We're all hurting. We all love Jason and it's very difficult to let go."

Nadia nodded her head and tried to compose herself.

"I feel so guilty for breaking down like this. I know Jason is going home. I rejoice with him Pastor that he's going to see Jesus face to face, but I love him."

Nadia stared intently into Pastor Willoughby's eyes. There was a moment of silence.

"He's my dearest friend, but I love him and I don't want to let him go!" Nadia said with a protesting tone in her voice.

Once again, Pastor Willoughby held Nadia tightly.

"I know it's hard, but you have to let him go, Nadia."

The words sounded harsh to Nadia's ears, but she realized Pastor Willoughby was trying to help her.

"I know. I know," Nadia confessed.

Pastor Willoughby handed Nadia a Kleenex.

"Jason is a wonderful, wonderful person Nadia and I can understand why it's hard to let him go. But Jason doesn't want you to grieve, Nadia. He wants you to rejoice with him in his soon homecoming."

Nadia began to calm down. She was trying to put the whole situation into perspective.

"I will miss him too, Nadia." Pastor Willoughby confessed.

"Why don't we pray-."

The tranquil atmosphere was suddenly, rudely interrupted by the ring of a cell phone. Nadia grabbed the cell phone out of her pocket. She got a horrified look on her face.

"It's Kathy! We need to go quickly!"

Pastor Willoughby grabbed his Bible and Nadia hurriedly followed him out the front door. They rushed into the car and sped off down the street, exiting onto 270-highway.

Nadia struggled to keep her composure. Thoughts of Jason dying before she arrived by his side, raced through her mind. She battled the vice-like thoughts of guilt and fear in her mind all the way to Jason's house. Yet Nadia remembered Jason's final wish to have his homecoming to be a time of celebration instead of despair and grief.

As the car pulled into the driveway, Nadia took a deep breath and stared over at Pastor Willoughby. His head was leaning back up against the seat. While Pastor Willoughby always looked calm and in control, at this moment, his face was filled with a look of sorrow.

Quickly exiting the car, Pastor Willoughby and Nadia rushed through the front door and quickly walked down the hallway and into Jason's bedroom.

The sound of labored and congested breathing gripped Nadia as she entered Jason's bedroom. Jennifer was busy evaluating Jason and listening to his heart. She stood up and stared back at Nadia and Pastor Willoughby. Her face told the whole story.

Nadia slowly approached Jason's bed while Pastor Willoughby stood next to the window holding his Bible. The soft and beautiful music of Jason's final composition, "Beyond the veil," was quietly playing in the background.

Nadia knelt down next to Jason's bed and gently took his hand. Jason responded by tightly clasping his hand into hers. Nadia fought hard to hold back the tears.

"I am here Jason," Nadia softly whispered. She thought she saw Jason open his eyes. She leaned closer, holding his hand a little tighter.

"I am with you, Jason. Pastor Willoughby is here, too."

Jason continued to struggle to breathe. Jennifer took her place next to Pastor Willoughby. Nadia closed her eyes and began to quietly pray.

Nadia finished praying and slowly opened her eyes. Suddenly, Jason began to cough. His chest rose up and then quickly fell. The congested breathing stopped. Nadia looked on with tears streaming down her face. With her hand trembling, she reached over and stroked Jason's hair.

Pastor Willoughby put his Bible down on the table. Nadia stood up. The chorus to "beyond the veil" had just begun to play. Nadia raised her hands into the air in worship with tears of sorrow and joy running down her face. Pastor Willoughby raised his hands in worship. Jennifer stood by emotionally moved by what was happening. Together, Pastor Willoughby and Nadia began to sing the chorus together in an act of worship.

You opened up the way when your hands and feet were nailed.

Now I can see your face beyond the veil

I want to touch your face with these hands that are frail

I want to see your face beyond the veil.

As Nadia and Pastor Willoughby both worshiped together, Jason was ushered into eternity to see Jesus face to face.

The song ended and the room became quiet once again, amidst the sobbing of friends with broken hearts. Pastor Willoughby began to pray out loud. Nadia opened her eyes and gazed down at Jason. He lay completely still and at peace.

Nadia wiped the tears away from her eyes and gently bent down over Jason and kissed him tenderly on his lips, saying good-bye.

"Peace be upon you Jason," Nadia whispered.

Chapter Twenty Two
The Reconciliation

Today was Jason's funeral. Nadia felt alone. It was her last day to spend at Jason's home. Pastor Willoughby would be picking her up in a few minutes. Then shortly after the funeral, Nadia would be flying back to Dhaka.

It all seemed so final today. There was a sadness, an emptiness and a brokenness that Nadia was feeling. Although it was not despair or depression, because she knew Jason was with Jesus, yet a loneliness surrounded Nadia like a dark cloud. She had just said good bye to her best friend and it hurt. It really hurt deep down inside.

Nadia laid the luggage by the front door. She had one more thing to do. Nadia walked down the stairs into Jason's studio. Jason's guitars were all standing upright on their stands. They would not be playing anymore beautiful music. They were ominously silent today. Nadia stared at the pictures on the wall. There was a very intimate picture of Jason standing next to his Mother. They were both smiling. It was a happy time. Down at the end of the wall, Nadia gazed at a picture of Jason standing next to her on the trip to Bangladesh five years ago. A tear began to trickle down Nadia's face. That had been a very happy time in her life.

When she could take no more Nadia ran back upstairs. She froze in the hallway. She didn't know if she could do it. Finally after mustering up the courage, Nadia slowly opened the door to Jason's bedroom. His bed was neatly made. All of the medical equipment was gone. The sun was beaming through the window. The room was quiet. Nadia stood still in the middle of the bedroom. She looked down at the bed. It was empty. It seemed like only yesterday when she had made a plate of sweet rice cakes for Jason and then had to wipe off the crumbs from around his mouth.

It was all she could take. Suddenly, she heard the sound of a car horn honking. It was Pastor Willoughby. Nadia ran out of the room and grabbed her luggage and headed out the front door.

The Church auditorium was filled to near capacity. It was a closed casket. Jason requested that everyone remember him when he was healthy. Nadia was relieved. She didn't know if she could look at him the way he was. As she mingled through the crowd, greeting everyone, her eye caught the sight of a young man in a wheelchair. He had a sad and gloomy expression on his face. It was Robbie.

Nadia walked over and knelt down next to Robbie. Robbie kept staring ahead. He didn't want to speak today. Nadia touched his hand and drew closer to him.

"Robbie. I'm really sad, too. I feel so broken inside."

Tears began to flow down Robbie's face. His face began to contort with anger and sadness.

"I lost my best friend, too, Robbie." Nadia gently said with compassion and understanding in her voice.

Robbie released his hand from Nadia's hand and wiped his face.

"He was like a brother to me," Robbie said, his voice cracking with emotion. "He was so patient and so kind to me. He taught me how to play guitar."

"Yes."

Robbie made eye contact with Nadia. His eyes were red and swollen from crying.

"I loved him."

Nadia reached closer and hugged Robbie tightly in his wheelchair. Today, they both needed each other as they let go of the pain and anguish that was tormenting them both deep down inside.

Nadia took a seat in the pew next to Robbie. The funeral began. Pastor Willoughby stood behind the pulpit gazing out into the vast Church auditorium.

"Today, we say good bye to a wonderful friend, a wonderful musician and a Godly Christian man. Today, Jason is singing the most beautiful worship songs face to face to his Savior, Jesus Christ. The Bible says, "absent from the body, present with the Lord." Our brother is with Jesus and all the saints and all the angels. One day, all of us will join Jason forever. Then, we will never be separated again."

Pastor Willoughby gazed down and caught Nadia's attention. Nadia's eyes connected with his. For a moment, Nadia felt the comfort and the promise of what Pastor Willoughby was preaching.

It was beautiful tribute to Jason and a time of worship to his Lord and Savior Jesus Christ. When the service was over, Nadia caught up with Jason's band members and gave them the final songs he had composed. The band was going to add some instrumentation to the tracks and have a fresh recording honoring Jason's music in the spring.

Shortly after 11:00 am, Pastor Willoughby drove Nadia to the airport and stood with her in the terminal.

"Nadia. Will you promise to stay in contact and come and visit us soon again?" Pastor Willoughby asked with a look of sadness in his eyes.

Nadia tried to fight back the tears.

"I can never thank you enough for what you did for Jason and me. I will never forget your kindness."

Nadia rushed into Pastor Willoughby's arms, hugging him tightly.

"Of course I will keep in touch. You are my family. I need your prayers, Pastor, because soon I will be on the mission field."

Pastor Willoughby smiled.

"You have them Nadia."

Nadia quickly embraced pastor Willoughby once again and headed toward the gate. She looked back and waved with sadness in her eyes and then started walking. Nadia was determined to fulfill Jason's last request.

After a short delay the 757 was airborne. Nadia relaxed back in her seat. In a few minutes the plane reached its cruising altitude and the flight attendants began serving beverages.

Nadia took a deep breath and picked up her Bible. A white piece of paper fell out from the pages and onto her lap. It was a letter addressed to her that had been tucked between the pages of her Bible. Nadia anxiously opened the letter and began to read it.

Dear Nadia:

I'm sorry if I never told you this while I was with you. I didn't know how you would take it, so I kept it to myself. When I first met you, I wished I could have been your Father. When I met you for the second time, I wanted to be your husband. You have grown up to be a beautiful woman. I wanted you to know this. I will miss you so much. I love you.

Jason

Nadia leaned back in her seat overwhelmed with joy and sadness at the beautiful last words from Jason. She held the letter against her chest and wept. Nadia closed her eyes and imagined standing at the altar with Jason. The images were too much for her to bear. It was much too early and much too painful to think about what could have been.

"Your will be done, Lord. I surrender to your will, "Nadia whispered out loud. Exhausted, Nadia carefully placed the letter back into her Bible and leaned back, drifting off to sleep.

Nadia kept quiet and to herself for the rest of the flight, thinking about how she was going to approach her parents after all of this time. What would she say? How would they react? What if they didn't want to see her? The questions plagued her mind until she finally landed in Dhaka the next day.

Weary and exhausted, Nadia made her way through the terminal until she spotted Pastor Ali and Leah. They were a delight to her eyes. Nadia ran to them in tears and embraced them together.

"Jason is dead," Nadia said while sobbing in Leah's arms.

"I'm so sorry sister," Leah answered back while hugging her tightly.

"I'm so glad to see you sister!" Leah exclaimed. Her beautiful green eyes sparkled with happiness as she looked into Nadia's eyes.

Pastor Ali came over and embraced Nadia.

"You're finally home, warrior princess!"

Nadia broke out into a smile and laughed.

"I'm so glad to finally be home!"

While Nadia was physically and mentally exhausted from the plane flight, she still insisted that she must see her parents before the end of the day. Pastor Ali and Leah agreed to let Nadia off at the entrance to the village project. They would spend the night in Dhaka and return in the morning to pick her back up. After a time of prayer, Leah hugged Nadia and she exited off the bus.

As the bus sped away, Nadia stood silently at the entrance of the village. The dirt road, the sign, the trees, the creek bridge, everything still looked the same after five years. Nadia reached deep down inside for courage and began to walk the long mile to her old hut. Her heart began to beat faster. Perspiration began to slowly drip down her face. She prayed as she walked, calling upon God for strength and grace. Then she remembered the night Jason had encouraged her to reconcile with her parents.

"If only you were with me, Jason." Nadia thought to herself.

Nadia walked across the wooden bridge and then ascended up the hill. She saw children having fun in the playground. She wiped the sweat from off her face . The sun was shining brightly today.

As she walked past the playground, a few children stopped playing and stared at her. They hadn't recognized her. She walked past some twisted, tall trees and stopped at the familiar picnic table. The moment of truth had arrived.

There it was! The hut was still there. It looked strangely quiet and unoccupied. Nadia felt a lump in her throat. She walked faster and came to a halt at the front door. Where was everyone? Nadia nervously turned the knob on the front door. It was locked. She began to panic. She knocked at the door.

"Father! Mother! Are you there? It's me -."

Suddenly, Nadia felt a hand touching her shoulder. She spun around and came face to face with Rochelle.

"Nadia. Is that you?" Rochelle asked with a shocked and stunned expression on her face.

"Rochelle!" Nadia cried out. She was almost speechless. She couldn't believe her eyes.

They embraced.

It was really Rochelle. She was still taller than Nadia. She was still slim with beautiful blonde hair and cut-off brown shorts.

"I don't believe it! " Nadia screamed.

"You're alive! You're alive!" Rochelle screamed back in tears.

"Where are my parents? Where are they?" Nadia insisted, her voice filled with fear.

Rochelle composed herself and smiled.

"They live in Dhaka now, Nadia. Your Father got a carpentry job and is making good money. They no longer needed the program, so they moved to Dhaka last year and got an apartment."

Nadia's face beamed with joy.

"A job. An apartment. That's great!"

"What happened to you?" Rochelle fired back, anxious to know her story.

"It's a long, long story. I promise to tell you all about it."

"I can't wait. You can tell me all about while I drive you into Dhaka to see your parents."

"Thank you. Thank you. "Nadia said.

Rochelle and Nadia had a lot to catch up on. They climbed into the gray suv and drove out of the village. Rochelle talked and drove, while Nadia filled her in on every detail of her life for the past five years.

The suv drove up a steep hill in the Dhaka district and pulled over to the side. Nadia looked up at a row of crowded, high rise apartment buildings. Rochelle gave her instructions and Nadia left the SUV in search of her parent's apartment.

Nadia walked up two flights of stairs and arrived in a hallway with tow doors a few feet apart from each other. She slowly walked up to the door with number three written above the peephole. This was it. Nadia nervously knocked on the door. Her heart was racing and her hands were shaking. Her whole body began to tremble. She knocked once again. Then she heard footsteps and the door slowly opened.

Standing in the doorway was Fatima. Her wavy black hair was peppered with a few strands of gray. She wore a few more wrinkles on her face.

"May I help you?" Fatima asked.

Nadia froze. Her lips began to tremble. She tried to speak and couldn't. Fatima stood still and then very slowly, the light came on. Her face turned white with shock. She shrieked and grabbed her face with her hands.

"Nadia!"

Nadia's whole body was shaking. Tears began to flood her eyes. "Mother!"

The door opened a little more. Fatima turned to look behind her. The door was now fully open.

"Rashid!! Rashid!" Fatima screamed. "Nadia's here!"

Rashid came flying around the corner of the room and stood behind Fatima. He was wearing a soiled white t-shirt, cut-off shorts and sandals. He stood staring in disbelief and shock.

"Father." Nadia said. She could barely speak amidst the emotion and tears.

"You're alive! You're alive!" Rashid shouted.

Fatima could hold back no longer. She reached up and hugged Nadia as tight as she had ever done before. Rashid burst into tears. He reached over and threw his arms around Nadia, lifting her off the ground in celebration that she had returned to them. The pain and the heartache was slowly beginning to melt away. The years of separation seemed so insignificant at this moment. Nadia felt accepted and loved by her parents for the first time. She sobbed loudly and couldn't stop hugging her parents or thinking about how glad she was for taking Jason's advice.

"Sit down, Nadia. Sit down!" Fatima insisted.

Nadia collapsed from the excitement into a cushioned chair. She gazed around their cozy little apartment. There were two more cushioned chairs, a small television and a kitchen. The apartment had a slick and shiny-looking hardwood floor with a polished look.

There were family pictures on the wall. Nadia's eyes stopped. Above the television was a picture of flowers she had drawn years before. She got up from her chair and drew closer to the picture. Below the picture was one of her poems. Nadia spun around and looked excitedly at her parents.

"My poems! My pictures!" Nadia exclaimed in disbelief. "But I thought that you hated me."

Rashid slowly rose up from his chair. His face frowned with guilt and shame.

"Nadia. We were wrong."

Nadia was stunned by her father's words. She gave him a perplexed look.

"Wrong?"

"Yes," Rashid admitted, drawing closer to Nadia. "A year ago, the Dhaka Police came to our apartment. They informed us that they had captured the men who had abducted you. We felt so terrible and so foolish!" Rashid began to break down. Nadia walked over and put her arm around Rashid's shoulder.

"We were wrong to not believe you."

Fatima rose up from her chair and stood behind Rashid.

"But, we didn't know where you were, Nadia. We prayed every day that you would come back to us. Now you're here!"

Nadia embraced Fatima as she began to loudly weep again. All of the pain and the anger began to slowly melt away. The healing had begun.

After a few moments, Nadia excused herself and ran back down to Rochelle. She told her what had happened and Rochelle rejoiced. She agreed to return and pick up Nadia tomorrow afternoon.

Nadia spent the rest of the evening rejoicing and explaining the last five years of her life to her parents. When Zak arrived home from school, Nadia reconciled with him. Jason had been right. God had incredibly blessed Nadia's reconciliation with her parents. Her prayers had been answered and now there was just one more thing left for her to do.

Chapter Twenty Three
Letting go

.

Nadia stood outside the door to her parent's apartment to say good bye. It had been an emotional but happy reconciliation. All night, Nadia explained the last five years of her life. There were tears and hugs and apologies and most importantly, a real respect and a rejuvenation of love once again. Rashid, Fatima and Zak did not share in the joy of Nadia's conversion to Christ. However, this time, they agreed to respect her decision and were happy that she had found real peace in her life.

Nadia promised to visit again real soon and started down the flight of steps to the ground floor. It was late in the afternoon and Rochelle was waiting outside in her suv.

"How did it go?" Rochelle anxiously asked as Nadia jumped in the passenger side.

She took a relaxing, deep breath and looked at Rochelle. Her eyes beamed with joy.

"Lots of hugs, kisses and apologies." Nadia began to tear up.

"Jason was right, Rochelle. I was able to forgive and so did my parents."

Rochelle reached over and hugged Nadia.

"I was praying for you." Rochelle said, smiling.

The suv turned the corner and headed out of Dhaka. Rochelle had agreed to take Nadia back to the old village for one last time. Then she would meet Pastor Ali and Leah right after sunset at the front entrance to the village.

It was 7:15 pm when Rochelle pulled up to the main entrance of the village.

"You must keep in touch girl!" Rochelle insisted.

"I will." Nadia agreed, hugging Rochelle. She stepped out of the suv Rochelle waved to Nadia and then drove off back down the highway.

Nadia stood at the entrance for a brief moment. She stared up toward the sign. Her mind was overwhelmed with the memories of living here since she was a young girl. The struggles, the trials, the difficult poverty-stricken days, until one day, her life dramatically changed.

Nadia slowly walked down the gravel road and crossed over the wooden bridge. A soft breeze was whisking through the tree limbs. The blazing, orange sun was beginning to dip below the horizon. Nadia walked through the playground and past her old hut. She paused for a moment at the picnic bench remembering all of the conversations about religion that she had with Jeremy. She gently touched the picnic table with her hand and grinned.

Memories.

Today was a special day filled with memories.

Nadia walked on. Her feet touched the trail that led to her secret prayer grove. "I made it. At last I made it." Nadia murmured to herself, breathing a sigh of relief. When Jason was at the point of death, she had longed to be back here at the prayer grove. Now at last she was here.

Nadia followed the winding trail into a thick grove of trees. The breeze whistled through the tree limbs and the limbs began to dance to its music. Nadia looked around with delight. Everything looked the same. The trail, the tree limbs, the flowers and the sound of running water quietly splashing over the rocks in the creek. It was just as she had remembered it. Quiet and serene and tranquil. The perfect place to be alone and commune with God surrounded by the beauty of His creation.

Nadia spotted a tall tree and its bulging trunk. The tree was only fifteen feet from the bank of the creek. This would be the perfect place for what she wanted to do. Nadia took a deep breath and filled her lungs with the sacred air of her secret place. She sat down up against the tree trunk and surrendered to the tranquil spell of the prayer grove. It felt like heaven. Nadia closed her eyes and stilled her mind. In the distance the soothing sound of water gently gushing over the rocks was mesmerizing and relaxing to Nadia's mind.

"I made it!" Nadia whispered out loud. "Thank you God, I finally made it."

After a few meditating moments had passed, Nadia picked up her Bible. She gazed down at the familiar inscription Jason had engraved on it.

> *Nadia, I have loved you with an everlasting love.*
> *Jeremiah 31:3*

Nadia remembered back to Jason's visit. This was the same inscription he had put on the journal he had given her. She treasured the Bible Jason had given her and treasured the meaning of the passage from Jeremiah. It was because of Jason that she had first discovered the unconditional love of God. Today she wanted to pay a special tribute to her dear friend.

Nadia picked up her pen. The words of a tribute flowed through her mind and soul. Her hand began to shake. Tears began to well up in her eyes as she began the painful process of letting go.

> *You mean so much to me*
> *And it's because of you that I'm free*
> *You changed my life*
> *When you told me about God's love*
> *Now there's no more strife*
> *Since I've been born from above*

The pen dropped from Nadia's hand. She felt an empty and painful void deep down inside. Yet, Jason had told her about God's love through Jesus. Now she wanted to say thank you once again in the most personal and meaningful way. She once again picked up the pen to write.

> *There's a time and a season for everything*

You were the greatest time of my life.
But now O Lord. I give you my life as an offering
Please come and take my life
I'm letting go. I'm so broken inside
But I know there's no turning back
I must go

Nadia once again dropped the pen. She knew she had to let go and follow Christ. She knew He had called her to the mission field. But it was painful, all too painful. Nadia needed God's strength to let Jason go and continue following Christ. Once again she picked up her pen.

I'm saying goodbye and it's just for a little while
Very soon one day I'm going to see your smile
You helped me to see beyond my veil
Now I can touch the face of God with these hands that are frail

I'm letting go. I'm so broken inside
But I know. There's no turning back I must go

Nadia laid her Bible aside and put the pen down. The written tribute was finished. Now there was just one more thing left to do.

Nadia recalled how every detail of the dream God had given her had been fulfilled by His sovereign purpose, except one. The public execution of the woman. She quietly pondered the last part of the dream and then relaxed her mind.

Nadia slowly stood up from the ground of the secret prayer place where it had all began over five years ago on a special morning after reading Jason's letter.

Nadia gazed up into the sky in awe of the beautiful streaks of purple and orange that seemed to dance together over the horizon.

Sunset was approaching. Nadia closed her eyes. Tears streamed down her face. The breeze quieted down and it became strangely still all around her.

Nadia carefully lifted her hands behind her neck. She began to unfasten the silver necklace that Jason had given her. As she tried to pry open the latch, suddenly the necklace broke and fell into her hands. She slowly dropped her hands in front of her and opened them up. A streak of sunlight beautifully reflected off of the silver necklace that lay crumpled in her hands.

Nadia walked toward the stream. Reaching the edge of the bank, she reverently knelt down on the moist and muddy ground. Her hands were trembling. Her soul was tormented with anguish. Nadia slowly opened up her palms and pulled them up toward her lips. She tenderly kissed the necklace and released it, watching it fall from her hands. The necklace quietly splashed into the gentle stream below and then disappeared from sight.

"Peace be upon you Jason. Thank you. Thank you for helping me see the glory of God beyond my veil. Goodbye my friend."

Nadia stood up on the creek bank. The brilliant orange and purple rays of the sunset were disappearing over the horizon.

It was finally time to go home.

Made in the USA
Charleston, SC
02 January 2011